BLINDSPOT IN AMERICA

BLINDSPOT
IN AMERICA

a novel

Elom K. Akoto

🐓 Red Hen Press | *Pasadena, CA*

Book design by Mark E. Cull.

Library of Congress Cataloging-in-Publication Data

Names: Akoto, Elom K., 1979– author.
Title: Blindspot in America: a novel / Elom K. Akoto.
Description: First edition. | Pasadena, CA: Red Hen Press, 2024.
Identifiers: LCCN 2024005994 (print) | LCCN 2024005995 (ebook) |
ISBN 9781636281827 (paperback) | ISBN 9781636281834 (ebook)
Subjects: LCGFT: Political fiction. | Novels.
Classification: LCC PS3601.K66 B58 2024 (print) | LCC PS3601.K66
(ebook)
 | DDC 813/.6—dc23/eng/20240208
LC record available at https://lccn.loc.gov/2024005994
LC ebook record available at https://lccn.loc.gov/2024005995

The National Endowment for the Arts, the Los Angeles County Arts
Commission, the Ahmanson Foundation, the Dwight Stuart Youth
Fund, the Max Factor Family Foundation, the Pasadena Tournament
of Roses Foundation, the Pasadena Arts & Culture Commission and
the City of Pasadena Cultural Affairs Division, the City of Los Angeles
Department of Cultural Affairs, the Audrey & Sydney Irmas Charitable Foundation, the Meta & George Rosenberg Foundation, the Albert
and Elaine Borchard Foundation, the Adams Family Foundation, Amazon Literary Partnership, the Sam Francis Foundation, and the Mara
W. Breech Foundation partially support Red Hen Press.

First Edition
Published by Red Hen Press
www.redhen.org

To my mother: Adzo Jeannette Tsedevia, my wife Asséyé, and my children Enam and Keli.

BLINDSPOT IN AMERICA

Prologue

Kamao had been waiting for his trial in Virginia's maximum-security prison Red Onion State for months now. The thick wall, the tiny window secured by four iron bars that let sunlight into his cell were all real. The bruises on his knuckles were a brutal reminder of the reality that surrounded him. At 4:00 p.m., two armed guards accompanied him to the small yard outside his cell, where he enjoyed the fading daylight of late February. He glanced into the void, attempting to hear the voice of his parents and friends telling him to be brave and not to lose hope. He thought about his parents; how were they handling his situation? They were denied a visa to the United States to be present at his trial. His father's status as a government official didn't help.

"This is a national security matter. We cannot allow a foreign country to meddle in a case that concerns the safety and the integrity of the United States," a spokesperson from Homeland Security told reporters, answering the question about their visa denial.

At 5:30 p.m., a female kitchen helper brought his dinner to the secluded area of the facility. All his food and personal items were inspected by the guards on duty before they delivered them to him.

"All clear! I will take it from here." The guard took the tray, opened the small window in the door, and placed the plate on the hard wood under the window. "Time to eat."

"I am not hungry," a voice replied from the back of the room. Kamao was sitting on the floor, his back to the wall, his knees bent, and his arms crossed.

"Look, man," the guard said, "you need to eat. None of us knows what is going to happen to you in a few months, but we all know what will happen if you don't eat." He waited for a few minutes and continued, "Come on, man, just try to eat something, all right?"

The prisoner got up, walked to the window, and took the plate.

"Thank you, Sam," he said.

"You're welcome," Sam replied. He looked at the poor guy from the window. Kamao looked pale. He had lost a lot of weight. His sadness was muting into despair. Would he ever be found innocent?

"Your lawyers will be here on Monday; you don't want them to see you like this, do you?" Sam asked. "It would look like you're giving up the fight. And if you're giving up on yourself, how can you expect them to fight for you?" Every time Sam saw Kamao like this, he tried to cheer him up without exposing himself as showing compassion to the prisoner, which could result in his losing his job.

Sam was born in Louisiana to a Haitian father that immigrated to the United States. His mother was from New Orleans. He was the only guard who never tried to give the prisoner a hard time. The others were usually rude to him, throwing his food on the floor for him to pick up the pieces and eat "like the pig that you are." One of the guards, Mitch Garvin, from Alabama, lost his job after he made that comment and was heard by one of the supervisors.

Kamao sat on his bed and ate his food: some mashed potatoes and gravy, with two pieces of fried chicken thigh. Within a few months, he had become the most covered individual in the news across the country. CBS, CNN, ABC, even newspapers like the *New York Times* and *Washington Post* all had a story to tell about the case. For several weeks following his arrest, there had been demonstrations in many cities, some in support of his innocence and others calling for the application of the most severe sentence against the most infamous prisoner in the nation.

"It is time for your visit," Sam said outside Kamao's cell. The prisoner got up, put his hands together, and stretched them out to be handcuffed. The guard opened the door and led Kamao to the visitation area where he usually met his attorneys.

"You don't look too well. Are you sick, Kamao?" Mr. Vivaldi asked.

"I am OK," Kamao replied in a desperate voice. "I just can't sleep well."

"I understand that," Mr. Vivaldi said, "but you need to eat and get as much sleep as you can. If you keep losing weight like this, you will get sick, and that can't happen; you need to be strong for the trial."

Mr. Vivaldi was accompanied by two other attorneys who were also representing the suspect. Many civil rights activists and the suspect's supporters were delighted when the prominent attorney who had won the nation's admiration by successfully defending some high-profile suspects agreed to represent Kamao. One of the cases he won involved the internationally renowned heavyweight boxing champion Tommy Johnson. Tommy Johnson was accused of raping and murdering Nathalie Stevens, a nineteen-year-old prostitute, in a hotel room in Las Vegas. Clark Vivaldi won the case, to the surprise of many.

Money was not an issue in Kamao's case; he could afford the services of the most expensive lawyers in the country. After his arrest, nationwide fundraising for his defense went on for months. Besides Mr. Vivaldi, a dozen other criminal defense attorneys came forward to represent the suspect, each with different expertise.

"The jury has been selected, and the trial is set to open on April 11, which is a month and a half from today. Do you have any questions for me?"

"No, sir," Kamao replied.

"OK then! Try to get some sleep, and please eat as much as you can; you need the strength," Mr. Vivaldi added. He pushed his chair back, gathered his folders, and said, "I will let you know if there is anything new, and remember: don't talk to anyone about your case when I am not around."

"Understood, sir," Kamao replied.

PART I

KAMAO—COMING TO AMERICA

Chapter 1

Kamao was born in Kpando in the northern Volta Region of Ghana. His father, Nana Attawa Ofando, was a successful chemist and pharmacist who had made a name for himself with the publication of several of his articles in the popular Ghanaian academic journal *The Corridor*. He was a respected scholar when he was a lecturer and researcher at Legon, one of Accra's most renowned universities. His family was from royalty and was respected in Kpando. Upon his retirement from the university after three decades, he relocated to his hometown. He opened some drugstores and a few other businesses that employed local residents.

Kamao's mother, Mama Agatha Olate, was one of Nana Ofando's three women. They were not his wives—because polygamy is illegal in the country—so they were simply called "his women." He had several houses in Accra and a large compound with four villas in Kpando. One for himself and one for every woman and her children. He had twelve children in total, boys and girls. They were pretty close, and so were their mothers. Nana's friends always praised him for keeping his family together.

Kamao had two sisters: Lassay, his mother's oldest child, and Nadu, her youngest. Mama Agatha was well known for her sales skills. She started as a yam and *kente* cloth retailer at the Kpando bus station and became one of the town's most prominent wholesalers for the most consumed goods like rice, soap, beauty products, and much more, in less than a decade.

Kamao grew up in Kpando, where he lived with his mother, and moved to Accra after obtaining his high school diploma. He became a political science student at the University of Legon. He had dreams and goals, one of which was to become a parliament member like his dear uncle, Nana Atana Okufuor, an influential member of the Ghanaian legislative body and a skilled politician. Kamao had a great admiration for his mother's older brother, who loved Kamao like his own son.

Another one of Kamao's goals was to work for an international organization, especially within the United Nations. An alternative—which also was his favorite option—was to live and work in the country of Uncle Sam. He always thought he would have more chances to have his dreams come true if he had the opportunity to study in the United States. He was fascinated by America and loved anything that was American. He would spend hours watching and reading news, from CNN to CBS. He watched TMZ and news about famous movie stars and singers.

"You will make a smart politician with your delicate approach to different issues and your eloquence and ability to convince people," Dansu said. He was one of Kamao's university friends. They were on their way to campus. Kamao usually gave Dansu a ride, as they lived in the same neighborhood.

"I don't understand this issue with the gold that is causing a big debate in the parliament," Kamao said. "How can the government tell people they can't have ownership of the gold they find on their land unless they receive permission from the authorities? Does that make sense to you?"

"I think it does," Dansu replied. "If everybody can do whatever they want, what will this country become? And it is only for tax purposes; you know that!"

"Of course I do! And that is exactly the problem," Kamao continued. "By continuing to raise taxes on the precious metal, they are trying to discourage people from doing their business and building a decent life."

"Don't worry, chief. Your uncle is on the case, right? Those new tax laws would struggle to pass with him around, that's for sure."

Dansu decided to put an end to the conversation to avoid upsetting his friend further. He hated taking a taxi to class when he couldn't get a free ride from Kamao. Cabs were so expensive in Accra. Besides, Dansu knew that Kamao was upset with the new law because his uncle was a gold mine owner and had left the business in the hands of other family members when he became a member of the parliament, but still had his hand in the industry discreetly. Kamao's reaction was simply in defense of his uncle.

As they arrived on campus, class had already started. The midterm exams were fast approaching and soon Kamao would complete his second year of college.

It had been almost a year since he submitted his application for the Diversity Visa lottery. The results had been out since May, but Kamao had not received any answer from the Kentucky Consular Center. He was anxious, but refused to lose hope. His dream to study and possibly live in the United States was still alive, and nothing could make him give it up. It was his third attempt with the DV program, and he had not been lucky so far. He was obsessed with the American immigration program that allowed citizens from developing countries around the world to immigrate to the United States.

As he was going through his email to see if he could catch a glimpse of anything related to the DV lottery, Kamao came across an email from George Washington University congratulating him on his admission to the university. He had indeed applied to a few universities to multiply his chances of seeing the land of the free, the home of the brave. A college admission was not what he was hoping for, but at least that was a relief: he still had a chance to see his dream come true. He would not have a quick start like his friends who won the DV lottery, but he would be starting somewhere nonetheless.

Cecilia was waiting for him on a bench in the same area they usually met before or after class.

"Good morning, my darling, you look stunning this morning." He put his arms around her waist and pulled her closer, giving her a tender kiss. Cecilia responded, but was a bit suspicious.

"What is with you this morning?" she asked, surprised by his great mood. "Did you win the lotto or something?"

"Almost," he replied, adjusting the collar of the burgundy dress he bought her. "I love seeing you in this lovely dress, my doe."

As he continued to joke around with her, Cecilia lost patience and pushed him away.

"Seriously, what is it?"

"OK! I'll tell you after class; come on, we're going to be late."

"So you want me to suffer through the test and torture myself, wondering about what could be your great news? Thanks for the great affection and for caring so much for your 'doe.'"

"Come on, Ceci, don't be like that," he said. Cecilia was still not happy. She turned her back to him.

"You made a valid point," he said, "so I will tell you."

Cecilia turned back, ready for the big news. He pulled her closer again and kissed her. She tried to push him away, losing her patience. "Stop that."

"OK! OK!" Kamao said. "I've been accepted to George Washington University."

"Wow! That's great news!" she said. "But that means you are leaving," she suddenly realized. "I knew this would come one day or another." She hurried to go to class.

"Come on, Ceci, don't be like that!" Kamao yelled behind her. "I haven't even told my parents yet, and I don't even know if they can afford it!"

"Of course they can afford it. Your family is rich!" Cecilia yelled back.

The subject of Kamao's study in the United States quickly became a matter that concerned the extended family. Besides his father and mother, who could cover most of his tuition and other expenses, his uncles and great-uncles joined in, offering to open a college fund for their nephew.

"I will take care of the room and board," Nana Atana Okufuor said proudly. Many people were present at the family meeting. Kamao hadn't seen some of them in a long time.

"I will cover the books and supplies," David Amati said. He was a cousin of Kamao's father and worked for the Central Bank of Ghana. Kamao had met him a couple of times, but they'd never had any other conversation besides simple greetings, and now he would owe him for a very long time, if not for life.

"We are blessed to have all your support," Nana Attawa Ofando said. "You all have proven again today what a family is all about. All I hope for is that our dear son makes good use of all of the support you are showing him and makes us proud." Hearing these words reminded Kamao of a dire reality: the journey he was about to embark on was not only for his good, but also for the good of his entire family, including the extended one, and he would have no excuse to screw it up. There would be many people who would be disappointed if that happened.

After his father raised the glass of palm wine with a "To Kamao!" and "To the family!" and sent everyone away, the future George Washington University graduate decided that there was another important meeting he needed to have, one where excitement might not be around.

Cecilia let Kamao say what he had to say before she replied.

"I told you what happened to my cousin, Asiedu; I will not let the same thing happen to me. I have read too many books and watched too many movies to let it happen to me. No matter what you say now, once your plane lands there and you start admiring the Yankee girls' delicate contours, Cecilia will be ancient history."

"I am not going to New York," Kamao said, an intensity in his voice.

"New York or Washington, they are all the same. I am not going to sit around waiting for you while you are having a good time over there."

"What about you? What proof do I have that you will not move on right after I am gone, huh?" Kamao retorted.

"You don't know what would happen and neither do I," Cecilia calmly continued. "That's why we just need to call it quits so that everyone can be free and we don't hurt one another."

"Do you have someone in mind that you want to date or something? Because you are giving me ideas." As Kamao started to question his girlfriend's motives, she looked at him from the corner of her eye and released a tongue click familiar to Western African girls as disapproval of someone's thoughts.

"Don't be silly, my dear, I am proactive and realistic," she said. "I am sure you know how I feel about you, but I won't sit around waiting for you only to see you come back with an American woman to rub in my face. I won't do it." Kamao knew that Cecilia was making a point; he knew that she was right. There was no need to try to fight her about the position she was taking. He resolved to take a more diplomatic approach.

"How about visits," he said. "Regular visits. I will come to see you anytime I have a chance: Christmas holidays and summer vacation will be a must, and there will be phone calls, FaceTime, Facebook, and WhatsApp. We would be in contact all the time; you won't even know that I left."

"Just drop it, Kamao; you know I am right."

"I am trying to see how we can make this work, but you're not. You just want to end everything," Kamao said, a stern look on his face. It was clear Cecilia had made up her mind; there was no chance he could make her reconsider. He couldn't feel the cold air of the AC in his girlfriend's room anymore. It turned into a furnace that was now blowing suffocating hot air in the room, and he needed to get out before he couldn't breathe anymore. He got up and opened the door.

"I will come to the airport," Cecilia said. He didn't turn back or utter a sound.

It was 9:00 p.m. on a Friday night in September. The front entrance of the Kotoka International Airport was crowded with people who came to bid their relatives and friends farewell. About thirty people came to say goodbye to Kamao. He didn't expect to see all those people, but he was not surprised either. He knew that certain things could hardly remain a secret. After hugs and kisses, Kamao waved at everyone, and they all waved back.

He looked around, trying to locate Cecilia in the crowd but couldn't find her. He was longing to make a final appeal to his sweetheart. His mother approached him.

"You did not forget anything, right?"

"No, Mama, I believe I have everything I need," he replied. His mother hugged him and refused to let him go. Nana Attawa came and gently pulled her away, rubbing her back as she wiped her tears away.

"God will be with you, my son. Take care of yourself and stay out of trouble," she said and walked away, still wiping her tears.

"Do you have your jacket? Don't forget it. It will be freezing when you get off the plane," Nana Attawa said with authority. "You can't imagine how cold it is over there this time of the year," he added, raising his voice this time to let everyone know he was talking from experience. "A bird can fly high in the sky and can go very far, but it always remembers its nest and how it looks." He used the old adage to tell Kamao never to forget home, never to forget where he came from, his people.

Nobody left, even after Kamao entered the lobby to check in and complete the formalities for departure. They all wanted to see the plane take off, the only way to be sure that he was gone. After he completed all the required steps, Kamao looked through the window as he entered the departure hall via the escalator. He saw Cecilia waving at him; she looked sad. He waved back slowly. At 11:00 p.m., the whooshing noise of the Boeing 747 tore the sky of Accra, waking up the residents who lived near the airport.

Chapter 2

"How long are you going to sleep for, man? Even astronauts who came back from space don't sleep like that. Wake up now, ah, what's the matter with you?"

"Do you know any astronaut who came back from space?" Kamao asked his roommate, readjusting his blanket on his shoulder.

"Wake up now, ah, what's the matter with you! This *abolo* is so good!" Adeomi said, chumping the bread like he hadn't eaten anything for days. *Abolo* was Ghana's famous soft butter bread that young girls, and even some women with their babies on their backs, secured with a cloth, tried to sell to passengers through the windows of cars and buses on roads. The bread was so famous that it was an expected gift from visitors who traveled by cars, buses, or trains. Kamao packed a few in his luggage to eat for breakfast for his first few days in America, and his roommate had no trouble finding them.

"It is called *abolo*, and stop going through my stuff like that." Kamao was talking to Adeomi with his back turned. His roommate was very annoying. It'd been two days since Kamao arrived in the United States, and classes would start in less than a week. He needed to rest, and that meant to sleep as much as he could, but his new associate would not let that happen.

"Don't you have some paperwork to complete at the admission office today?" Adeomi said. "They are not going to wait for you! That place gets busy like Kamala Market."

"It is only eight o'clock. I have time," Kamao replied.

"You don't know what you're talking about, broda. Don't say I didn't warn you." Adeomi left the room with a big chunk of *abolo* in his hand, munching it with pride. Kamao got up, closed the bag that Adeomi had opened, and took a shower. As he left their room and started going down the stairs, he heard some voices murmuring behind him; he turned around, and a door was quickly shut before he could see who it was. He heard someone say, "I told you he has a new roommate," but he couldn't figure out what that was about. He kept going down the stairs and almost bumped into a student who was coming out of his dorm. "Oh, sorry, I didn't see you there," the stranger said, closing his door and making sure it was locked by trying to force it open. As he finished, he turned to Kamao and shook his hand.

"I am Ayefumi."

"My name is Kamao."

"Nice to meet you, Kamao. Have a nice day,"

Ayefumi started his car, and as he was getting ready to back out of the parking lot, Kamao waved at him; Ayefumi rolled his window down. "I just got here a few days ago, and I have no idea where to start. I have a lot of things to do before school starts. Could you please help me? I don't know where the immunization office is."

"Come on, get in. I will take you there," Ayefumi said, as if he was expecting the request. "You are Adeomi's new roommate, right?"

"Yes, how did you figure that out?"

"Everybody was talking about it in the building; I was just wondering if that was you."

"Is it a big deal? Why so much interest?"

Ayefumi turned off the ignition. "Look, you must be from somewhere in Africa . . ."

"Ghana," Kamao said.

"You're a brother, I will be straight with you. Adeomi is a particular guy. He doesn't have a good reputation around here."

"And why is that?" Kamao quickly asked.

"Let me just say he is a crook and many other things. Just be careful, and whenever it is possible for you, find another place. You're the seventh roommate he's had in less than eight months."

Kamao thanked his driver without mentioning that Adeomi had already been going through his stuff. He changed the subject. "This place is huge," he said, looking at the tall buildings and the nicely cut grass all over the campus.

"Here we are," Ayefumi said, as he parked the car in front of the student services building. It was a red brick building that looked more like a cathedral with an impressive spire that quickly caught the attention of visitors.

"Thank you very much, Ayefumi! It is very nice of you," Kamao said as he exited the car.

"It's nothing," Ayefumi replied. "You can call me Aye. Look, I was going to run some errands, but I can do that later. We all had our first day in this country, and you're going to need some help, so I will stick around. Do you have all the papers you need?"

"I think so," Kamao replied.

"Let me take a look." Ayefumi took the pile that Kamao had in his hand and started to go through it as they entered the building.

"It was quick and easy," Kamao said, impressed, as they left the immunization office. "The people were nice too."

"Yeah! It wasn't too bad," Ayefumi said, nodding. They were not as lucky when they entered the financial aid and campus housing office. It was crowded, and the line was very long and moving very slowly. Ayefumi pulled a ticket from a box and handed it to Kamao. He found an empty chair, sat down, and told his companion to stand in the line and wait for his number to be called, which Kamao executed without delay. He waited patiently for his turn. Thirty minutes had passed, and he heard, "Now serving ticket number B75 at window number seven." He looked at his ticket; it was his turn. He walked to the window and sat down. He was a bit nervous, as the lady sitting on the other side of the window was still busy running her fingers over the keyboard, her eyes glued to the computer in front of her. The silence bugged Kamao, and he wondered if he should be the one to start the conversation, but he wouldn't dare. So he waited.

"Sorry about that," the woman said. She stopped typing on the keyboard. She took the file from Kamao and asked, "Are these your documents?"

"Yes, ma'am."

"How are you today?"

"Pretty good, how about you?"

"Not too bad, thank you for asking. It is a bit crazy today; we are trying to keep up with a couple of people gone. I am not even sure I will be able to go to lunch." Was she complaining to him? Kamao had no idea; all he knew was that she was courteous, friendly, and kept a reassuring smile on her face. She seemed very professional. She looked pretty. Her curly black hair made her look a little older, although she might only have been in her late twenties. Her black hair looked fake, maybe tinted, because it didn't match her skin tone, which looked too pale for a brunette. He wondered if she was a redhead who hated her appearance. "You are from Ghana?" she asked.

"Yes," Kamao said, interested in carrying on a conversation with the lovely, pretty lady.

"It must be a nice place. It is in Africa, right?"

"Yes, it is," Kamao answered.

She continued to ask simple questions as she was filling out Kamao's student profile on her computer.

After Kamao completed his enrollment for the fall semester, Ayefumi took him to an all-you-can-eat Chinese restaurant. Kamao knew a lot about the United States before coming into the country. Still, he was impressed by everything he saw—the size of the roads and their cleanliness, the size of the buildings and their delicate architecture, the attitude of the people who seemed to mind their own business, mostly—he liked it, not all, but most of it. As they sat down, ready to start with their entrée, Kamao saw an opportunity to learn a little bit about his new friend.

"So, you're from Nigeria?"

"Yes," Ayefumi said.

"From which state?"

"Oyo State, Ibadan."

"And Adeomi, he is from Nigeria too, right?"

"Yes, he is from Enugu. You'll learn about him without my help, that's for sure." Kamao liked Ayefumi; he seemed very mature and poised, confident but polite, full of good manners.

"What are you studying?" Kamao asked.

"Accounting. I'm in a master's program."

"Wow, that's great. I have a long way to go before I get there," Kamao said.

"How old are you?" Ayefumi asked.

"Twenty-three,"

"Don't worry, just stay focused and you will get there. It's true what they say about America: this country is full of opportunities. There are some obstacles for us—the race, the accent, and other things—but there are many of our brothers and sisters who are doing very well. Sometimes you get some help that gives you a boost, and sometimes you don't. You just have to be ready and know where you want to go. Do you have somebody here?"

"I have a few friends in different states, but I don't know anybody in DC."

"Wow, that's going to be tough."

"Yeah! I figured."

"Well, I'll try to help as much as I can, but I can't promise anything, and I can't be around all the time."

"I appreciate your help today; I can't ask for more."

"How are you going to pay for your tuition?"

"My parents will help with that, but I don't think they can afford all my expenses here for all the years I'll be studying."

"What are you, a sophomore?"

"Yes, I was a junior back home, but not all my credits were transferred. And I want to continue with the master's right after I complete the bachelor's."

"You have, what, an F-1 visa?"

"Yeah!"

"Well, it will be tough to get a job with that. But you can figure a few things out once you get to know the system." Ayefumi did not want to say too much to get Kamao's hopes up. He stopped and took a sip of his cold Sprite. "As for me, I am twenty-seven, and I have a son back home with my wife. I can't wait to bring them here." He got up, took his wallet out, and grabbed a fifty-dollar bill. Kamao reached for his billfold. "This one is on me, don't worry about it," Ayefumi said.

Kamao got out of the car as they got back to the students' building.

"Thank you very much, Aye, for your help today. If you hadn't been with me, it would have been a big struggle."

"No problem!"

Kamao entered the building, and went up the stairs to the second floor where their dorm was. The door was cracked open, so he pushed it and entered. Adeomi wasn't around. Kamao's heart started to beat very fast. He looked around; all his belongings seemed to be exactly where he left them. He put his backpack and folders on his study desk. He opened both doors of his armoire and scrutinized the inside. Nothing seemed to be missing. He took one of his suitcases out; the lock was intact. He put it back and took the second one out. He quickly noticed the broken zipper that left the bag open from the middle to the bottom. He opened the lock, and the suitcase opened flat on the floor. He threw everything out, as only one item mattered to him at that moment: his waist satchel that contained the five thousand dollars his family gave him to live on for the first few months. He picked his clothes back up piece by piece to make sure he would not miss the satchel. It was nowhere to be found. Kamao scratched his head with both hands to see if he would feel the pain, proof that he wasn't dreaming. It was not a dream; the money was gone. "What is this!" he said.

A voice was telling him to tear his roommate's belongings apart to look for his money, but Kamao couldn't do that; he was a considerate and peaceful young man. His family and friends used to call him the "the peacemaker." Others called him "Annan 2.0" because of his diplomatic approach to various issues. He never got into a fight, and it wasn't that he couldn't fight. He was a well-built athlete who had competed in different sports since he was seven; a black belt in *Gōjū-ryū*, he had also taken some private courses in handgun use. On his bedroom wall in Accra, he hung the Latin quote from the Roman general Vegetius, *Igitur qui desiderat pacem, praeparet bellum*, something close to: "He who wants peace prepares for war." He had a great admiration for revolutionary nationalists around the world who he believed died for the love of their people. So he wanted to be able to defend those who couldn't defend themselves. As he kept walking around in a circle, trying to figure out what to do, Adeomi entered the room with a grocery bag in his hand.

"Hey, broda, you're back," he said. Kamao, furious, rushed to him and grabbed the collar of his shirt with both hands, so firmly that Adeomi could pass out if he held on longer. Adeomi, who was five foot two, could only feel the tips of his toes on the ground as the five-foot-eight Kamao pulled him closer. Adeomi grabbed Kamao's hands and tried to push them back. "What is this now? Ah, why you attack me like this, ah, let me go now."

"Where is my money?" Kamao asked. "My five thousand dollars, where did you put it?"

Adeomi was finally able to push Kamao back and started to readjust his shirt. "Are you *wahala*? Are you mad? What makes you think I took your money?"

"You left the door open to make it look like someone else came in and took it. Do you think you can make a fool of me?"

"Maybe I forgot to close the door when I was going to the store and someone came in."

"You're taking me for a fool. That person knew exactly where my money was. You've been going through my stuff since I got here, that's why I kept my suitcases locked and moved them away, but you already knew where the money was." Adeomi tried to walk away, but Kamao grabbed the back of his shirt and pulled him. Adeomi almost fell, but Kamao held him firmly, turned him around, and once again grabbed him by the collar, nearly strangling him. "I will ask you one more time: where is my money?" Before Adeomi could utter a word, Kamao delivered a sharp kick to his stomach, let go of his shirt, and punched him. Adeomi fell on his back. Kamao jumped on him and gave him a few blows all over his face. To escape, Adeomi used all his strength and threw Kamao over using his arms and legs. Kamao landed against the wall, and the commotion alerted the neighbors, who rushed over to see what was going on. As the fight continued, a girl called 911 and reported the disturbance. Nobody attempted to break up the brawl, and it went on; Adeomi was overpowered and lay on the floor half-unconscious. Blood covered his face, his upper lip was open, and his nose broken. Metro police arrived within five minutes. Two officers—a male and a female—responded to the call. As they saw Adeomi laying on the floor, his face covered with blood and Kamao standing with swollen knuckles, there was no need for anyone to tell them what happened. Kamao was handcuffed, and one of the officers called for an ambulance. Some residents of the building came outside, some looking from their window wondering about what happened. Ayefumi came out as Kamao was escorted to the police car.

"Kamao, what happened?" he asked incredulously. Kamao turned around but couldn't utter a word. The officers took him to the station. Ayefumi got into his car and followed them.

"Could you spell your last name please, sir?" the judge asked Adeomi.

"O-M-O-T-O-L-A, Your Honor," Adeomi said. His accent had changed. He did not speak with his strong Nigerian accent. His English was almost perfect. He was barely recognizable. He was wearing a mask for his broken nose, and a brown Band-Aid that was hiding a dozen stitches was protecting his upper lip.

"Tell me what happened, Mr. Omotola—is that how you say it?" the judge asked.

"Yes, Your Honor. Yesterday, I came back from the store, and as soon as I entered the room, he," he said, pointing at Kamao, "assaulted me. He said I stole his five thousand dollars."

"And did you steal the money?" the judge asked.

"No, Your Honor. I didn't steal the money," Adeomi replied with confidence.

"OK, sir, would you state your name and tell me what happened?" the judge said, turning to Kamao, who looked exhausted after a night in jail. He did not get any sleep and he hadn't taken a shower. He was wearing the same clothes he had on the day before. He couldn't believe what was happening to him. He arrived in the US only a few days ago, and he already found himself in jail and in front of a judge. He had never appeared in court back home and had never been in jail.

"O-F-A-N-D-O—B-I-R-A-M-A, Your Honor."

"OK, tell me what happened."

"I was going into our dorm on Tuesday and saw that the door was open. I looked through my stuff and noticed that my money was gone."

"How much was it?" the judge asked.

"Five thousand dollars, Your Honor." Kamao knew how to address a judge from watching Hollywood movies and American TV shows. Adeomi had helped a little too.

"And how did you know it was your roommate who took the money?"

"He had been going through my things since I arrived without asking me, and he knew where the money was."

"He claimed that the door was left open and anyone could have entered the room. What do you say about that?"

"People told me that he's a crook and a scammer. I am sure he left the door open on purpose so that he would not be blamed for what he did."

"Mr. Birama," the judge said calmly, removing his glasses and putting them in front of him. "I am sure there are laws in your country that forbid you to attack people and hurt them based on assumptions. In your country, in"—he looked through the documents in front of him—"Ghana, in Ghana, you don't just jump on people because you think they took something from you, right? Or is that what people do over there? If that is the case, it's unfortunate. Well," the judge said and put his glasses back on, "in this country, we have laws that forbid physical assault. If you have proof that someone took your money, you call the police, and that person will be arrested and will have to return it. In your case, you have no proof, only assumptions, and you are at fault because you have assaulted him. If you had seen him taking the money, things may have been a little different. You have violated a few of our laws. However, I am going to be lenient considering that you are new here. I am going to sentence you to two weeks in jail, and you're going to pay for Mr. Omotola's medical expenses." Kamao was furious, but he knew that any adverse reaction to the judge's decision would not work in his favor.

"Do you have anything to say?" the judge asked.

"No, Your Honor," he replied.

Two weeks passed, and Kamao was released. He received a restraining order and couldn't share the room with Adeomi any longer. He wasn't looking forward to that anyway. Ayefumi picked him up and took him to his dorm. His roommate, an Indian engineering student, had agreed to take him in for a few days.

"What are you going to do now?" Ayefumi asked. "Classes have already started. You have missed the first week."

"I don't know," Kamao said. "I need to call my parents and ask for another allowance if I want to stay in this country."

"You're also going to need a job unless your parents can pay for all your expenses, especially now that you will need an apartment. You are an F-1 student, right?"

"Yes."

"Yeah, you can only work for a few hours a week on campus with that status. But we will think about something else later. What about your credits, how many did you transfer?"

"I was a junior at Legon, but they only gave me credit for two years here. My major was political science with a minor in French, and I took some other courses, but the university didn't accept those credits."

Kamao had only been in the United States for a month, and already things had turned upside down for him. He didn't lose faith or hope. He still believed that he had come to a great country. He was not going to let what happened to him affect his morals and distract him from his goal, from his dream. He decided to think of the situation with Adeomi as a minor disruption that should not stop him from looking forward, and that should make him stronger. He thought of himself as lucky to have a family that cared about him and that was willing to support him abroad. Many of his friends, like Dansu, were not as fortunate, and he should be thankful. He resolved to make his time in America a real success, and nothing, nobody, was going to stop him—not Adeomi anyway.

The phone rang. Mama Agatha was in a meeting with a couple of her retailers; her phone was in her office. She called one of her maids. "Adjoa, go fetch my phone for me in my office, please." Adjoa, a sweet girl, one of Mama Agatha's favorite helpers, whom she was hoping her son would fancy, quickly obeyed and brought the phone to her *apeno*, her boss. Adjoa was the daughter of one of Mama Agatha's childhood friends who had died a few years earlier, and Kamao's mother decided to take the young orphan under her wing and teach her the trade and help her become an independent businesswoman. Adjoa's humility, positive attitude, and respect for everyone brought her the admiration of most people who knew her. She was always clean and nicely dressed. She liked to wear traditional colorful dresses made by local seamstresses who used different fashions and designs. She was what one would call a medium-sized girl, with dark and shining skin. She would have no reason to envy Nubian princesses if it wasn't for their wealth. She had the beauty and the youth that made many boys and older men buzz around her like a colony of bees fighting to gain access to the nectar. She graciously turned them down. Even when they lost their chance, they didn't hate her; she was that adorable. Kamao liked her, but he didn't think his mother's plan would work. "She is too young for me, Mama, and she's like my sister; she's been living with us for years." That's what he'd said to his mother when she tried to make sure he didn't leave without any girl to think about after Cecilia broke up with him.

"Allo!" Mama Agatha said.

"Mama," a trembling voice said on the other end.

"Eh! My sweetheart, my dear son. Is this how long it took you to call your mother? I've been worried about you. I asked your father if he had heard from you, and he said 'No.' How are you? Is everything OK?"

"Yeah, everything is fine. It's just that I encountered an unfortunate situation a few days after I arrived, but things should be back on the right track, so . . ."

"What happened?" Mama Agatha asked. She got up and asked her associates to excuse her. She went to her office, closed the door, and listened to her son's story.

"Why don't you just come back? Just come back and forget about that America."

"Mama, it is not America's fault. It is one guy, and it was an unfortunate situation," he explained.

"I don't want you to be there by yourself and struggle like that."

"Mama, it'll be all right. It is very nice here; I like it very much. It is everything I thought it would be. I just need to know where to get the right information to know what to do in every situation. It will take time, but it should be all right."

"I can't even see you. I want to see you."

"If you want to see me, that can be arranged. I want to see you too. I can video call you on WhatsApp. Wait for a second. I will call you back." He hung up, went to the app on his phone, and video-called her.

"Sweet Jesus! What happened to you? Why did you lose so much weight? And your face"—she was referring to the few bruises he got from his fight with Adeomi—"I don't like it. I don't like it. I don't want to lose you like this. Come back home. I will buy you a ticket."

"Come on now, Mama, don't be like that; I told you, I like it here. It is not that bad. Everything will be fine, I promise." Mama Agatha sighed and calmed down.

"How is everybody? Starting with Papa," Kamao asked.

"Your father is fine. He opened two new pharmacies: one in Ho and another one in Ashaiman. They want him to join the government, you know! The president wants him to be the next Minister of Health. He doesn't want to, but everybody thinks he should."

"Do you want him to?" Kamao asked.

"He doesn't belong to me alone. It doesn't matter what I want or think; it's about what he wants and what he thinks is good for him and his family."

"That's a good answer, Mama, well said." His mother told him about everybody else, his two sisters, and other siblings on his father's side.

"How about Adjoa? How is she?"

"She is fine. Getting prettier every day, and boys won't leave her alone."

Kamao quickly changed the subject, knowing exactly where his mother was going with that comment. "I will call Papa later. Mama, look, I am sorry to ask you like this, but all my money is gone. I don't have anything."

After Kamao told her about the incident with Adeomi, she asked, "So you mean he took the whole five thousand dollars? What kind of African boy is that? Who raised him?" Mama Agatha could not contain her indignation. "You know we worked together, your whole family, to get that money for you. We will go broke if things keep up like that."

"I promise you, it won't continue like this, I'll work something out," Kamao said, trying to reassure his mother.

"I don't want to go to your father and tell him the money we gave you is gone and that we need to send you more. He'll be disappointed, and everybody will know."

"Mama, you don't have to tell anybody; I don't want you to tell anybody, not even Papa. Mama, please, I know I am asking you for a lot, but please help me." Mama Agatha remained silent for a moment.

"All right," she finally said. "I will send you two thousand tomorrow and some more later. But know that if it continues like this, it won't be long before I go broke."

"I will not let that happen, Mother. I will not let you go bankrupt. I will find a solution."

"OK, my dear boy, take care of yourself and please, stay away from that evil boy the devil put on your path. He is a liar; the devil is a liar." Mama Agatha's wish for her son turned into a feisty prayer aimed at the devil and his little messenger Adeomi. The devoted mother invoked the intervention of the Holy Spirit and Jesus Christ to shield her son and to protect him against all evil. Kamao patiently stayed on the phone and went through the prayer with his mother, making sure to add an "Amen" to every invocation of the Holy Spirit and Jesus Christ. As he hung up the phone, Ayefumi entered the room.

"I need to do something about my situation," Kamao said. "My mother will send me some money, but I will become a serious burden to my family if I don't do something, if I don't get a job. Can you help me, please?" He looked at Ayefumi with an expression of despair on his face.

Chapter 3

He had missed three weeks of school, but Kamao was able to catch up with most of the coursework. In one of his classes, he sat next to a nice girl on his first day who shared her notes with him. The Violence/Revolution and Terrorism class was one of Kamao's favorites. For the midterm, they had the choice to do a presentation on great revolutions, patriotism, and nationalism, or take an exam. Kamao chose to do the presentation. As he was getting ready to get into Ayefumi's car to head to the campus library where he usually did his research, a Honda Accord pulled into the parking lot and Adeomi got out, looking like a famous rapper that just won a Grammy Award. His all-matching Air Jordan outfit invited everyone to take a second glance at his new look when passing him by.

"You know whose money paid for all of that?" Ayefumi said in a mocking tone.

"Did my money buy all of that?" Kamao asked back, astonished.

"Yup," Ayefumi said.

"Even the car?"

"Oh, yeah! With three or four grand, you can afford a nice Accord like that."

"Wow, is that how he makes his living? Robbing people?"

"Yup," Ayefumi said. "But let me tell you: people like that, they always pay for their actions one way or another. So you don't have to worry about what he did to you. If he doesn't end up in prison for a very long time, he is going to die young. He is going to mess with the wrong people, and they'll kill him."

"I wonder if he grew up like that," Kamao said.

"There is a guy in Philly who knew his family back home," Ayefumi said. "He is a member of the Organization of Nigerian Nationals, and I met him in Connecticut during one of our conferences. He told me about Adeomi."

"How did that happen? Was Adeomi with you guys?"

"No, he wasn't. We were talking about him, and the guy asked if he could see the picture of the person we were talking about, that our story reminded him of a family he knew back home. It only took him a split second to recognize

Adeomi on my phone. He said Adeomi was not his name. He said his name was Eweka Okpara."

"How did he end up with the name Adeomi?" Kamao asked.

"I don't know, but the guy said he wouldn't be surprised if he learned that he was using someone else's identity. Maybe a Nigerian student's, who has curiously disappeared while visiting his family back home."

"You think that could be possible?"

"I don't know. What I know is that he is not a typical student. He doesn't have a student life. He is rarely seen on campus, and no one ever sees him studying."

"But you can't fool the immigration services like that! You can't fool America like that!" Kamao insisted.

"You can fool anybody if you know what you're doing. The guy at the conference said Adeomi's entire family is a family of crooks. His father was a master scammer. He had all the jobs in the world you could think of—from taxi driver to college professor—he even tried to pass for one of the government members, a minister or something, before he was arrested and sentenced for life. One of his brothers was burned alive in the middle of Ashaiman Market. They said he stole a motorcycle and they caught him, put a tire around his neck, and burned him right in the middle of the market in broad daylight and in front of police officers who stood there and did nothing. Another one of his older brothers was a member of Lawrence Anini's gang."

"I remember Lawrence Anini," Kamao said. "Wasn't he executed with some of his members in 1987 or something like that? It was in Benin state, right?"

"Exactly!"

"There was a newspaper with a picture of his execution that was all over Accra a few years ago. It was telling some story about him."

"The guy at the conference said Adeomi's brother was in that picture with Anini."

"Really! Wow, that's unbelievable."

"Well, this is the kind of guy we are dealing with. Just stay out of his way, or he will sell you whole or in pieces, and alive if he could."

"That's sad. That's really sad," Kamao concluded, after a moment of reflection.

Ayefumi dropped Kamao off at the university's library. "Call me when you finish."

"OK, thank you!" Kamao said.

Ayefumi and Kamao lived together in the college dorm for a few weeks after the Indian engineering student moved out. Kamao knew that he needed to get a job, and Ayefumi was willing to help him with that, although according to his visa status he was not authorized to work—not legally anyway.

"I'll talk to Lazo. He can help us, I am sure of it," Ayefumi said.

"Who's Lazo?"

"He's someone I would like you to meet. I'll take you to his place sometime later. He's a very good friend. He said that Ali, our former boss, was looking for someone last week in one of his gas stations. I'll check and see if the position is still available. I'll ask Lazo to talk to Ali. They are very close. If things work out, you might start working soon."

"That's exciting! Thank you, Aye. I can't wait to meet Lazo."

"I told him about you too. He can't wait to meet you as well."

Ayefumi took Kamao to one of Ali's gas stations, a Texaco on Spencer Street. Lazo was able to convince Ali to hire Kamao. As they entered the store, a guy standing behind the cash register, protected by bullet-resistant glass, greeted them. "How are you, Peter?" Ayefumi said.

"Good!" the guy said, with a broad smile that revealed his dark brown teeth, probably rotten by the excessive chewing of snuff or some other kind of smokeless tobacco.

"Where is Ali?" Ayefumi asked.

"He's in the cooler," Peter answered. Ayefumi and Kamao went to the cooler, and Ayefumi called Ali. A dark-haired Middle Eastern guy came out of the cooler. He was wearing a light blue long-sleeved shirt, professionally ironed, with black pants. He looked like he'd just come back from the mosque and likely stopped by to fill up the beer section of the cooler before going home.

"So, you are the good friend Lazo and Aye are talking about," Ali said in his Arabic accent.

"Yes, sir!" Kamao answered with assurance.

"OK! You don't have any experience, right?"

"That's right. I've never done this before."

"If you are an honest guy like your friends, I will hire you, and I will train you. I'll pay you in cash. There will be no tax withheld since you are not working legally. During your training, you will get seven dollars an hour, and when you know everything, it will go up to nine dollars." Kamao knew he had no other choices.

"Thanks, Ali! I knew I could count on you," Ayefumi said.

"No problem, Aye! Now, I need to warn you," Ali continued, turning to Kamao. "This is a very dangerous area. Have you heard of the ghetto before? This is the ghetto. It is a Black people's neighborhood. These people say their ancestors worked for this country for free and now they don't have to work but only profit from their fathers' work. All they do is sell drugs and shoot everybody. They have problems with rednecks, Indians, and everybody else."

"But I've seen some Black people with good jobs," Kamao said.

"Only a few of them," Ali quickly objected. "So there are a lot of drugs and gunshots in this neighborhood. Even though it is a dangerous area, there is money here. They spend a lot of money here. All the drug money, they give it to us, so what can you do? Just pray that you are safe. You see that?" he asked, pointing at the safe area of the store. "That is bulletproof glass. When you stay there, you are safe. And there is a button under the cash register; if you think it is too dangerous, you push it, and police will be here in two minutes. I will tell you more when you start, OK?"

"OK!" Kamao replied, wondering if he was getting a job or was being drafted into the army in the middle of a war. Overall, he was excited about his first job in America.

"When can I start?" he asked anxiously.

"Today is what, Thursday? Come back on Saturday; I will introduce you to Peter, and you can start your training. You can come at 10:00 a.m."

"OK, thank you!" Kamao said, firmly shaking the hand of his future boss.

They left the store, and Kamao scanned the area. He saw two Black guys in their late teens standing next to the store entrance, smoking what appeared to be a dark cigarette with a white tip in the form of a kids' whistle. He would later learn that those were called Black & Mild cigars. One of the guys was wearing an oversized white T-shirt that reached his knees, and the other was wearing a dirty white tank top that revealed his muscular upper body, a signal to the girls in the neighborhood that he was in good shape. His jeans were falling to his knees, and he was holding them with one hand while smoking his cigar with the other. Kamao knew that was called "sagging pants," but he never understood the point of it—to show the whole world your dirty underpants? A little further, closer to the street, a group of kids were riding their bicycles, joking, and making fun of each other. A white couple was walking, some grocery bags in their hands. So it wasn't an all-Black neighborhood after all. There were a lot of apartment complexes in the area. That could explain why Ali's business was flourishing. The plan was that after his training, Kamao would take over the evening shift, and Peter would start the night shift. Having a store open 24/7 meant more business coming in.

On their way back to the students' residence, Kamao and Ayefumi visited a few apartment complexes to see which ones offered a better deal, as they were planning to find a larger space that offered more privacy. Now that Kamao could afford to pay rent, there was no need to wait. Ayefumi was also planning for his wife and kid to join him, so having a room for himself was a step toward getting ready to have a family life in America.

As they got back to their dorm, Ayefumi thought it was necessary to warn Kamao about some challenges that were awaiting him in his first job in America. "One thing I can tell you about the job you are getting is that you have to be very careful. You can't trust anybody, including Ali himself. Everybody's goal in this country is to make money, as much as possible, and they don't care who gets hurt in the process. People would walk on your dead body to meet their goal if they had to. Don't expect anybody to care about you; you have to do it yourself. The glass door that is protecting the cash register area is not bulletproof; it's bullet resistant. There is a difference; don't depend too much on that glass. You have to be vigilant."

"Can you tell me a little more about Ali? He seems to know a lot," Kamao asked.

"He said he was an anesthesiologist in Yemen. I know he is well-educated; I just don't know if that's what he was. He also served as an interpreter for some American envoys in Yemen from USAID and other humanitarian services. By doing this, he was targeted as a spy for the United States by local community leaders. After the strike of a wedding convoy in 2013, all Yemenis working for America were targeted by their own people. He fled to Pakistan with his family and later applied for asylum."

"I remember that strike," Kamao said. "The news said twelve or thirteen people were killed, and wasn't Clinton the secretary of state at the time?"

"I've heard the news, but I didn't pay attention to the whole thing. Ali will tell you the story himself and even more. He likes talking about how much America owes him."

Saturday came, and Kamao was excited about his first job in the United States. As illegal as the situation was, it was a starting point for independence in his new country. The cold rain in the October morning made the wait at the bus stop feel longer than it was. Kamao was prepared nonetheless. He was dry under his large umbrella. He felt sorry for some of the other people who were also waiting for the bus and did not have anything else to protect themselves besides the jackets that no longer kept them warm, as they were soaked. Next to him, a woman and her daughter were standing, shivering, as the rain kept pouring, adding to the torturing effect of the cold wind. Kamao wanted to invite them to share his umbrella, but Ayefumi's words sounded in his ears: "This is not Africa. Things that we usually do out of kindness are easily misinterpreted here and can get you into serious trouble." So he gave up the thought. The bus finally came; it was on time. Everybody got on, greeted by the driver, who kept smiling at them, revealing his newly bought golden teeth. When he arrived at the store at 10:05 a.m., Ali was stacking some chips on a shelf.

"My friend, come, come," he said with excitement. "You are on time; that's very good, that's a good sign. Come, come." He invited Kamao to enter the secure area of the store where the cash register was located. "This is Feruza; she works morning shift. She will start training you, and Peter will take over at 2:00 p.m. You can have lunch at noon, and today, I will pay for your lunch." Kamao was impressed and puzzled at the same time by Ali's enthusiasm and unexpected kindness.

"Good morning," Feruza said with a smile. She reached out and Kamao shook her hand. Her netela was covering most of her upper body, only revealing her face, a true-beauty princess from Ethiopia. For a few seconds, Kamao was carried away by the ravishing creature standing in front of him. He managed not to stare at her, but couldn't hear the rest of what Ali said.

Before he could enjoy some time with Feruza, Ali summoned him to help fill up the shelves on the floor. "This is a great country, you know! It has so much to offer. But never forget this, my friend: America has a lot to give but much more to take from you. You have to find the balance, a way to lose, but not too much." Kamao found out later—after working for Ali for several months—that what he meant was he had to find a way to cheat America "just like it cheats you." He made most of his fortune from gambling machines that he kept in secret, to entertain his privileged customers, among whom were college professors and police officers. He made sure to do them favors when they needed him to, and Kamao understood that the items in the store were just a show, and the real business was behind closed doors. Only the store employees and some VIP customers had access to the unique restroom next to the back room where the machines were. Ayefumi knew Ali's secrets, but he was a discreet person; he preferred to let Kamao find out on his own.

"He's making a killing," Kamao exclaimed, after discovering how Ali made his money a few weeks after working for him. "Some nights he makes two to three thousand dollars just from the machines. If you multiply that by the stores he owns here and in Virginia, this guy is making a lot of money!" Ayefumi smiled, none of that new to him.

After helping Ali fill up the shelves, Kamao went back to the cash register area where Feruza showed him how to handle money in the store. He learned a lot of things; Feruza was a great teacher, and he enjoyed her company a lot. They talked about politics, religion, and marriage. No matter what the topic was, Kamao was not bored, as he enjoyed the company of the beautiful and gracious twenty-two-year-old woman he just met and would be working with. Although Feruza wasn't indifferent to his charm, he didn't want to get his hopes up. He imagined her body under the netela and her long purple robe. He thought it was unfair not to be able to contemplate her attractive physique, which he believed must be close to perfect. Peter came in at 2:00 p.m., and Feruza had to go home. Kamao hoped for Sunday to come fast so that he could see her face again, the only part he was allowed to admire.

Peter was from Nepal, a refugee who was living in the US with his wife and three children. His real name was Patak. He thought it would be too hard for Americans to pronounce it, so he made it easy for them. "Peter, that's my name," he said when he was hired. He was a funny-looking man, with a pointed nose like a fully grown zucchini detaching itself from the rest of the plant. He was only in his early fifties but had the appearance of a wrinkled older man with a withered face and dry, wrinkled skin, the result of a life full of hardship. He spoke in broken English and repeated most of his words, but wouldn't stop until he finished his story. He told Kamao about how he and his family fled their homeland, Bhutan, to escape ethnic cleansing and joined the refugee camp in Nepal, and how eleven of his relatives died on their journey. He never complained and never sought sympathy, and Kamao admired his resilience. He couldn't get some details of Peter's story out of his head. One that struck him was that his six-year-old daughter, Sangita, died of stomachache and exhaustion after the family ate plant roots and dragonflies for dinner in the swamps next to a large rice field between Bhutan and Nepal. They spent five days in the swamps with fifty other families before they were granted refugee status and entered the camp in Nepal, and the next day, Peter's younger sister, Suskita, and her two-day-old baby died. Kamao learned everything about the job in three days. He was a fast learner.

"I am impressed, my friend. You can start working by yourself next week," Ali said. Kamao smiled and nodded with an expression of gratitude on his face.

Chapter 4

Ayefumi took Kamao to meet Lazo on a Sunday afternoon. It was Kamao's first weekend off since he started working at the gas station. A tall, muscular Latino with tattoos on his neck and arms opened the front door to the apartment. Kamao didn't want to reconsider his first impression of Ayefumi—his candor, good manners, and selflessness—but he wondered what kind of people he'd been hanging out with. The last thing he needed was to be introduced to some gang member, which could bring another trouble that he knew wouldn't help him in America.

"Kamao, this is Lazo. Lazo, this is Kamao," Ayefumi said.

"Kamao," Lazo said, and shook his hand with a firm grip, "Ayefumi told me about you." Kamao turned to Ayefumi with a thousand-questions look. "Oh, no worries, good things," Lazo said. "It's nice to meet you, and welcome to the United States."

"It's nice to meet you too," Kamao said, making himself comfortable on a soft brown sofa. He couldn't take his eyes off the strange tattoos on Lazo's body.

The latter caught him staring and said, "I know, the first impression most people have of me when I first meet them is never a positive one, but I will tell you everything, don't worry. I believe that first impressions are deceptive most of the time."

"I was a bit shocked; I won't lie," Kamao said. "After hearing the great things Aye said about you, I . . . I didn't . . ."

"I know, and I understand. You don't need to explain anything. Some people told me straight up that I look like some bad guys they see in movies who just hurt people and destroy everything on the streets."

"The first time I met Lazo," Ayefumi said, "I tried to stay away from him as far as I could. But behind that mountain of muscles and all those tattoos lies a caring, generous, and sympathetic heart." Lazo chuckled.

"I want to thank you for helping me get the job," Kamao said. "I appreciate it."

"No problem," Lazo said. "It's just so you can start somewhere. Aye and I have been there as well."

Kamao looked at the family pictures on the walls and on the TV stand. A girl with long dark hair stood next to Lazo in most of them. She looked short standing next to Lazo's imposing stature. Lazo brought some tortillas chips with salsa and placed them on the center table. Kamao declined the invitation for some liquor. He was content with the orange juice next to the snack.

"Is she your wife?" Kamao asked, pointing at one of the pictures.

"Oh no," Lazo said. "That's my cousin Dania. We grew up together. Her mother raised me, pretty much. You see, after my mother died, Dania's mother took me under her wing. She was my mother's younger sister. If your first impression of me was that I was probably a gang member, you were not totally wrong. I started hanging out with those guys when I was fifteen; that's how I got all these tattoos. The only difference is that I didn't take the oath that would have tied me to a specific gang. My aunt, Dania's mother, got me out before I went too far; I am here today thanks to her."

"Where is she now?" Kamao asked.

"She died. M18 killed her. That's the gang I was going to join. I owe her my life, but since I can't do anything for her now, I owe her kid. That's why I need to get Dania out before it's too late. Her life is permanently in danger. If I don't get her out soon, she will be dead just like her boyfriend, who got killed a couple of months ago. I've been sending her some money, so she's OK for now, but I don't know how long that will last."

"Why? They just kill people like that?"

"Gangs are very powerful, Kamao. When they are well organized, they can become a deadly war machine. There is a system in our country called *la renta*, where you pretty much pay to stay alive."

"What!" Kamao said, almost choking on his juice.

"Yeah. You won't believe it, but it is true."

"Wow! I can't believe it. Poor Dania," Kamao said.

"She's handling all of that pretty well. She's very strong. Here is a picture of them." Lazo reached for a photo on the TV stand. "This is her, her boyfriend Manuel, and her son Junior. I've tried different ways to get her here, but her visa has been denied every time." As Lazo continued with Dania's story, his phone rang. "Oh, speak of the devil," he said. The screen showed a video call. "Hi, *prima*. Guess who's with me?" Lazo said.

"Kamao and Ayefumi!" Dania said without hesitation.

Lazo turned to Kamao and said, "She knew you were coming today; we talked earlier, and she remembered."

Ayefumi greeted Dania and went to the kitchen, and Lazo gave the phone to Kamao.

"Hello, Dania," Kamao said.

"Hi, Kamao. Lazo told me you were coming today, and I wanted to say 'hi.'"

"I appreciate that very much. It's nice of you."

"How do you find America?"

"Oh, you know, everything looks bigger than I thought, the buildings, the cars"—he lowered his voice—"even some of the people. Shh, don't tell anyone." They both laughed. Kamao kept moving the phone around to catch a better connection, as Dania's image and voice were unsteady. "Lazo told me a little about you and your story. I am sorry that you're going through all of that."

"Thank you!" Dania said.

Kamao and Dania chatted while Ayefumi and Lazo were getting the food ready in the kitchen.

"She seems really nice," Kamao said after Dania hung up.

"She loves talking to my friends. Every time Aye comes here, they talk until I take the phone away."

In a serious tone, Kamao turned to Lazo and said, "Don't hesitate to let me know if there is anything I can do to help in your effort to bring her here."

"Thank you," Lazo said.

PART II

FRESH START

Chapter 5

"Thank you, Brandon," Senator Brad McAdams said, as his chief of staff handed him the folder that he needed for his meeting with members of the Senate's subcommittee on border security and immigration. He flipped through the pile as Brandon went to get him a cup of Colombian black coffee, one of his favorites. "Thank you very much," he said. He took the coffee and headed to the conference room on the same floor as his office. Brandon followed closely behind him like a dog on a leash. The senator wasn't ready to back down from his effort to promote and help pass the new immigration laws proposed by President Reynolds's administration. On his last attempt to convince his colleagues of the good intentions of the proposed laws, he had faced fierce opposition from Senator Dale, a Democrat from New York.

McAdams's family was one of the wealthiest families in San Antonio and one of the richest and most influential in Texas. Brad was born Bradley Robert McAdams; his father, Robert Ashford McAdams, was the heir and owner of Rockwell Oil Company, LLC, an affiliate of two internationally known oil giants. As he started to gain popularity as a skilled politician, Brad began to break away from the family brand. He wanted to create his mark so that no one would—perhaps even during a presidential debate—call him "a spoiled brat who only profited from his family's wealth and renown." He started to divert his investments into real estate, and as years passed by, he became the owner of several hotels and golf courses across the South. His brother and sister were in charge of the family company from which he got his share, but he grew his own business that he ran with his son, Philip. When Philip died in a plane crash in Colorado with his mother, Eileen, Brad was left with his daughter Lindsey, who he raised alone. She was going to be a sophomore in college. She didn't need a college degree—she was already a millionaire—but Lindsey didn't care that she was a rich girl whose father was an influential US senator. She was quite a simple person: she liked to mingle with regular people and enjoyed simple things. She wanted to learn because she liked school. She loved to read. She was compassionate and sympathetic. She favored spending money on meaningful things like helping local charities and volunteering with her friends in community services. She liked fairness and hated politicians. She thought they only worked for their own interests and couldn't care less about citizens. She loved her father, but hated him as a politician.

"Why are you a political science major then, if you hate politicians so much?" her best friend Megan asked her one day on their way to class.

"You do know that studying political science doesn't necessarily mean that I am going to become a politician, right?" Lindsey asked back.

"I know that," Megan said.

After the death of his wife and son in the crash of their private jet in the mountains of Colorado, the senator named his daughter the sole beneficiary of his business empire. Two reasons motivated this move: first, he wanted to make sure her future was secured, at least financially. Second, since he was a public official, a US senator eyeing the White House, he planned to transfer the business into her name when the time came. To prepare her to take control of the affairs in the future, he invited her to join the management team, which she declined. She had no desire to run the business; someone else could be in charge of that. She would simply be the owner. She wanted to focus on college, she said. She didn't lack anything; however, her father made sure a portion of the real estate revenue was transferred to her account regularly. She was grateful to her father for securing her future, but Lindsey wasn't a spendthrift; her mother had taught her to be generous, compassionate, and kind, qualities she never hesitated to demonstrate whenever the opportunity allowed. She liked to go shopping with her friends from less fortunate backgrounds without showing off, and whenever she felt like any of them tried to treat her differently or wanted to make her spend money just because she could, she would distance herself or end the friendship. She had helped pay the scholarships of a few people she learned were struggling via her accountant. She managed not to let people know who she was. The only thing that gave people an idea of her family's wealth was the BMW M6 convertible her father had given her on her twentieth birthday. She enjoyed fancy cars more than clothing and jewelry. She liked doing her chores, but her father insisted she let the housekeepers do them. Despite all the residential properties the senator owned in DC, he preferred that his daughter lived with him in their most protected one. It was McAdams's principal residence in the capital. The security system at the senator's home was impressive. Sitting on sixty acres of land, about fifteen miles from the White House, it was protected by tall wrought-iron fences with a large black gate controlled by a security post that could hold up to six guards, and three large screens that showed the view from all the surveillance cameras.

The senator had enlisted the service of Agent Corey Murdock, one of the best Secret Service agents at the White House. The agent was at the senator's service during his days off and free time, and he was well compensated. He was in charge of building the senator's protective service by hiring old companions who needed a job or extra cash. A former Navy SEAL and team leader, Agent Murdock was respected and well regarded by his peers and superiors. Some people who knew his affinity for Senator McAdams said of him that he was the senator's watchdog and did his dirty work. The senator had indeed pulled a few strings to secure a position for him as a White House Secret Service agent.

The relationship between the two men started several years back when the senator took on the defense of the leader of Bravo Team after a federal investigation was opened into him for potential war crimes committed during a high-stakes mission in Tajikistan. He was cleared on all counts and was later awarded the Purple Heart. He knew that he owed the senator not only his career, but also his life, and for the senator, the ex-Navy SEAL was the right man to take care of some business he couldn't handle himself. Not only was Agent Murdock the senator's informant at the White House, but he also was the mastermind and executor of his secret missions, and his bank account was well funded for his services. He knew what needed to be done for the senator and would get it done even without the senator's permission. He always got the senator's praise and a reward. Murdock's new ambition was to get a position as a lead agent at the White House. The senator told him, "I will see what I can do, Corey." He knew it wouldn't be easy, but he also knew that the sixty-three-year-old senator was capable of a lot of things and should never be underestimated. All members of the senator's personal security detail were ex-special forces or ex-Navy SEALs; Agent Murdock made sure of it. His impressive security detail often raised questions about the senator's life and intentions at the Capitol. Some of his colleagues, who were less fortunate and could not afford a private army, were jealous. When asked by some close friends why he needed all that security, he replied, "I need to be alive to make my dream come true."

Chapter 6

As midterms were fast approaching, Kamao found himself very busy, working and studying. His research for the presentation was taking most of his time when he wasn't at work. He wanted his PowerPoint and the entire presentation to be perfect since it was all about one of his favorite revolutionary leaders of all time. When the time came, Kamao inserted his flash drive into the computer and opened his PowerPoint. The title read: Thomas Sankara, a Man of the People. Under the title was the image of a man in military uniform with three golden bars on each shoulder. It was a man with a thin mustache and a smile that was both reassuring and menacing. He was carrying two pistols on his waist, one on the right and one on the left.

"This is Thomas Sankara, former president and revolutionary leader of Burkina Faso, a French-speaking country in West Africa," Kamao announced. The entire room became quiet, all eyes on him. The professor took a seat in the back of the classroom to make sure not to miss anything. Kamao depicted the man as a revolutionary leader who cared about his people more than anything else. "He wanted his people to be proud of who they were. He wanted them to thrive and achieve authentic independence." Kamao informed his class that Thomas Sankara led his country to food self-sufficiency during his first three years in office. He also vaccinated two and a half million people against meningitis, yellow fever, and measles within a few weeks. The World Health Organization also congratulated him on the extraordinary success of the vaccination campaign. Kamao showed a clip of the documentary entitled *Thomas Sankara: The Upright Man*, in which the leader encourages his people to consume their products and to stop begging and waiting for help from the West, particularly from the former colonial power, France. The video also showed him as a strong advocate for women's rights. He was said to be the first African leader to appoint women to strategic positions in his government.

Lindsey was carried away by the passion with which Kamao presented his project. Until now, she hadn't paid much attention to the guy who had been in her class for two quarters. She lent him her notes when he started class late.

He was just a classmate who needed her help. But all of a sudden, she didn't want to miss any movement of his lips, any gesture he made. She forgot about her two friends sitting next to her. All that mattered for her at that moment was Kamao. She had never heard the name of the revolutionary leader before and found the presentation fascinating and full of great information. Above all, she found something extraordinary in Kamao that she couldn't explain. She felt a sudden attraction. It wasn't love at first sight, as Kamao had been in that classroom for months and she'd barely noticed him. But what had changed now? Lindsey couldn't explain it to herself. She cared about the guy all of a sudden. He seemed sincere in the opinion he was sharing with the class. He talked about how great leaders who care about their people don't last and how developed countries kept managing to make the poor ones more miserable. Lindsey shared most of Kamao's views. She was happy that someone was saying things that made a lot of sense to her. She heard a call for fairness, a request for the respect of human dignity in Kamao's presentation. She was heartbroken when she learned that Thomas Sankara was assassinated in a plot by the French that involved his best friend, the number two in the regime.

"I used to think of the word 'revolution' as a term that symbolized bloodshed, chaos, and confusion. But the Burkinabé revolution marked a period where the people learned about themselves, realized who they were, and learned to accept and celebrate their identity and strived to achieve autonomy and total independence from the developed nations. I've learned that although many historians labeled Sankara a nationalist, he did not seek to exclude other nations nor did he think that his country was or could be better than others. He promoted Pan-Africanism, and other countries, like Ghana, followed his example. He was also open to collaborating with other nations, including the Western world. All he wanted was to help his people see their potential and embrace their uniqueness and stop accepting the status of inferior and alienated beings." As he was finishing his conclusion, loud applause rang through the classroom, a demonstration of how captivated the class was by Kamao's passionate presentation.

"It is now time for questions and comments, ladies and gentlemen," Mr. Andrews said. "Go ahead, Kassidy," he said as Kassidy Sanders raised her hand.

"I liked the presentation very much. I think it is very informative. I've never heard of that country before: Beurkanian Fasco? But I've learned so much now. Thank you."

"You're welcome," Kamao said and added with a smile, "The country's name is Burkina Faso."

"Would you say President Reynolds is a nationalist or a patriot? Some people call him a white nationalist. What label do you think would fit him better?" Dan Sandquist asked, without raising his hand and cutting Annie Hanley off as she was commenting on Kamao's presentation.

"Please remember that you need to raise your hand before asking questions or making comments, Mr. Sandquist," Mr. Andrews said in a polite but admonishing voice. Dan remained quiet and waited until Annie finished, then raised his hand and repeated his question.

"Well, it depends on what motivates his decisions, his policies, and it also depends on the definition you give to patriotism and nationalism," Kamao said.

"Well, he's defending his country and is protecting it from all those immigrants; I don't know why they can't stay in their own country."

"I am sure you know that this is a country of immigrants just like our forefathers, and just like your family," Megan yelled, as she couldn't take Dan's rudeness any longer.

"Calm down, Megan, don't start a fight!" Lindsey said to her friend in a low voice, gently tapping the back of her hand. Mr. Andrews tried to get the class back in order, but it was too late, he could not stop the commotion.

Everybody was mumbling something, and Dan, raising his voice, continued: "Yes, our forefathers might have been immigrants, but they worked very hard to build this country, and we can't just let other people take it away from us."

"Yes, they built this country with the blood of African slaves; don't ever forget that part of your history," Kamao interjected. A silence took over the classroom.

As he noticed that everyone seemed to have calmed down, Mr. Andrews said, "Any more questions or comments? Thank you, Kamao, for your presentation." Another applause followed, and Kamao rejoined his seat. Lindsey didn't understand how Kamao had sat close to her the whole time and she never really paid attention to him or took the time to have a conversation with him.

"Nice work!" she said as Kamao returned to his seat.

He turned around, smiled at her, and said, "Thank you!" Dan was staring at Kamao with anger and a look of defeat on his face.

Mr. Andrews usually encouraged discussion during the presentations. Some political topics drew passionate comments that generally led to intense discussions, but they were never this stormy and uncomfortable. "OK! If there are no more questions or comments, one of your classmates has an announcement to make. Kaitlyn, go ahead please," Mr. Andrews said, turning to a frail girl with a green dress that looked so light that the fall wind would not face any resistance raising it.

She got up and said, "Hi, everyone," in a trembling voice, waving a hand. "I would like to invite all of you to my engagement party this coming Sunday at 5:00 p.m. I would like to know who would be coming, so if you can stop by when leaving class today to confirm that you will be coming, that'll be great, and I will give you the address. Thank you!" She sat back down quickly. She talked fast and was shaky the whole time.

"Are you going, Kamao?" Lindsey asked. She understood that to get his attention, to get him to be interested in her, she needed to start talking to him.

He turned around and said, "Me? No, I don't think I will be able to. I don't have a car and I don't know if my friend can give me a ride."

"It will be fun; you should come," she insisted. "I can give you a ride if your friend can't." She tore a piece of paper from her notebook, wrote her number on it, and gave it to him. "Here! Call me if your friend can't give you a ride."

"OK! I will see," Kamao said with a smile. He turned back to his notebook and wrote down some notes for himself.

The Sunday evening was free for Kamao. He had an arrangement with Ali, who allowed him to work in the morning so that he could be free in the evening. Ayefumi dropped him off. "You're gonna have to find a way to get back home," he said.

"I know," Kamao replied; "I saw a bus stop not too far from here. I will leave before eleven so I can catch the bus."

"This place is incredible," Ayefumi said. "This girl must be wealthy."

"Yeah, I imagine," Kamao replied. He got out of the car, thanked his friend, and headed to the party. There were two security guards at the gate to Kaitlyn's residence. They asked Kamao's name, found it on the guest list, and welcomed him to the party. They were very polite. Kamao imagined some loaded Glock 17, 9mm under their dark vests. The decor of the residence was breathtaking. A fifty-yard pool in the form of a crescent with clear blue water was in the middle of the front yard. Trees that looked like date trees surrounded it. The vast green lawn that extended throughout the estate was evenly cut and looked healthy, a sign that it was cared for daily. The two-story house with a balcony was crowded with guests. A tent was raised on the east side of the residence for extra space. In the reception room, Kaitlyn and her fiancé were the objects of all attention. They were chatting with several people at the same time, glasses of champagne in their left hands, the right one free for constant handshakes. They had to; everybody wanted to talk to them. Two singers that Kamao did not know were taking turns doing their best. One sang some pop songs, and the other played some country music and R&B.

A waitress approached Kamao as he entered the room and offered him some snacks, a smile on her face. She invited Kamao to pick whatever he wanted, and he felt obliged. He didn't know what it was, but the snack was delicious: some baked pastry with meat. Another waitress approached him as he was savoring his food with a collection of beverages in clear glasses, artistically arranged on a silver platter. Kamao picked one, probably attracted by the light blue color of the Alizé. He smelled it and gulped it down quickly to get another, but he had to find the girl who was long gone. He held the empty glass in his hand until he found her again. She smiled at him and asked, "Would you like another one?"

"Yes, please," Kamao said. He had mastered the American good manners. He was a good student, and Ayefumi was a great teacher. But he knew a lot of things about America before coming to the land of the free. He was called "America boy" back home for a good reason. He had an almost accurate answer to most questions about America from politics to the economy, healthcare to celebrities, and "Who names their baby 'North West'?" His laptop always had several browser tabs opened. Some were news, others sports and celebrity reports. When anyone who knew about his obsession with the United States asked why he had so much interest for the country of Uncle Sam, his answer was always jokingly imitating American slang: "USA is the real thang. You don't know about the USA, you don't know nothing." Although he knew a lot about the United States, he had realized that he had a lot more to learn when he finally entered the country. He walked around the room and spotted a few classmates and said, "Hi, how are you?"

As he walked past the newly engaged couple, he heard Kaitlyn's voice behind him: "Kamao, I am so glad you came. Let me introduce you to my fiancé. Nate, this is Kamao; Kamao, Nate."

"Hi, Kamao," Nate said. "I've heard a lot about you. I liked how you put that arrogant bastard back in his place. You rock!"

"Thank you," Kamao said, surprised that his classmate's fiancé knew so much about him.

"I am lucky to be in the same class as you, Kamao. You have a lot of great ideas and a lot of information to share. You say a lot of things that I've never thought of and have never heard of before." Kaitlyn seemed sincere and more relaxed than she usually was in the classroom.

Kamao said "thank you" and moved on. He walked around for a while, stopping to say "hi" to people and engage in some small talk, practicing his American social skills. He saw Lindsey chatting with some people in a small group about twenty feet away but did not think it necessary to interrupt them. He went outside, longing for some fresh air.

He walked around the pool, contemplating the clear blue water while drinking some more Alizé. He was tired of walking. He sat on a bench in front of the pool and leaned back, allowing his legs to dangle a little. He wasn't bored, quite the opposite. He was enjoying the party. He just wanted to make sure to fit in by not showing too much enthusiasm, which would have probably revealed that he was new to American high society gatherings. He tried his best to play it cool. Kaitlyn was a rich girl. Kamao met her parents; they were friendly and shook his hand and engaged in the usual small talk, asking about where he was from, how long he had been in the US. He answered all their questions, making sure to ask a few back. They looked like millionaires with all the fancy things they had in their residence, which they would be transferring soon to Kaitlyn as a wedding gift. Kamao kept the top button of his blue shirt open to reveal a shining golden necklace.

As he was going through his thoughts and contemplating his surroundings, he heard a voice behind him: "I am glad you came, Kamao." It was Lindsey. She looked lovely in a blue velvet dress. "May I sit with you?" she asked.

"Yes, of course!" Kamao said, scooching over to make room for her on the bench. "I like your dress; it is beautiful," Kamao said.

"Thank you. You look nice too," she said, a little shy. After an awkward moment of silence, she said, "I enjoyed your presentation; I learned so much. I liked what you said about people considering their neighbors family in your country."

"Yes, pretty much," he said. "Although I don't think it's the case everywhere." She nodded and smiled.

"And every child belongs to the entire community?"

"Practically. For example, when a parent is not around, the neighbors automatically fill the void. They take care of the child's needs and even punish him or her when necessary. I remember my mom thanking one of our neighbors who tied me to a tree because he thought I was mistreating trees and not showing respect to the environment."

"Oh! My goodness, you were a bad kid," Lindsey said, laughing.

"Not really," Kamao replied. "I was just a normal kid, doing normal things."

They were lost in their conversation and forgot about time and their surroundings. Lindsey said a few things about herself and her childhood, making sure to leave out some sensitive topics that could lead to Kamao wanting to know more about her family and could possibly have led to her revealing who her father was. She laughed at Kamao's jokes, contemplating his beautiful white teeth, his handsome face, and athletic body. Kamao suddenly looked at his watch; "Shoot!" he said. The time was 10:46 p.m. The last bus would leave at 11:05 p.m. "I have to go." He jumped off the bench. "I will miss my bus if I don't leave right now," he said, readjusting his suit.

"You're taking the bus?" Lindsey asked.

"Yes," he said, starting to walk toward the front gate. "It was nice talking with you."

"Yes, I enjoyed talking with you, too," she replied. "I can give you a ride home if you want," she added, almost yelling as the distance between them grew with every step he took.

"I'll take the bus. It's OK! Thank you," he said, turning back and waving at her. Lindsey waved back, disappointed. She stood there, watching him disappear in the shadow of the night. She felt something; the cadence of her heartbeat during their conversation was, in itself, a revelation of that feeling. She held her breath a couple of times in an attempt not to forget any detail of his appearance or of the beautiful convincing words that had been coming out of his mouth. She wondered if what she was feeling was real. She had felt it before, but this time it was different; it was stronger. She wanted to follow him; she wanted to go everywhere with him; she wanted to be with him. She knew it: she was falling in love, she was sure of it. She wanted to; it felt good.

It was almost midnight when Kamao got back to the apartment. The bus ride was about forty-five minutes from Kaitlyn's residence to Windsor Gardens apartments. Ayefumi was awake in his room. He was talking to his wife in a tender, loving voice. Maybe he was trying to reassure her of his love, considering the long distance and the years apart from each other. When he could no longer hear his roommate's voice, Kamao knocked on the door.

"You are finally back; I was starting to worry, man! It's almost midnight," Ayefumi said in a parental voice, almost admonishing his protégé.

"Yeah! Sorry about that, Aye," Kamao said. "Thank you for caring for me so much. I was enjoying the company of a beautiful girl to the point that I forgot how late it was."

"Oh yeah? A girl, huh? You're the man!"

"Nothing happened, man! We were just talking."

"Everybody just talks, of course. There is nothing wrong with that. Why didn't she give you a ride? She didn't have a car or something?"

"She offered to give me a ride, but I declined."

"You declined? Why? You said she is beautiful!"

"She is. She is gorgeous: blue eyes, beautiful face, nice body."

"You saw all of that and you walked away?"

"Man, I don't wanna get into that right now."

"You met her at the party?"

"She is actually in one of my classes."

"Well, good luck with whatever your plan is with that girl."

"There is no plan, but thanks!"

Kamao went into his room to get ready for bed. He planned to get up early in the morning to go get his passport photos to apply for the DV lottery that had started a few days ago.

Kamao left the campus at 2:00 p.m. He enjoyed going to the library after class to get some work done. He liked seeing all the people that crowded the library. The discipline that reigned there fascinated him. The absence of noise in a room full of people revealed the imposing impression of the place. As he was walking to the bus station, he heard someone call him and turned around; it was Lindsey in her convertible BMW.

"You're just leaving campus?" she asked.

"Yes," Kamao replied. "I went to the library to get some work done." He was still walking while talking to her. Lindsey drove alongside Kamao with a speed that annoyed the other drivers, who guessed that she was a VIP offering herself the luxury to do what she wanted. They trailed behind her for a while then, with rage, zoomed past her in a whirlwind. She didn't pay them any mind, as her focus was on the good-looking guy walking on the sidewalk.

"Where are you going now?" she asked.

"I am heading home to get changed and go to work."

"I don't have anything to do right now; I wouldn't mind giving you a ride. You wanna hop in?"

Kamao stopped, looked at Lindsey, but couldn't really see her eyes, nicely protected behind her sunglasses, and asked, "Are you sure?"

"Yes, of course," she said, leaning over to open the door for him. Kamao got inside the car and comfortably installed himself on the black leather seat.

"Your car smells nice," he said.

"Thank you," Lindsey replied. He had noticed a change in his classmate. She seemed more daring now, taking the initiative; she was no longer the reserved, cautious girl Kamao talked to at Kaitlyn's party.

They arrived at the apartment complex, and Lindsey pulled into a parking spot. Kamao got out, and she said, "I will wait here for you, and I will take you to work."

"You don't have to do all of that, Lindsey!"

"I want to. You don't want me to?"

"I do. I enjoy your company a lot. I just don't want you to feel sorry for me or obligated."

"I don't feel that way, Kamao, don't be silly," she retorted.

"OK! Thank you very much," he said. "I will be right back." He made a few steps, then turned around and said, "You can come and see where I live if you want." She jumped out of the car as if she were waiting for the invitation. "You just gonna follow a stranger into his apartment like that?" he teased her as they went up the stairs.

She laughed. "You are no stranger to me. I trust you." They both laughed. As they entered the apartment, Ayefumi was in the living room, getting ready to leave for work.

"Hi!" Lindsey said.

"Hello!" he said back.

"This is Ayefumi, my roommate," Kamao said. "He is my mentor and my best friend."

"Yeah, whatever, man!" Ayefumi replied.

"This is Lindsey, a classmate," Kamao continued. "She is a good friend of mine."

"OK!" Ayefumi replied, nodding in approval. "Nice to meet you, Lindsey," he said to his mentee's new friend.

"It is nice to meet you too, Ayef . . ." Lindsey replied, a little uncomfortable.

"Ayefumi. But you can just say 'Aye' if that's easier."

Kamao excused himself and went to his room to change. Ayefumi finished getting ready and yelled, "I am gone, man!"

"OK! See you later," Kamao yelled back from his room.

"Have a nice day," Ayefumi said to Lindsey as he opened the front door,

"Yeah, you too," she replied with an awkward look on her face, imagining what Ayefumi might think would happen after he left. She wanted to walk around, but there were no pictures on the wall, nothing to see. The living room was almost as empty as the tomb of a famous painter. An old TV was facing the couch, alone on its stand. The dining room was in the kitchen, a small wooden table with two metal chairs that gave the impression that the two friends furnished their apartment with whatever they had found here and there when they were moving in. Lindsey was not disappointed. She knew Kamao was still adjusting to the country; she knew nothing about Ayefumi, but it didn't matter to her.

One thing that drew her attention was the cleanliness of the place, no dust to be seen on the TV nor its stand. The couch looked old but well maintained, with no stains, no tears, and mostly no smell. She wandered into the kitchen and saw no dirty dishes, not that she was expecting any, but she was impressed with the way they kept their apartment clean and welcoming. Kamao came out, buttoning up his shirt. "Sorry I left you here alone."

"No, that's OK!" she replied. He went to the kitchen and packed his dinner. She followed him. "Your place is very nice and well kept," she said.

"Thank you," he replied. They left the apartment. Kamao let Lindsey get out first and followed her, allowing himself to admire her contours. Her tight blue jeans revealed a firm, athletic, and appealing attribute. The light blue shirt that matched her jeans reflected the essence of elegance, her knowledge of fashion. Lindsey would have made a great model. Her brown hair that fell to her shoulders was blowing in the wind as she came down the stairs. Kamao was gratified by the beauty of the woman who was fascinated by him. He was, however, a gentleman, and would not misinterpret Lindsey's friendship and jeopardize their proper relationship.

They arrived at the gas station. Lindsey recognized the place. "I know this place; I get gas here sometimes," she said. "There is a guy who used to work here, hmm . . . Ali, I think his name is. Is he still here?"

"Yeah! He's the owner," Kamao said. "Thank you very much, Lindsey! I appreciate your help."

"Don't mention it," she said. He got out and entered the store. She waited a few seconds to watch him disappear behind the glass door, like a worried parent making sure her child was safe behind the school walls after dropping him off. As he went behind the counter, he waved at her. She waved back and left.

Chapter 7

He had been in the United States for almost a year now. It seemed like the life Kamao had dreamed of was starting to turn into reality. He'd had several good fortunes in the past few months. The turning of the year had brought a lot of changes, positive changes, in his life, and the good fortunes kept adding up one after the other through the middle of the year. In early May, he came back from work one Sunday night and wanted to check his email before going to bed, and that was when he found out that he had won the Diversity Visa lottery. The United States logo, the eagle in the middle of a circle with a white background, quickly drew his attention when he opened the email. When he saw the word "Congratulations," his heart started pounding. He tried to focus and read the email entirely and sighed in disbelief. He got up, went to the kitchen, grabbed a bottle of cold water, drank some and poured the rest on his head, and said to himself, "I am not dreaming about this, I can feel the cold water." He took some paper towels, dried the water up from the kitchen floor, went to the living room, sat on the couch for about ten minutes, trying to calm himself down and make sure he still possessed all his senses. The same question kept turning over and over in his head: had he just won the DV lottery he had been attempting to win for years? He got up, went back to his room, and reread the email several times to make sure he had not misinterpreted any information. All was clear for him. It was a fact; he had won the DV lottery. He knocked at Ayefumi's door, and as his roommate was not responding, he looked at the watch on his wrist and realized that his mentor was still at work. He went back to his room but couldn't sleep that night.

"You are a lucky bastard, man!" Ayefumi said when Kamao announced that he had won the DV lottery. "That's awesome, Kamao! God really cares for you!"

"I know! I can't believe it myself."

"So you can buy a car and do your own thing now that you are going to have a green card."

"That's right!" Kamao said, rubbing his hands, moving his head from left to right, wetting his lips like a rapper who had won an award and was getting ready to give a speech.

"Since you are already in the US, the process will be expedited, right?"

"Right. I should get the green card in a few weeks, and my status will change. I am going to be a real Yankee, bro," he said, slamming Ayefumi's hand.

"You're not from New York! And nobody says that anymore."

"Who cares! I am going to be an American. Do you know what that means?"

"I do. I am very happy for you. I felt the same way when my status changed and I got my green card. Are you going to celebrate with Lindsey?"

"Of course. She was very happy for me when I told her this morning. We have a big plan for tonight."

"So I am going to need my noise-cancelling headphones then."

"Sorry, man!"

"I don't blame you guys. I just wish my wife were here so I don't have to struggle after hearing you two."

"I understand. Sorry about that, man! I love that girl, Aye; I am crazy about her!" Kamao continued.

"I know you do. You guys look great together. Things are going well for you, my brother. I am happy for you. Just stay the same, remain decent and humble, and God will bless you even more."

"I appreciate it, man! Thank you! Your wife and kid will join you soon too; I am sure of it. You deserve happiness on your own. You are a real big brother."

"Don't mention it. Let me know when your status changes so we can start practicing for your driver's license."

"OK! Thank you. I need to bring the good news to my mom."

"Of course!" Kamao left his friend in the living room, went to his room, found his phone, and dialed his mother's number.

Mama Agatha's BMW stopped at the traffic light at Nkrumah Square in the center of Accra. It was a busy Monday afternoon. She had just left a meeting with the local vice president of the First National Bank at the Achimota Retail Center. The meeting was about an investment opportunity. The loud sound of klaxons was ringing from every direction, like the sound of a mediocre orchestra playing in the absence of the concertmaster. The unbearable heat of the sun that was hitting the pavement was burning the faces of the street merchants who were running between the slow-moving cars as the light turned green on one side, then red on the other. A little girl, about seven years old, was quietly staring at Mama Agatha, a basket of Pure Water on her head. Sweat was dripping from her face.

Kamao's mother was starting to feel uncomfortable with the little girl, whose stare was begging her to pull down her window and buy a bag of her merchandise. Mama Agatha hoped for the light to turn green very soon so she wouldn't get recognized. As the red light was not turning green, she lowered her window and waved for the girl to come closer.

"Why do you look so sad?" she asked her. "Do you want me to buy some water from you?"

"Yes, Mama," the girl said in a trembling voice. Mama Agatha handed her a fifty-cedi bill, took a bag of Pure Water from her basket, and told her to keep the change.

She was rolling her window back up when silent tears started to flow down the girl's cheeks as she said, "Thank you, Mama Agatha! God bless you."

Mama Agatha rolled the window back down and asked the girl, "You know me?"

"Yes, Mama, everybody knows you," the girl said. "You help people all the time. We see you on TV." The girl was right. Mama Agatha was seen on TV several times, taking food and other necessities to orphanages, hospitals, and many other places where there was a need.

"This is what I was avoiding," she said in a low voice.

Her driver, Osofo, heard her and said, "That's what you get for being so nice, Mama. Do you think you can hide? That would never happen." They both laughed.

"Is that how you talk to your boss now? You will be fired soon, don't worry," she teased him. They both laughed again. She gave the girl three additional fifty-cedi bills and told her, "This is for you, OK? Tell your mother I gave it to you so she doesn't think you stole it, OK?"

"OK, Mama Agatha. Thank you!"

"Here! Tell your mother to call me or to come and see me next Saturday if I don't answer the phone, OK? My address is on the card." She gave the girl her business card as the light turned green and the car started moving. Her phone rang. "It is my son," she said. "Turn the music down."

"Hello, darling, how are you doing?"

"I am doing very well, Mama. How about you, how are you doing?"

"I am doing OK, my dear. God is taking care of us. How is your girlfriend?"

"She is OK, Mama."

"I told you before you left, I don't want you to get into white people's business, but you didn't listen. They mess with people's heads."

"Mama, you know Lindsey is not like that; you've talked to her. You told me you like her."

"I do; she sounded like a sweet girl. I just want you to be careful in dealing with her people. You know what they think about us; you know how slick they can be."

"OK, Mama. I heard you; I will be careful." Kamao paused for a few seconds and said, "I have a great announcement for you."

"What is it?" Mama Agatha asked impatiently.

"I won the visa lottery that I've been trying to win for years."

"You won what?" His mother asked.

"The visa lottery, the thing that helps you become American if you win, that I've been trying to get for years."

"Oh yeah! Where you sent your pictures and other things?"

"Yeah, that," Kamao said, all excited, trying to get his mother to exult. An effort that seemed fruitless, as his mother asked: "So you are going to become American and stay there forever?"

"Well, I will visit you regularly, like every year if necessary, and you can visit me too, or even stay here with me if you want."

"Nonsense! I am fine where I am. And I am happy with what I have. I am happy for you, but I don't want you to stay there forever and forget your people."

"That's not gonna happen, Mama. You know that."

"I know you have been dreaming about America for a long time, and I am very happy for you. I just didn't think you wanted to stay there forever. But if that's what you want, I will support you. Make sure you call your father to tell him. I am not going to do that for you. When are you coming back to see us?"

"Next year, Mama. Next summer."

"OK! That's good. We will be expecting you. Take care of yourself, OK?"

"OK, Mama. I will call again soon."

"OK, my dear, goodbye."

"Bye." Kamao was surprised by the lack of enthusiasm from his mother when he told her he won the visa lottery. She used to encourage him not to give up and to keep trying. Now, she seemed not to care at all. He wondered for days about what was wrong, why his mother didn't celebrate his good fortune.

His father, on the other hand, exulted and told him not to come back and to work hard and build his wealth. "America is a country of opportunity," he said. "You have to go as far as you can and try everything you can to get where you want to be." He was happy to have an American in the family.

When Lindsey asked Kamao later that evening, as they were having dinner at the Lombard Garnier Restaurant, about how his parents received the news of his good fortune, he replied, "They were delighted and couldn't wait to have an American in the family." He felt terrible for lying to her but couldn't accept the idea of telling her that his mother was somewhat disappointed. He wanted to enjoy his time with his sweetheart. He looked at her with particular attention as she gulped a half glass of a Manhattan cocktail.

"Why are you looking at me like that?" she asked, embarrassed by his strange stare.

"I just can't tell you how happy I am that we are together. I am so delighted to be in the presence of the beautiful woman sitting across from me." She smiled, flattered, blushing a little. "You are beautiful, Lindsey. I love you so much, it hurts a little." She laughed, with a look of innocence in her eyes as if it was their first date. She was melting to the words of the *galant Bonhomme*, the gentleman. She didn't want to say anything, longing to dwell as long as she could on the sweet melody that Kamao's words brought to her ears. His thoughts took him back to when and how it all started.

One Monday afternoon, a few weeks after Kaitlyn's party, Kamao approached Lindsey after class. She didn't drive to school that day; one of her father's guards dropped her off. "I am heading to Frankie's ice cream shop and then to the library to do some work. Do you feel like eating some ice cream?" he asked her.

"Sure," she replied, delighted that he finally invited her to something. They crossed the street together, waving to some acquaintances that were going in the opposite direction. They arrived at the ice cream shop. Frankie greeted them with a broad smile and took their order. Lindsey put her phone on the table as they sat down to relish in their ice cream.

"That will be nineteen dollars and sixty-eight cents," Frankie's helper Tony said as he brought the order. Kamao grabbed his wallet from the back pocket of his blue jeans and found a twenty-dollar bill that he gave to Tony.

He quickly grabbed another five-dollar bill and said, "Here, this is for you."

"Thank you!" Tony said, taking the additional bill.

Lindsey looked at Kamao and smiled, thrilled to be in the company of a courteous gentleman. "Mmm! This is good," she said, as she took the first bite.

"Yup!" Kamao replied. "That's why I come here all the time." Lindsey picked up her phone, checked something, and put it back on the table. Kamao recognized the man standing next to her in the picture on the home screen. The phone rang, and the caller ID showed Dad.

"Would you excuse me for a second?" Lindsey said. She got up and took a few steps from the table.

"I didn't know that you were an acquaintance of Senator McAdams," he said as she got off the phone.

"You know him?" she asked back.

"Who doesn't know Senator McAdams?"

"You're right; everybody knows him."

"Although I disagree with most of his positions, I like him. He is not a hypocrite like most of the other politicians are. He gets straight to the point, and he's real. You either like him or hate him. I admire his stren—"

"He's my dad," Lindsey said quickly, shutting down his monologue before it turned bitter and made her uncomfortable. Kamao lost his words, dumbfounded by the news. He tried to put the pieces together and wondered how he hadn't find out sooner. Mr. Andrews had referred to Lindsey's affiliation with some people in Congress during a class discussion, but he didn't make the connection. Maybe it would have helped if he had paid attention to her last name.

"You're Senator McAdams's daughter?"

"Yup, he's my dad," she said, starting to feel uncomfortable. "I should have told you earlier. I'm sorry!" she added.

"Oh! No, it is not a problem. You are just different from what one would expect from a person like you."

"What do you mean?" she asked, terrified by the outcome of her revelation.

"You are so simple, so amiable, and not full of yourself." They both laughed. She felt relieved.

"I hope this doesn't change anything between us."

"Between us?"

"I like you very much, Kamao. I feel happy every time I am around you. I've been hoping that our friendship can turn into something else." She couldn't believe herself, talking to a man about her feelings with such boldness, but she was happy she did. She had let it all out now—*Que será, será*. She was amazed by her own courage, although her heart was pounding in her chest while she was talking, and she couldn't keep her eyes steady on him. As Kamao was about to respond, a black Suburban, all windows tinted, with a US GOV plate, pulled up. A tall muscular guy with thick black sunglasses jumped out of the front passenger seat and opened the back door for Lindsey to get in. Kamao noticed that someone was sitting in the back of the car, but he could only see the bottom of their pants and their shoes. Senator McAdams was waiting for his daughter. They were heading to the party of a friend of the senator in Miami Beach, Florida, on their private jet.

Back in the apartment that evening, Kamao wanted Ayefumi to help him with his situation. "I don't know what to tell you, man. Really, I don't," Ayefumi said. "This is a decision you have to make on your own. Now that you know how she feels about you, it is up to you to decide what to do. You had girlfriends before, right? It is not like this is your first time."

"But this is different, Aye. I can't believe she's Senator McAdams's daughter. One of the most influential members of the United States Senate, a close friend to the president. What would I be getting myself into if I go out with her?"

"Don't go out with her then!"

"You know how I feel about Lindsey, Aye!"

"I am going to bed." Ayefumi went to his room and closed the door.

Kamao remained in the living room, his head spinning. He couldn't sleep that night. He knew he had feelings for Lindsey—strong feelings. He was, however, a cautious guy and a gentleman who would not take advantage of a woman. He knew all along that Lindsey liked him, but he didn't want to take advantage of that, and he wasn't sure what the outcome of an interracial relationship would be. Seeing how quickly racial tensions were rising in the country due to the administration's new immigration policies, Kamao understood that caution was the wisest approach.

It had been almost a week since the end of the semester, and Lindsey hadn't heard from Kamao. He had her number, so why hadn't he called? The week that followed the ice cream shop encounter was review week, and Mr. Andrews made class attendance optional. Kamao used the opportunity to accumulate overtime hours at work. He missed the final and had to make it up, so he didn't get the chance to meet with Lindsey to finish the conversation they started. The truth was that he wasn't sure what to do.

Lindsey couldn't sleep; she was tossing and turning in her bed. To spend two whole weeks without seeing Kamao, without talking to him, was torture. She tried not to overwhelm him. She told him how she felt about him; now it was his turn to make his move, but nothing came. He had her phone number. Why wasn't he calling? She looked at the time on her phone. It was 10:15 p.m. Kamao's shift was almost over. She got up, got dressed, and took her keys. The drive to the gas station seemed longer than usual. When she pulled into the parking lot, Kamao was doing his shift report before Peter took over.

"Your girl is here," Peter said as Lindsey got out of the car. Kamao looked outside through the window. He didn't show any reaction. Lindsey came in. There were no customers in the store.

"Hi, Peter," she said.

"Hi, Lindsey," Peter replied.

"Can we talk outside for a minute, Kamao?" she asked him, then went back out.

"I'll be right back," Kamao said to Peter.

"Don't worry, I will finish everything," Peter replied. Kamao followed Lindsey outside.

"How are you?" she asked him.

"I am OK!" he replied. "How about you?"

"I am not OK! I haven't heard from you for two weeks. Did I do something wrong?"

"I was busy. I am sorry."

"Did I say or do something wrong? Was I wrong to tell you how I feel about you? Kamao, I am falling in love with you. I can't help it. I can't stop thinking about you. I can't find interest in anything else." She began quivering, a vibration in her voice. "Why haven't you called me?"

"I am sorry, I . . . I don't know what to say."

"Say something, please!"

"Lindsey, I . . ." He couldn't find the right words.

"I am sorry I was too bold. Forgive me," Lindsey said. She got in her car, started the engine, and drove off. She managed not to shed any tears, however devastated she was. Kamao stood there, dazed and confused, staring at the taillights of the black BMW that faded away in the night.

The wait for the 11:00 p.m. bus seemed longer than usual to Kamao. The cold wind of December seemed colder, particularly that night, although it was only forty-nine degrees outside. For a winter in DC, that was tolerable, but not for Kamao. He couldn't wait to get home and fall asleep. He was distraught. On the bus, he wouldn't look at anyone. He kept his head down during the trip to the apartment. An old Black lady he chatted with often was waiting for the usual signal, a glance from Kamao, their conversation starter. He always saved a seat for her in front of him using his backpack. He saved her the seat that night, but didn't look up to smile at her and ask her how her day was at Burger King as he usually did. She knew something wasn't right, but she wouldn't dare to disturb him. She didn't know him that well and felt that it would be wiser to leave him alone. He didn't have his headphones in—something was undoubtedly bothering him. During one of their conversations, Kamao told her that in Africa, there is no place for the word "alone," that people always jump in to help when someone felt abandoned or sad. People would help without being asked, and if they messed up while trying to help, they were often forgiven because of their good intentions. She was happy to know that about Africa, but that night she resolved to cling to her American way: you leave people alone when they don't want to be bothered.

Kamao's thick leather jacket wasn't doing a good job keeping him warm. He was shivering when he got to the apartment. He turned the heat on and went straight to bed. He lay on his bed, shoes and jacket on. He wasn't mad at anybody—certainly not at Lindsey, as she was the bravest to have expressed her feelings openly, waiting for him to respond.

Kamao knew that what Lindsey was feeling was reciprocated. He couldn't understand his hesitation. He was a gentleman; he didn't like to take advantage of people. He knew that for some of his friends, dating a girl like Lindsey would be a treat. Kamao couldn't give up the thought that people would think of him as an opportunist for dating a white girl in America, let alone the daughter of a millionaire US senator. For him, no one would see that he loved her. Lindsey had seduced him with her pleasant manners and her beauty, but he resolved to keep his head straight, worrying that any misstep on his part might jeopardize any chance he may have with her. He spent several sleepless nights thinking about her and all the adventures they could have together. Now that she had made a move and declared her feelings for him, he found it hard to decide what he wanted. He saw several interracial couples in their apartment complex, and they seemed fine; no one was bothering them. Regardless of the racial tension caused by President Reynolds's immigration policies and the open support he enjoyed from white supremacist groups, the American openness to diversity was everywhere, and Kamao knew that.

Kamao's first Christmas in America was not pleasant. He didn't have any family in the country to spend Christmas and New Year's Eve with, and he declined the few invitations he received, preferring to work through the holiday season. He did a double shift on both Christmas and New Year's Day, as Peter called out both nights.

"You're going to kill yourself working like this," Ayefumi said when Kamao was getting ready to work on Christmas evening. "Do you owe somebody money? Why do you work so much? You don't even have credit cards that would make you work this much to pay them off. What do I tell Lazo? He's expecting us for tonight's party."

"Just make up a story, Aye," Kamao said as he opened the front door. Ayefumi knew very well what was going on with his friend. He knew what was going on between him and Lindsey, but he decided to stay out of it, not even attempting to advise his roommate. First, because he knew—and he was certain Kamao would agree with him—that there are certain things in life you have to let people figure out on their own, no matter how much you love them or care for them. Second, he remembered his grandfather's wise words: "Never put your finger between a tree and its bark." Kamao and Lindsey needed to figure out what they wanted. Well, mostly Kamao—Lindsey had already said what she wanted. She wanted him; she wanted to be with him. Now, it was up to him to decide, and he needed to make up his mind quickly before it was too late.

A new semester had begun. It was the second week of January. Kamao made up his mind: he had a New Year's resolution, and it included Lindsey. He wanted to call her on New Year's Eve. He picked up the phone; he wanted to call her to wish her a happy New Year and possibly talk about what mattered to him, but he couldn't. He didn't have the courage; he didn't think the timing was ideal. Lindsey had missed the entire first week. Kamao dialed her number after class. The phone rang, but no one picked it up. He was worried. He didn't know where Lindsey lived. He wouldn't dare to show up at Senator McAdams's house unannounced anyway. He called her phone all day but still couldn't talk to her. When she finally showed up the following week, she sat in the back of the class quietly. Kamao turned and glanced at her at times during the lecture. When class ended, he ran to her as she was leaving the building. He called her, and she turned around waved at him with a smile but kept walking.

"Lindsey, wait for a second, please!" he begged. She stopped, turned around, and waited for him.

"I called you many times; you didn't pick up."

"I saw the calls; I didn't want to talk to you over the phone. I wanted you to tell me what you have to say in person. And I was in Texas for two weeks anyway. When you were calling me, I wasn't in DC."

"And you didn't even want to pick up the phone so I knew that at least you were OK?"

"Nope, I didn't!"

"Lindsey! I . . ." He paused and touched her elbow. "Can we go somewhere else?" They walked to a shadowy area outside the building, away from the crowds.

"Lindsey, I am sorry that I caused you pain. When you left that night at the gas station, it felt like the world was crumbling around me. The truth is, Lindsey, I have feelings for you too. Strong feelings. The truth is, I am falling in love with you too, but I was too scared to admit and show it."

"Scared of what?" she asked.

"Do you want me to be honest with you?"

"Yes."

"I was anxious about what an interracial relationship in this complicated time in the country would be like. I was wondering about what it would bring upon us. Upon you."

"Kamao, there are interracial couples everywhere, and they are fine!" she said, almost laughing at him.

"I know, I know! That's why I decided not to worry anymore. I didn't know what people would think about us."

"Let them think what they want," she said, getting closer.

"I also didn't want to do anything that would look like I was trying to take advantage of your kindness and . . ."

"You're a true gentleman, Kamao. It has never crossed my mind, and never will, that you are taking advantage of me," she said. He put his arm behind her back, gently pulled her toward him, and kissed her tenderly.

Kamao's room looked nothing like the abandoned city the living room resembled.

"Wow, your room looks amazing!" Lindsey said as she patted the wings of a crystal glass angel standing on the dresser. There were some posters on the wall. "Who is this?" she asked, pointing at a man with long thick black dreads.

"That's Tiken Jah Fakoly. He's a popular reggae singer from Côte d'Ivoire."

"What about this one?"

"That's Abedi Pele, a famous soccer player from Ghana. He played in some major European leagues."

"You like soccer?"

"Oh yeah! That's our favorite sport in Africa," Kamao said, rearranging the place—not that his room was a capharnaum, but he was almost a perfectionist. He liked his environment to be clean and organized. The closed blinds, the dimmed light, the crisp smell of an air freshener mingling with the cold air blowing from the ceiling made Lindsey ecstatic.

"Sorry for the mess," Kamao said.

"Are you kidding?" she replied. "Your room looks perfect and beautiful." He went to her and pulled her toward him. She let herself go. He kissed her on the cheek, hugged her firmly, rubbing his cheek against her.

"You smell so good." He gently took her light green jacket off, gaining access to a buttoned beige blouse. He unbuttoned the shirt, one hole at the time, starting from the top. She stood still, self-conscious, as if she were afraid of making any sudden movements. For Lindsey, this was a moment she didn't want to end. The enjoyment of her garments coming off one at a time, the touch of Kamao's hand on her soft, fair skin, nearly took her to climax. She closed her eyes to lock in the feeling. She felt a burning flame rise inside at his touch. She started to respond to his kiss. When her jeans finally came off, she kicked them away with one quick move of a leg. Kamao knelt and kissed the white rose design on her light blue underwear. Lindsey tilted her head back, knocked out by the sensation. She pressed his head against her with both hands and started breathing heavily, shaken by the spasmodic waves that were taking her to the island of pleasure. He was no beginner, of that she was sure. She realized he knew what he was doing; the feeling was unimaginable. Lindsey fell on the bed, unable to stand any longer. He followed her, picked up his phone from the nightstand, and called Ali to let him know he would not be able to come to work that evening. "I will make it up to you, I promise," he said.

They lay on the bed, their naked bodies covered with a comforter; Lindsey enjoyed his embrace.

"You were amazing, my love. Where did you learn to do all of that?"

"I can't tell you my secret," he said. They both laughed.

"Well, I am glad I can enjoy all of that now." She kissed him. "You know you kind of look like Tom Sank?"

"Who's that?" he asked, surprised.

"Sankara!"

"Oh! Wow! Is that what you call him?"

"I read that people called him that too."

"I didn't know that."

"Yeah! You kind of look like him, with your nose and your mustache."

"You are seduced by a deceased president?"

"No, you are better looking, and you are mine." She got on top of him and kissed him seventeen times.

"I am hungry," Lindsey said. "I need some energy before the next round." Kamao got up, put on his jeans and a T-shirt, and went to the China One restaurant half a mile down Mercer Street.

"Mmm, this is delicious," she said, gobbling down the spicy teriyaki noodles.

"Be careful. You don't want to choke, talking with your mouth full." Kamao said in a paternal voice. Lindsey chewed her food slowly. When Ayefumi got home, it was almost midnight. He saw Lindsey's car in the parking lot. He quickly knew what that meant. He entered the apartment, managing not to make any noise. He went to his room, got changed, and went to the kitchen. He saw a Chinese takeout box on the dining table; Kamao must have left it for him.

"How was work?" Kamao asked as he came out of his room.

"Same old, same old, you know," Ayefumi said, enjoying his pork fried rice and buffalo wings. Kamao knew what he liked.

"Hello, Aye! How are you?" Lindsey asked, coming out of the room, only covered with a white bed sheet.

"Hi, Lindsey! I am good. How about you?" he replied, fixing his eyes on his food. Lindsey drank a glass of water and went back to the room.

Chapter 8

"I chose to study not only international conflicts but also domestic ones because I am a genocide survivor, if I can put it that way." Professor Bresensky was the favorite instructor of many students who took his class. He always received compliments from the department chair after instructors' evaluations at the end of every semester. He spoke with an accent that made it easy for his audience to guess his origins, Eastern Europe or Russia, with sentences like "Zis is vat ve vil do in zis class zis semester." His introduction was always fascinating to students. He earned their respect the first day after revealing his struggles and how he found security and healing in America. He emigrated to the United States from Sarajevo during the Bosnian genocide.

A captain in the Bosnian Serb Army, he disobeyed the order to execute a couple dozen civilians in a village near Srebrenica. He deserted after being labeled as a traitor and a sympathizer of the enemy. He tried to get his family out of the country but got to his villa too late that night. His wife, Mamuda, and his two children—Nasr, sixteen, and Talia, thirteen—were lying in their own blood when he got to them. Their bodies were torn up by bullets. One of his closest friends told a high-ranking officer that he refused to kill the villagers because he was from the same region and had hidden his real identity. A price was put on his head, dead or alive. A CIA operative who he had worked with in the past helped him get out of the country. He wanted to stay alive to tell the story of his wife and children. He became known after publishing his book, *Forgiving Bosnia*.

"When I first came to America, I never left my AK-47," he said. "I went to bed with it and drove around with it. But now, I don't need to. I have told my story, and I have fulfilled my dream. I have no more fear." Kamao found the professor's story sad but fascinating.

"We are going to be very busy this semester. The spring semester is always busy. So you should tell your friends what to expect when they choose this class for spring. We are going to have a seminar with two guests from Rwanda: two friends of mine. You should prepare a lot of questions for them. They will visit us after the conference on ethnic and international conflicts here in DC next month. An important assignment this semester is the interview report. You are to interview a politician, preferably a state or federal government official. Your questions will revolve around the reasons why they chose their career, what motivated them, and what challenges they face. You will then submit an interview report paper. You can conduct the interview individually or in a group of two. I will post details of the assignment next week. In the meantime, you should start establishing contacts." Kamao and Lindsey looked at each other and smiled. They already got that part covered.

"Wow! This is amazing!" Kamao said, as they entered the Capitol, taken by the sight of the large building that hosted the United States Congress.

"Hi, Lindsey!" the senator's secretary said as she welcomed them in the office.

"Hi, Margot!" Lindsey replied.

"The senator is in a meeting right now and will be with you shortly."

"Thank you, Margot."

"Can I offer you anything? Tea or coffee?"

"Do you want anything?" Lindsey asked, turning to her companion.

"No, I am good. Thank you!" he said, nervous. Kamao was almost shaking. He couldn't believe he was in Senator McAdams's office, one of the most feared US senators: belligerent at times, a formidable adversary, and a staunch ally when needed. Kamao had grown to admire the senator as he had followed American politics since he was in middle school from TV news, newspapers, the internet, or the library. One of the oldest members of the Senate, Mr. McAdams would be running again to preserve his seat in the coming year's election. Tenacious and combative, he hated to lose an argument and would eagerly turn a political issue into a diatribe against fellow senators, Republicans or Democrats. A die-hard conservative, he benefited from the untiring, resolute support from the party's base.

"Who are those in the picture?" Kamao asked. He pointed a finger to a framed photo on the desk next to the senator's computer, trying to distract himself from the noticeable agitation that his trembling feet were causing as they shook in an uncontrolled rhythm. His heels pounded on the carpeted floor.

"That's my mom and my brother. They died in a plane crash. Are you OK?" Lindsey asked, noticing the tottering of her partner.

"I am OK! Just a little shaky."

She got up, opened a drawer on her father's desk, removed two pieces of gum, unwrapped one, folded it in her mouth, and handed the other one to Kamao. Kamao squeezed the piece of gum under his tongue as if he were afraid it would jump out in defiance.

"Sorry I kept you waiting for so long," the senator said as he entered his office. He hugged Lindsey, then shook Kamao's hand and installed himself in the large brown leather chair. He unbuttoned his suit jacket, revealing a protuberant belly under his striped white shirt. He readjusted his tie, ready to get into business. Kamao was impressed by the large man in front of him. The senator looked stout and hairy in person, the back of his hands covered with tufts of black and gray hair, all his nails proportionally trimmed. Nicely shaved, he looked tired but undefeated, offering a complacent smile.

"Thank you for agreeing to meet us, Senator!" Lindsey started. "My partner Kamao and I are in your office today to interview you as part of our class assignment. Kamao will ask the questions, and I will take notes." Kamao stole glances at the senator during Lindsey's introduction to avoid being spotted by the man who was captured by his daughter's professional exhibition and had almost forgotten that there was someone else in the room. But it didn't take Kamao long to find out that the senator was purposely ignoring him as he answered most of his questions, looking at his daughter and paying him no attention.

"What made you decide to become a politician, Senator?" Kamao asked.

"I wouldn't say I decided to become a politician. It wasn't my plan in the beginning. I would say it just happened. I saw that our country had some problems and still does, and I started talking about them and taking action. And that led me here." The senator spoke with an ease that showed his interviewers that he had no intention to rush through the questions and was willing to answer each one as fully as he could. Kamao was careful not to upset him, managing to keep his comments and questions in line with a perpetual smile. Lindsey stuck to her note-taking job, giving her boyfriend a chance to interact with her father. The senator, however, only looked at him when he asked a question and turned to his daughter to give his answer.

"Would you agree that some of the policies of the current administration, policies that you show support for, for the most part are motivated by a racist view of immigrants and minority groups?"

"Well, first of all, you don't have to be a racist to do what is right for your country. And if people think that of you, well, what can you do to change that? Would you do anything to protect your homeland?"

"Yes, Senator," Kamao replied.

"Well, we are just doing the same here, and if implementing policies to keep our country safe makes us racists, well, so be it. Now, do you think I am racist?" he asked, facing Kamao this time.

"I can't say, Senator, but what I know is that some of the comments you have made in the news seem to label you as such."

"What comments?" the senator asked abruptly, seeming angry suddenly.

"When you were presenting your argument in support of the cancellation of the DV lottery program on the floor last month, you mentioned that most of the immigrants who come to the US don't even have the skills that this country needs and instead come here with many problems that their own governments wouldn't solve that become your mess and—"

"And what is wrong with that?" Mr. McAdams asked, fuming with rage now that Kamao had brought up a sensitive topic that kept crossing his path. "What is racist about that?"

"In your argument, you said that"—Kamao looked on his notepad and read—"'those people that we allow into our homeland from those sick countries are just a bunch of rapists and murders.' Some commentators labeled that statement as racist and xenophobic. I just wanted to know what you want to say about that."

"There is nothing to say about that." The senator leaned back in his chair, fixing Kamao with a look of anger and disdain. He managed to remain calm. He didn't want to make a scene that would embarrass his daughter. Lindsey got up and shook her father's hand.

"Thank you for your time, Senator."

"You're welcome," he replied in a low-pitched voice with the sudden look of a tired, defeated gladiator.

He nodded and said nothing when Kamao got up and said, "Thank you, Senator," shaking his hand.

"You came out bold in there all of a sudden. What got into you?" Lindsey asked Kamao as they were going down the stairs outside the Capitol.

"I'm sorry. I didn't know your father would be offended by my questions."

"Not all the questions, just the last ones. I am impressed you planned this well, like a real journalist with quotes and comments he made in the past. Great job."

Kamao, noticing a sarcastic reproach in Lindsey's tone, held her by the elbow, gently turned her to face him, and said, "Lindsey, I am sorry. I thought that showing your father that I am interested in what he does by referring to his comments would impress him and trigger an interesting discussion. I am really sorry that I hurt you."

"You didn't hurt me, but I think my father took it hard, and it was because of me that he didn't throw you out or dump his anger on you. Not that he didn't deserve what came at him. I mean, the whole nation knows about his disdain for immigrants and his racist attitude toward minorities. And yet he always acts like he is the one being persecuted, and he sees it as a provocation and an attack whenever someone brings that up. I am just tired of all of that." She turned and continued walking. Kamao followed, ashamed of himself, like a guilty dog that had its tail between its legs.

The amphitheater was full during the seminar with the two Rwandan officials. Professor Porter, another political science professor, also wanted his students to benefit from the visit of the guests. On the stage, two men sat between the two professors. One was a frail man with a thin nose and round glasses that dangled with every movement he made. He would simply readjust them with his index finger. His name was Félicien Mziwana, an advisor to President Kagame on foreign relations and a lecturer at the School of Law of the University of Kigali. The other man, Anastase Ramaphoze, was the deputy minister of foreign affairs of Rwanda, a dark-skinned man with a well-groomed afro and a large nose with a pair of rectangular glasses. He continuously scanned the room as if he were trying to spot a disguised spy hiding in the crowd of students. He looked severe and fearsome.

Professor Bresensky introduced the guests. He emphasized that they had allowed him to reveal their ethnicity, something the post-genocide Rwandan government managed to discourage by making sure all citizens only identified as Rwandans and not as Hutu or Tutsi. Kamao quickly guessed that Mr. Mziwana was Tutsi and the deputy minister was Hutu, and he was correct. The two men were friends—at least, that's what the professor said of them. It was said that in his effort to reconcile the country, President Kagame asked the victims, mostly Tutsis, to forgive their former persecutors and executioners, the Hutus, and work together to rebuild the nation. Félicien and Anastase's friendship became the symbol of that politic of reconciliation when they appeared together on national TV to bury the bitterness and to promote unity and harmony. During that event, Anastase revealed that his older brother killed Félicien's mother and that he witnessed the scene. His brother wanted to show him how to kill a "Tutsi cockroach." Then he gave him the machete to kill Félicien, to demonstrate what he had learned. He instead hid Félicien in a toilet pit when his brother and other Hutu killers started running after some captured Tutsis who had been escaping. The two men reconciled in a ceremony broadcasted live on national TV, sponsored by the government to invite the population to bury the hatchet. They both joined the government and later created the Rwandan Youth Organization for Unity and Progress (RYOUP). They also joined efforts to open an orphanage in Kigali, sponsored by UNICEF.

After Professor Bresensky introduced the guests, both men took turns and talked to the audience. They gave an account of their lives during the three-month tragedy that began in April of 1994, then answered questions from the audience.

At the end of the seminar, Lindsey and Kamao approached the two guests on the stage. "You said you run some youth programs that involve orphans and others in need?" Lindsey asked Anastase.

"Yes, indeed!" he said, "Félicien can tell you more about that, as he is more involved than I am."

"We have different programs," Félicien said. "We don't just provide materials that those kids physically need. We also have programs like youth clubs, camps, and other activities where they learn to accept and tolerate people who are different from them."

"Are those programs also sponsored by UNICEF?"

"Not directly. UNICEF is an international organization that relies on donations as well, and what they get, they spread among different programs around the globe. So we are always in need of sponsors. If you want to help us, you can advocate for our cause and help us find new sponsors."

"OK! I will see what I can do," Lindsey said, managing not to make any promises.

"Thank you very much, miss!" Félicien said.

"The seminar was amazing, wouldn't you say?" Lindsey asked Kamao on their way back to his apartment.

"Oh, yeah! It was unbelievable. I mean, I watched a lot of documentaries about the Rwandan genocide and read a lot about it, but I've never met any survivor or anyone who lived through it until today. I am very proud and grateful to Professor Bresensky for giving us a chance to experience this. By the way, I am glad you didn't make any promises back there."

"I just felt like doing something, you know?"

"I know, but I am glad you didn't make any hasty decisions. You can help when you know the time is right and after you take the time to think clearly about what you want to do."

"I can't agree more, my love. You are such a wise man," she said. She caressed his head with one hand while holding the wheel with the other.

Chapter 9

It was mid-July, and Kamao got out of his Toyota RAV4 in front of Smart Cuts barbershop. Lindsey had invited him to meet her father at their residence to introduce him as her boyfriend. He wanted to look as elegant and classy as one could be for the occasion. He wanted to start with a nice haircut and go to the mall later to shop for a nice smoking jacket.

Kamao entered the barbershop. A thick smell of ganja welcomed him. He almost suffocated. He held his breath for a few seconds, composed himself, and said, "Hi, how y'all doing?"

"Good, bro. What's up with you?" JJ, one of the barbers, replied.

"Just chilling, bro." After watching hundreds of Hollywood movies growing up, including *Boyz n the Hood*, Kamao had often imitated the slang of Black Americans when the occasion allowed it. Now that he found himself in a Black neighborhood, he deemed this imitation the best way to blend in. Four large black hydraulic reclining chairs were facing a large mirror on the wall with a long table and cabinets between them. The setup suggested that four barbers shared the shop. Three were inside cutting their clients' hair while the fourth one was outside on a smoke break. It was Kamao's first time going to a barbershop in America. He and Ayefumi cut each other's hair, usually. But he was going to meet Senator McAdams the next day, and he needed a professional touch. The shop had a dozen small chairs, and seven customers were waiting for their turn. Kamao joined them and wondered who his barber would be. There was a basketball game on the forty-two-inch TV.

"That nigga keeps missing the hoop, bro," one client with golden teeth said.

"Yeah, man. Andre ain't having a good time this season since the breakup with Aliya," another with a teardrop tattooed below his left eye said.

"But it's been like three months already, though. He should be over that already," the first one objected.

Kamao listened to the gossip, preferring to remain quiet. He didn't want to betray his "cool" image with his thick, no-flow African accent. The fourth barber came in.

"There is a new customer, Tony. You wanna do him?" JJ, who had three customers waiting for him, said.

"Yeah, I got him," Tony said. He walked to Kamao and shook his hand. "What's up, bro? I am Tony, I'll take care of you."

"OK!" Kamao said and got up.

His phone rang; it was Mama Agatha. "Sorry, man! Can you give me a second, please?" he said.

"Yeah! No problem, bro," Tony said. Some customers looked at Kamao, and he could read "You ain't one of us, bro" in their eyes. He sat back down.

"Allo! *Babamu*, can you hear me? Why is there so much noise? Where are you?" Mama Agatha called him by his particular name: her "sweet little boy."

"I am at the barbershop, Mama. How are you?"

"I am OK! We are all OK! Did you hear the news?"

"What news?" Kamao asked.

"Ah! You don't watch TV anymore or what? Or do you only watch the American *wahala* all the time now? You don't care about your country anymore, huh."

"What is it, Mama?" he asked again, impatient, ignoring his mother's complaint.

"Your father is now the Minister of Health. He was appointed yesterday."

"What? Wow! Really? How did that happen?"

"What do you mean, 'how did that happen?' You know he has been turning the position down for years."

"Yes, I know. That's why I asked: what happened this time?"

"He said the president himself called him and asked him to take the position and help him run the health department."

"Wow! That's great news. My father is the Minister of Health of Ghana!" Kamao said and quickly lowered his voice, looking around to make sure nobody heard him. He was unsure of what the people in the neighborhood could do if they knew that he was the son of a government official, even if it was of a foreign country.

"I will call him and congratulate him later."

"OK, my dear. How is your sweetheart, Lindsey?"

"She's fine, Mama, thank you."

"Tell her I say hi!"

"I will, Mama. Thank you."

"And I hope you are using a condom. I don't mind being a grandmother again, but I don't want you to be a father yet. You need to finish school first."

"Mama, you shouldn't be talking to me like that. That's a private business."

"*Anh*, now that you are in America, you are talking about private business. When I was bathing you, was that a private business?"

"I was a young boy, Mama; stop that."

"OK, OK! Bye-bye." Mama Agatha hung up.

"Sorry about that, man."

"No problem, bro. I understand," Tony said, shaking the cape to remove the hair trimmings from his previous customer. Kamao stared in the mirror at times to make sure Tony was doing what he told him. The phone rang again; it was Lindsey this time. He picked it up.

Tony stopped, smiled, and gave him a thumbs-up.

"Hi, baby. Are you still at the barbershop?" Lindsey asked.

"Yes, I am getting my hair cut right now."

"OK! Can I go to the mall with you afterward? It seems like I'm going to finish my errands earlier than I thought."

"I thought you were meeting Megan and Trish."

"Yeah, but I told them we will meet another time. I miss you. I want to be with you this afternoon. Is that OK?"

"Yeah, of course, baby! I'd be delighted. I can come and pick you up at my apartment."

"OK!"

"I should be back in about . . ." He turned to Tony and asked, "How much longer?"

"Twenty more minutes should be enough," Tony replied.

"I will be back in about half an hour," Kamao said to Lindsey.

"OK! See you then. I love you."

"I love you too."

Since they started dating, Lindsey had tried to explore Kamao's world. She wanted to know about his culture, his country, his people. She began to enjoy African foods. One of her favorites, *fufu*, was a sticky, tender dough made from yam or plantain flour. She ate it with her bare hands, following her boyfriend's lead. She liked it better with peanut or red palm sauce, garnished with goat or chicken meat.

"Mmm, this *fufu* is good," she said. "Where did you learn to cook like this?"

"My mother made sure all her kids learned how to cook," Kamao said. "We always had housemaids, but she never let them cook for us. In our part of the world, it is a common belief that a girl must know how to cook, or she would become a useless woman, and her own family would not encourage anyone to marry her. That implies that boys don't have to learn how to cook as they would expect their wives to do it for them. My mother had always been against those social norms. She vowed that all her children, male or female, would know how to cook, how to clean, for themselves. She didn't like the special 'boy treatment' my father gave his sons; she made me do the same chores as my sisters, and I never minded that. I believed that was fair. For me, everyone must be treated equally." Kamao poured some liquid soap in a plastic basin in the sink. He started to wash the dishes. Lindsey finished licking her fingers and washed her hands in the soapy water Kamao made. She poured some clean water in another basin and started to rinse the dishes next to him.

"I always thought your childhood was fascinating with the stories that you tell," she said. "I would love to know more about your childhood."

"Just ask me, and I will tell you everything I remember," he replied. Kamao watched how Lindsey dried up the clean dishes with a towel and artistically arranged them inside the cabinet.

"Where did you learn to do all that as a spoiled rich girl?" Kamao asked.

"Just like your mom, my mother didn't let my father spoil me the way he wanted either. She let Margarita, our housekeeper, teach me a few things. I enjoyed doing my chores too. But my father hates it whenever he sees me do anything that looks like a chore around the house. He would say something like, 'Honey, you should be paying someone to do this for you.'" She tried to imitate her father's voice, which cracked Kamao up.

"What? Don't I sound like him?" she asked.

"You always amaze me with your decency and humility for a person of your standing. A rich and pretty girl, the daughter of a United States senator; I did not think you would be so down-to-earth." She smiled and did not reply. He cleaned his hands and went to the living room. He sat on the couch, grabbed the remote, and turned the TV to the National Geographic channel. Lindsey joined him on the sofa. She lay down and put her head on his thigh. He started weaving her hair like a skilled artisan.

"I have an announcement to make," she said.

"Really? I hope it's a good one."

"Oh yeah, it is! I am officially a sponsor for the Rwandan Youth Organization for Development that Félicien and Anastase told us about during the seminar."

"That's amazing, babe. So you have decided to help them."

"Yes."

"That's great! That's kind of you." She waited to see if he would ask her how much she sent. He didn't. She knew he wouldn't, but she wanted to tell him anyway.

"I sent ten thousand dollars."

"It is very nice of you, baby," Kamao said. He leaned over and kissed her.

"I talked to Félicien after I sent the money. He continues to amaze me. I mean, what a resilient man! He was smiling during the entire seminar like he didn't live through hell. I mean, can you explain that?"

"I can't, unfortunately. I know I could not do what he did. I don't think I have the strength to forgive like that."

"So it is not like an African thing or a cultural thing to be resilient?"

"It might be a cultural thing particular to Rwandans. It is not something I am used to. I honestly don't think I can forgive like that. I would have killed Anastase's entire family."

"You would do that?" Lindsey asked, shocked by his blatant honesty. She got up and turned to him, waiting for an answer.

"I would probably not kill the entire family, but I would hurt someone, that's for sure."

"I understand," she said, reassuming her previous position.

There was a short moment of silence, then Kamao said, "I have an announcement to make too." Lindsey turned around and faced him, making sure not to miss a word.

"You remember what I told you about my father turning down the position of Minister of Health several times?"

"Yes, I remember," she said.

"Well, he accepted it this time. He was appointed yesterday. He is the new Health Secretary of Ghana."

"That's great news, babe!"

"Yeah, it is."

"What changed this time?"

"My mom said he had received a call from the president himself, asking him to join the government to help solve some difficulties that the department is facing."

"Wow, that means your father's competence is without question. Well, now we both have important dads who work for the government. Yours is a health secretary and mine a senator."

"Yup," Kamao said.

"What does that make us? VIP kids?"

"I guess. That means we have some privileges. I wish he were a member of the government when I was a kid; that would have made me the boss of the other kids in our neighborhood."

Lindsey laughed. "Really? You would have liked that?"

"Oh yeah. Why not?"

"What is special about your dad being a member of the government?"

"Don't you feel special that your father is a senator?"

"Not really. I mean, he is just a regular guy who happens to be in that position. He will be gone if he doesn't win the next election."

"That's true, but while he is a United States senator, doesn't that make you feel special? Or doesn't that give you some pride?"

"Nope. It doesn't."

"Wow, you're unbelievable. Your family is wealthy and your father is powerful, and you just feel like a regular person."

"Yup. I'd rather see everybody happy, or at least do what I can to make them happy."

"Your decency and sympathy are contagious, Lindsey. That character makes me fall for you more every day."

"I am still curious about why people feel special or more important than others when a parent or a family member holds an important job," she said.

"I don't know about other continents, but in many African countries, people don't necessarily get to important government positions on merit, not even through elections, because most elections are rigged. So it is rare to see regular people in such high positions. You either know someone who can help you get there, or you work your way up using various connections."

"Can I ask you a sensitive question?" Lindsey asked, sitting up to face him.

"Sure. I will answer the best I can."

"Is there that much poverty in Africa, just like what we see on TV: children malnourished, people starving? Are the governments that incapable of helping their people? I want to know because my father and people who think like him use the example of struggling governments to defend their agenda against immigration."

"Wow, that's a tough one! Well, I don't necessarily disagree with everything your father and other people on his side say and try to do. I certainly don't wish that they succeed in their effort to cancel the Diversity Visa, because thanks to that program, I am now a green-card holder. Now, to answer your question directly, Africa is actually rich, very rich. Almost any natural resources you can think of you will find somewhere in Africa."

"OK," Lindsey said.

"There is poverty and misery all over the continent until this day because, in my opinion, our leaders are corrupt and self-centered. They don't care enough to implement important economic and political changes that could make people's lives better."

"That's interesting to know," Lindsey said. She looked at the time; it was 10:17 p.m. "I have to go now. I haven't seen my father in two days, and I want to remind him in person about our dinner tomorrow." She kissed him tenderly. He held her tight, refusing to let her go.

"Are you sure he would want to see me?"

"Of course. Why wouldn't he?"

"I don't know. I am just a little nervous."

"Everything will be fine. I will make sure of it. You don't have to worry." She got up. He held on to her waist and got up too. She turned around, put both arms around his neck, and kissed him passionately. "I love you so much. I've not felt this happy in a long time," she said.

Chapter 10

When Lindsey got home, her father was still awake. He was in his study, going through some paperwork, his reading glasses misadjusted on purpose so he could see above them when he needed to.

"Good evening, Dad," she said and kissed him on the cheek.

"Hi, honey. How are you?"

"Not too bad. What are you doing?"

"I am having lunch with the president tomorrow. I am just going over some things we are going to discuss. How about you? How is everything?"

"Good. I hope you didn't forget about the dinner tomorrow night with my boyfriend?"

"No, I didn't. But you haven't told me anything about him yet. I know you wanted it to be a surprise, but you know I don't like those types of surprises. So, who is he? Do I know him?"

"You have met him, yes."

"Oh yeah? What is his name?" Lindsey hesitated, imagining the consequences of her revelation. But it was too late. Backing away would not be a good idea.

"It is Kamao," she said in a trembling voice.

"Kamao? Who's that?" the senator asked, frowning and surprised. "Where have I met him?"

"In your office, at the Capitol," Lindsey said, visibly shaking. "We interviewed you together."

The senator slowly removed his glasses, struggling to retain his anger. He managed, however, to remain calm.

"He is your boyfriend? That scumbag?"

"He is not a scumbag, Dad."

"You brought him to my office to patronize me?"

"It was just a class assignment . . ."

"Didn't you see how he talked to me? The questions he was asking?" The senator got up and loosened his tie that suddenly felt too tight. "What are you doing with that guy, Lindsey? How long have you been seeing him?"

"A few months."

"A few—" He almost exploded in rage but collected himself. "Did I do something that you are trying to punish me for? All I have ever done, everything I am doing, I do it for you."

"Dad, Kamao is a decent, honorable guy. If you can just take the time to know him a little, you'll see that he is a great guy."

"Is he even in this country legally?"

"Yes, Dad, he has a green card."

"How did he get the green card?"

"Why does that matter?"

"It matters to me."

"He said he won that Diversity Visa thing."

"That's exactly what I've been talking about. What did he do to deserve a green card, huh?" The senator could no longer contain his fury. "We can't just give out citizenship to people like you hand out candy on Halloween. Has our country been reduced to a charitable organization?"

"Dad," Lindsey said calmly, "we both know what your problem is. If he were an immigrant from some European country, like Norway, Sweden, or France, you wouldn't be outraged. But because he is a Black guy from a 'shithole country in Africa,' you can't stand it."

"That's not what this is about," the senator objected. "This is about a merit-based immigration plan. We want people who can contribute to this country's economy with the skills and training they already have so we won't have to waste money on them. Do you know how many of these people are on multiple government assistance programs, like food stamps, Medicaid? A lot! And they haven't contributed to anything."

"Those would be the elderly, the disabled, and the kids, Dad. People who are able to work do, and they pay their taxes."

"These people bring their problems from there, and they become our problems. They bring violence, drugs, and other issues to our homeland, and we have to spend our taxpayers' money to fix them.

"Are you playing a trick on me or are you that ignorant of the reality? The statistics are available for everyone to see. Check them, and you would see the percentage of 'these people' who earn college degrees, compared to 'your people.'"

The senator removed his tie; the room was getting too warm. He hated to get angry at his daughter. He tried not to get mad at her, but he couldn't accept that she would end up with someone like Kamao.

"Dad, you always say you want me to be happy. I know you love me and that you will do anything for me. I need you to believe me when I say that I find my happiness with Kamao." He bent over, both hands on the table, looking at his daughter with raised eyebrows. She walked to him, put a hand on his shoulder, talking in a pleading voice. "He makes me happy, Dad; he truly does. He doesn't drink or smoke. He doesn't even like clubs. He is the right guy for me, Dad. I love him. And he loves me."

"How do you know that? Didn't it occur to you that he might simply be with you because of . . ."

"Because of what? Because of money? I don't think so. I don't see any sign that suggests it."

"Probably because he is good at hiding it. I mean, how can you trust someone like that?" The senator sat back down in his large rocking chair.

"I just trust him. It's not hard."

"Well, I don't want to see him. I don't want him in my house." He tried not to raise his voice at his daughter again. He tried to get busy again, looking through his paperwork.

"If you cancel the dinner tomorrow," Lindsey said, after a moment of silence, "you can forget about the trip to Brazil next month."

"That trip was already planned, and you were looking forward to it. You can't blackmail me with this."

"That's what I said, Dad, and I will stick with it. If you cancel the dinner, forget about the trip. I will not go anywhere with you." She waited for her father to respond, but he said nothing. He tried to focus on his work but couldn't.

"What do you say, Dad?" she asked. He remained quiet.

"All right, then. We'll be here around 6:00 p.m. tomorrow. Elvira and Martin will cater for us. I've already talked to them." She left the room and closed the door. The senator leaned back in his chair, put his hands behind his neck, and rocked himself back and forth.

Kamao was ready before 5:30 p.m.

"Wow, babe! You look like a movie star on the red carpet. You look stunning!" Lindsey exclaimed.

"Thank you," he said. "You look terrific yourself, as always. Come here." He pulled her closer and kissed her. She always loved that. She put her arms around his neck, holding him for more kisses. Kamao looked elegant in his new white smoking jacket with a black bow tie.

"I've never been this nervous in my life," he said.

"You'll be fine. Just try not to say anything that you know might provoke him. You should know him quite well already."

"All right. Let's do this," he said, forcing himself to smile.

The McAdams' residence was imposing, and Kamao was impressed. But he managed to conceal his excitement in fear of giving the senator the idea that he was not used to such luxury. Lindsey parked the car on a curve in the large driveway. She couldn't go any further; several cars had filled up the passage. She turned the ignition off, wondering what was going on. As they got closer to the front door, she could hear a lot of chatting and laughing, with soft music in the background. She rushed ahead of Kamao, looking tense. Kamao ran and grabbed her by the elbow.

"What is wrong, my love?" he asked, looking concerned.

"I don't know what is going on in there, but I am going to find out and—"

"Calm down, baby, please. Let's make a good impression on your dad tonight, OK?"

"This was supposed to be our dinner night: you, me, and my father. Just the three us."

"It's OK, baby. Whatever is going on in there, let's just enjoy the party."

As soon as Kamao and Lindsey entered the living room, the senator's guests started greeting him all at once with constant questions and comments. They were all smiling; some were so close that he could feel their spit on his face. Their breath smelled of alcohol and something else he couldn't figure out.

"I was in Uganda in June," Analise Goddard, the wife of one of the senator's attorneys, said. "My son Jeffrey is working with a charity there. They are building wells for some villages. He studied engineering and runs most of the projects for the organization."

"You could have simply said he is an engineer," Kamao thought, still smiling, accompanying each one of their comments with a "Wow, that's really great."

"So, where are you from again? Gabana, right?" the oldest man in the room asked. It was Mr. Norwick, a die-hard Republican and the RNC finance chairman. At seventy-nine, he was the oldest serving member of the Republican National Committee. He said he would only resign when his heart told him so. He walked with his fists swinging to the right, then to the left as though he was fighting an invisible force that was trying to slow him down.

"I am from Ghana," Kamao said with a smile.

"Where is that at again? The Caribbean?"

"It's in West Africa." Kamao managed not to appear overwhelmed by the repetition. Mr. Norwick nodded, turned, and walked away. He would be back, probably with the same question or a more annoying one.

"Dad, can I see you for a second, please?" Lindsey said, leading her dad to the study.

The senator put his drink on the glass table, said to Mr. McPherson, his financial adviser, "Would you excuse me for a second, Dave?" and followed his daughter.

"What's going on?" Lindsey asked once they got into the study.

"What do you mean? We have guests."

"This was supposed to be a dinner night for only three people: you, Kamao, and me."

The senator said nothing.

"What are all those people doing here? How did you manage to invite them all so fast?"

"You said I couldn't cancel the dinner. You didn't say I couldn't invite other guests." Lindsey looked furious, and that worried her father. "Look, honey, this is just a small party. I am sorry if I disappointed you, but I will make it up to you another time, OK? I promise."

"You truly are a politician," she said. "You're good at your game. But be careful, Dad, you might end up losing me if you keep this up." Lindsey left the room. She found Kamao, who was still fighting against the odds.

She pulled him away from the guests and said, "Let's get out of here. I am truly sorry you have to go through this. I will never forgive my father for this."

She started pulling him toward the front door. He stopped and gently pulled her back.

"What are you doing, baby? We can't just leave like that! What would that say about me? That I am quitter, that I can't handle tough challenges. I know exactly what is going on here. Your father doesn't want to talk to me, so he invited a bunch of annoying guests to embarrass me or whatever, but I can take this. I will accept the humiliation; I will take whatever your father throws at me because I love you. I cannot run away; that would mean I am not worthy of you." Lindsey felt like kissing him right on the spot but knew that wasn't a good idea.

Kamao wasn't a stranger to high society. His father had always held parties at their family residence in Accra. Ambassadors and other foreign dignitaries, including local government officials, usually attended. His father made sure his older children were in attendance to make connections. So Kamao knew about the manners of people in high society. He just needed to get used to the American way. Table manners were not an issue; he passed that test with flying colors as the senator was peeking to see if the other guests would call him out for something he was doing wrong. The roast duck with baked asparagus, one of the senator's favorite dishes, was delicious, especially when it was accompanied by a Château Margaux, one of the most popular red wines from Bordeaux.

"Have you tried caviar before?" Analise asked, in a pretend friendly voice, leaning toward Kamao.

"Yes, I have had it on many occasions," he replied.

"Really? What occasions?" she asked again, making it sound like an innocent inquiry.

"We used to receive several dignitaries in my father's residence."

"What does your father do?" Pat McPherson asked, as though it were her turn to interrogate Lindsey's new friend.

"He used to teach at a university, but now he is the Minister of Health."

"What is that?" Pat asked, genuinely confused.

"The Health Secretary," her husband quickly said.

"Oh, OK!" she said. "That's very good. You are from an important family, then." The senator sat at the table, smiling at Kamao whenever their eyes crossed, but managed not to engage in any direct conversation with him.

He asked him at times, "Is that enough? Would you like some more?"

Kamao answered, "No, thank you." Lindsey participated in the small talk and answered a few of the gossiping ladies' questions.

"He is so cute. How long has it been?" Mrs. Goddard asked, leaning over to talk to her. "Have you been to Africa yet? It's so beautiful. Just be careful with the mosquitoes, they are merciless. And they give you this thing called *palu* in Senegal. I don't know what that is."

"It's malaria," Dave McPherson completed.

"It wasn't too bad," Kamao said when Lindsey was driving him back to his apartment.

"I am sorry, baby, but I am not in the mood."

"It's OK, my love. Don't let what your father did put you down like that."

"How come you are not upset about this?"

"To be honest with you, you are all that matters to me. Yes, your father's approval would be a blessing, but you truly are the only person who matters to me in this relationship."

"You are truly special, baby. You are an amazing guy. But my father can make life difficult for us, for you, and I am worried about that. That's why I wanted him to show me that he won't cause any problem, and it seems like things are not going the way I hoped."

"I love you, and your father cannot stop that. You can be sure of it," Kamao said after a moment of silence. Then only the humming of the engine could be heard. They spent the remainder of the trip wondering what was going to happen to their burgeoning love.

PART III

DANIA: ROUND TRIP

Chapter 11

Manuel's funeral was short. Only a few people attended, mostly family members, as several of his friends feared for their own life if members of M18 discovered their acquaintance with the deceased. Dania was dressed in all black, her face covered with a black veil. Junior sat next to his mother, quiet, wondering what would become of him and his mother now that his father was gone. For a four-year-old, Junior was a brilliant kid; he understood things most kids his age didn't. He told his friends his uncle Lazo, who lived in America, sent him a tablet and video games, and that made his friends jealous. They would come over to play with him, and he would show them how to use different electronic devices. He clung to his mother and didn't let go of her hand throughout the ceremony. Dania's eyes were swollen from crying and mourning her boyfriend. She loved Manuel.

They met during Dania's medical lab technician internship at Rosales National Hospital in San Salvador. She went to Manuel's room to collect a blood sample for lab work. Manuel was awake and was going through his contact list on his phone, wondering who his next customer would be.

"Good morning, Mr. Rodriguez. I am Dania; I am here to get some blood from you for the lab. Dr. Sanchez told you earlier that someone will be coming, right?"

"I am relieved that I am going to suffer in the hands of a beautiful girl," he said.

Dania turned to him and said, "Thank you," with a courteous smile.

"What's your name?"

"Dania."

"You have a beautiful name, a beautiful face, and a beautiful smile. I am delighted to make your acquaintance today."

"You better stop making me blush. You know I have a needle in my hand, right?"

"Right," he quickly said. "I will be quiet." As Dania stuck the needle inside his arm, Manuel screamed. "Ouch! Ouch! She is trying to kill me! You are trying to kill me. You are evil. What did I do to you?" Dania burst out laughing as her attempt at getting ahold of herself failed. Her distraction didn't, however, prevent her from accomplishing her task with success. A nurse ran inside, alarmed by the howling, and quickly realized that the patient was just putting on a show to get the girl's attention and make her laugh. And he succeeded.

"Stop yelling! You are drawing too much attention!" Dania said. "You're going to get me in trouble if you keep that up. How did you get malaria anyway? I thought we didn't have that around here."

"I went to Guatemala last week," he said.

"What were you doing in Guatemala that you couldn't protect yourself from mosquitoes?"

"I took a car to a client. I sell cars, good cars. Sometimes I drive the car to the customer because that can get me more sales."

"So you are a good businessman," Dania concluded, pretending not to care too much.

"You can say that!" As she was getting ready to leave the room, he said, "Look, Dania, I like you, but I like to be a real gentleman, and I don't want to do anything to annoy you and make you hate me. I would like to keep in touch with you if that's OK." She smiled and wrote her phone number on a piece of paper, folded it, and put it on the table next to him.

"You could have handed it to me," he said.

"Don't ask for too much; you might ruin your chances," she replied, her back turned to him, allowing him to contemplate her small-sized body.

"Good to know," he teased back.

When Junior was born, Manuel couldn't contain his joy. He called all his siblings in El Salvador and elsewhere in Central and South America. He told them how happy he was to be a father and that his son was a healthy and robust baby who looked just like him.

"I would do anything for both of you, *Mamita*. I promise you: I will do anything to make you happy," he said to Dania.

"I know you will, Manuel, I know you will," Dania replied, cuddling the cooing baby. "I love you, Manuel. You're crazy, but I love you. I don't want anybody else." He kissed her on the forehead and kissed the baby on the cheek. "But I am scared," Dania added.

"What? What are you scared about?"

"What future does this baby have in this country? With the violence and the gangs . . . what is he going to become? Why don't we go to the United States? We'll have a better life there."

"*Mamita*, there are gangs everywhere, even in the Uni—"

"I know, I know that. But it's safer; it's better there. The United States is a country of law and justice. We won't have to fear for our lives every day. I can go to school and become a nurse, get a better job, and not worry about my life being permanently in danger. Before this baby, it was just a vague thought, but now, I can't stop thinking about it. I am scared for my baby; I am scared for us." Manuel had downplayed her plea to immigrate to the United States, insisting that he had a good business and could take care of them—until the death of Dania's mother, who had refused to raise the amount of her *renta*.

"How do we do it? How do we go to the United States?" he asked.

"Lazo can help us. He will find a way," Dania said. "There is no guarantee it will work for us, but people have tried and have succeeded. We can only try and hope that it works for us too."

"OK! But I bet that thing costs a lot of money; I heard that people lose money, a lot of it, trying to go to America."

"I know; it is true, but please! Let's try it."

Manuel's death came as a shock to many. He was a kind, genuine, and fun guy to be around. He knew how to deal with demanding customers. He knew how to convince a doubtful car buyer, who walked into his dealership uncertain, to leave with the assurance of getting the best deal ever. Drago, his associate, found him dead, a bullet hole in the side of his head, one morning as he entered the office at the dealership. Drago told Dania that he heard Manuel and some guys arguing the night before in the office, and he was telling them that things were tight and that he couldn't afford to give their boss more money.

"He told me after they left that he was saving money to buy a house and marry you and couldn't afford to pay one thousand dollars to the mobsters' boss. I am pretty sure they were not happy about his answer and came back." Dania knew that Manuel couldn't tell Drago he was spending the money trying to get them out of the country. She felt guilty for what happened to her boyfriend, the father of her son. If she hadn't convinced him about moving to America, maybe he would still be alive.

Dania's phone rang. "It is Uncle Lazo; I need to take it, baby," she said to Junior. "Let go of my hand so I can talk to him." Junior complied and let his mom pick up the phone.

"Dania, how did things go, my dear?" Lazo said.

"I don't know what to do, Lazo. I am all alone. I don't know what to do. He's gone; they took my love."

"Stop crying, please. Where are you right now?"

"We are just leaving the funeral home. They took my Manuel."

"Where is Junior?" Dania gave the phone to her son, unable to contain her sobs.

"Hi, Junior. How are you, my little man?"

"OK," Junior said, calmly.

"Be strong, OK, my man? Be very strong for mommy, OK?"

"OK, Uncle Lazo."

"All right, let me talk to your mom." Junior gave the phone back to his mother.

"*Prima*! Please don't give up. I am still fighting for you. Something will come up; I am certain of it. We have to keep the faith, OK? I'll call you later. Be strong, my dear."

"OK, Lazo, bye," Dania said, inconsolable.

Chapter 12

Kamao was at work when Ayefumi called and told him that they needed to talk when he got home, and when he did, it was almost midnight. Ayefumi was waiting for him in the living room with the TV on.

"What's up, Aye! Is everything OK, bro?" Kamao asked as he entered the apartment.

"Yes, everything is fine. It's about Lazo."

"What happened to Lazo?"

"Nothing happened to Lazo; he's fine. Do you remember what he said about him trying to bring his cousin Dania here with no success?"

"Yes," Kamao said. He put his backpack on the floor and sat on the couch.

"Well, he came across a new network and he believes it'll work this time."

"What makes him believe it'll work this time?"

"He works with this guy called Ramon, who said he knows some people in government who help people get their visa and become legal residents, even citizens."

"Really? People in the American government?"

"Yes, but apparently it's a secret network, and they do things very discreetly."

"And they just help people like that? With nothing in return?"

"Oh, no! There's money involved, all right! And a lot of it. That's why I wanted to talk to you. You remember when you told Lazo to let you know if he needed anything for Dania? This is it, Kamao. He couldn't come to you with something like this since you guys are not that close, and he said he didn't have many friends he could talk to about this. He told me, and I'm unable to help him with this all by myself. So I decided to tell you about it to see if you could help."

"I'm thirsty," Kamao said. He went to the kitchen, came back with a bottle of water, and sat back down. "So, you think this is legit?" he asked. "I mean, I want to help Lazo and Dania, I really do. But I have a problem with the secret network you're talking about. You don't know if it can be trusted."

"I believe it's legit," Ayefumi said, and as he sensed hesitation on his friend's part, he added, "Look, Kamao, you remember how I looked out for you when you came to this country? Lazo did the same for me. He helped me just like I helped you. He wasn't even from the same motherland as you and I. He found a job for me; he let me sleep in his apartment for months, rent-free. He gave me his food; he gave me money when I was broke. He is a real brother to me, just from another continent."

It was apparent to Kamao that Ayefumi wouldn't come to him with this boldness if he didn't take the situation seriously. He sighed and said, "OK! What do you expect from me?"

"I was wondering if you could talk to Lindsey to see if she would be willing to help. You've said a lot of great things about her, how sympathetic and caring she is, and I . . . I am hoping she could help us. And before you say anything, I thought about this thoroughly before bringing it up. I know you're not in the relationship for her money. I wouldn't even mention her name if I wasn't desperate."

Kamao shook his head, a smile on his face. "You knew exactly what I was going to say, so you said it yourself, very smart. Aye, I've never seen you come out this boldly. I always admire your sincerity, but I am disappointed that you think you can use me to get Lindsey to do you favors like this. Please don't ever do that again."

"Noted. I'm sorry," Ayefumi said.

"And what made you think I can't help you myself?"

"I didn't know if you could or would be willing to because this is a lot of money. But if you could, that would be great."

"How much is it?" Kamao asked.

"Five grand."

"Five thousand dollars?"

"Yes, that's the amount we are looking for."

Kamao squeezed the water bottle a couple of times. "I might be able to help," he said after a moment of silence.

"Wait a second!" Ayefumi said incredulously. "You have five thousand dollars right now?"

"Yes. I mean not right now, but I can gather it in a couple of days. And it is not Lindsey's money; it is my money."

"If you say it's your money, I believe it's your money." Ayefumi looked at his friend with attention and curiosity. "I know your family is rich . . . but five thousand just like that? You're amazing, Kamao. Thank you!"

Lazo could hardly restrain his emotion when he came over a few days later to take the money. "Thank you, Kamao," he said. "You don't know what this means to me." He took the brown bag from Kamao and counted the hundred-dollar bills. "I've been sending Dania six hundred dollars every month since Manuel's death, and I can't do it anymore, and they . . . they are getting impatient." Ayefumi and Kamao knew exactly who he meant by "they." Lazo looked at the bag in his hand, wiped some tears away, then continued. "Some of them know her connection to me. She's been OK until now because a high school crush, who's one of them, is holding off the move on her."

"Why can't she just move?" Ayefumi asked.

"They've moved a couple of times already with her aunt and Junior, but if the gangs are really looking for you, it's only a matter of time before they find you." He paused for a few seconds and said, "Thank you, Kamao. She'll start paying the money back as soon as she gets here and finds a job, and if she doesn't pay it back for some reason, or if this whole thing doesn't work, it'll become my debt, and I will pay you back." He took a folded paper out of his back pocket and handed it to Kamao. "Please read this and tell me if you're fine with it."

Kamao read the debt contract and nodded at Lazo with a smile.

Lazo was nervous, sitting in the large, nicely decorated office in downtown DC. There were pictures from different regions of the world. Lazo was able to guess a few: a large Indian tiger was chasing a gazelle on a brown and gray floormat. A picture on the wall showed the owner of the office on a safari in the Serengeti National Park in Northern Tanzania. Another photo showed him in the Amazon forest, posing in the middle of some half-naked indigenous women and children. Lazo wondered why Steve Bradford kept an office outside the White House and concluded that the Deputy National Security Advisor probably deemed it appropriate to conduct his private business away from the West Wing. He heard the door open behind him, and a middle-aged man entered the room with a broad smile on his face.

"Good afternoon. Sorry I am late. I was in an important meeting. How are you?" the man asked and shook Lazo's hand.

"I am doing well, sir, thank you for agreeing to see me," Lazo said, trembling.

"You are from Ramon's crew, right? You are Lazo."

"Yes, sir," Lazo said, worried that he was probably going to ask him for some documentation, take his green card away, and send him back home.

"Those people are powerful," Ramon had told him. "You don't mess with them. They will crush you like an annoying bug. You simply say 'Yes sir, yes ma'am' when they talk to you."

"You guys did a good job in my new house the other day," the man said. "All the cameras have good angles, and the images are high quality. Good job!"

"Thank you, sir," Lazo said, confused. He looked at the name plate on the table; it said: Don Ashton, Attorney at Law. It was clear the man he was talking to wasn't Steven Bradford, the man who Ramon said works with the president.

"Do you have a photo of your cousin?"

"Yes, sir, here it is." Lazo took a photo of Dania and Junior out of his wallet.

"This is nice," Don said. "Is that her kid?"

"Yes, sir."

"Well, that looks nice, but do you have other pictures of her alone?"

"I believe I do," Lazo said, and searched his bag.

"Ramon told you to bring some pictures, right?"

"Yes, sir, he did . . . here, here it is."

"Oh, this one looks nice. She is pretty," he said, staring at the picture of Dania in a white skirt with a blue top. "What's her name?"

"Her name is Dania."

"She's your cousin?"

"Yes, sir."

"Would you give me a second, please?"

"Sure," Lazo said.

Don got up, went to a room adjacent to the office, remained there for a few minutes, then came out and said, "I think we can help her out. Tell me a little bit about her and her situation." Lazo told him about Manuel's death and how Dania's own life was in jeopardy.

"OK, it looks like she has a strong enough case. This is how it's going to work," Don Ashton said. "She will be issued a visitor's visa for three months, then, once she gets here, we will start the process for her asylum application. Does that sound OK?"

"Yes, sir. Thank you very much," Lazo said, excited for his cousin.

"So you'll send her an invitation—and I will show you how to do that—then in about a month, she will receive a phone call from the embassy in your country for her interview. You will have to manage for her flight, and we will take care of her once she gets here."

"No problem, sir, thank you," Lazo said.

"Now, do you have the money?"

"Yes, sir, here it is." Lazo removed the brown bag from his backpack and took out the money Kamao gave him. Don counted the bills, zooming through them like a skilled accountant. "This is five thousand," he said. "It should be eight thousand dollars."

"Eight thousand?" Lazo exclaimed incredulously, disappointed.

"No worries," Don said. "We can still start the process, and you can bring the rest later; but you should bring it before the month ends. If not, come back and take your money."

"OK, sir, no problem. I will come back with the other three thousand."

"And remember: never talk about this to anyone and don't send anyone to me. If you need anything, you go through Ramon."

"I understand, sir. Thank you!" Lazo said and left the office, wondering what hellish chasm he gotten himself into. He called Ramon. "You didn't tell me I was meeting some else and not Steven Bradford."

"What do you think, man? That the Deputy National Security Advisor would meet you in person and talk to you about some illegal immigration shit? He operates through a middle person. I gave you his name just so you know this is legit, and you better not say a word to anyone. It's my life on the line, and now yours too. Do you understand, *amigo*?"

"Of course, Ramon. I understand."

"Don't worry, man! Your cousin will be here in no time. She is not the first one, you know! Bradford will just make one phone call, and she will be here with you safely. She will find a job. Did I tell you they will help her find a job too?"

"Yeah!"

"Then she can send for her kid once her papers are out. Just chill, bro: everything will be fine. You'll see."

"All right, man! Thank you." Lazo said. Since he lived in a one-bedroom apartment, he had arranged a place for Dania with an old friend, a girl from Zacatecas, Mexico. She had a two-bedroom apartment and agreed to have Lazo's cousin as a roommate.

Chapter 13

Dania was covering a shift for a friend at the hospital when her phone rang. "Hello," she said.

"Hi," the voice on the other side of the line said. "Is this Dania Morelo Rivera?"

"Yes," Dania said, nervous, as she suspected where the call was from.

"I am calling from the United States embassy. This call is to inform you that an interview is scheduled for you next Thursday at 10:00 a.m. Can you make it?"

"Yes . . . yes," Dania said, still nervous but excited. Her heart was still pounding after she hung up. Was this it? she wondered. Was she going to America this time? She had applied for visas in the past and was denied every time. What would be different this time? she thought. Would Lazo's new connection pay off? The questions kept zooming through her head; she sat down, bewildered.

Junior refused to let his mother go when Dania was getting ready to head to the airport. This time it was real; she was going to America. "Don't worry, my love. Once I get my papers, I will come back and take you with me to America, OK?" Her son wouldn't have anything to do with that promise. He hung onto his mother, crying as if he would never see her again.

"It's OK, Junior, let Mama go. She will be back; she will come back for you," Aunty Graciela said.

"Mama, don't leave me; I want to go with you," he cried out.

Dania couldn't hold back her tears, but she knew she was doing the right thing for her son's future. She had to leave; she couldn't take him, not yet. She only had a three-month visitor's visa. Once there, she would apply for asylum and get a legal status; that's what Lazo said. The trip to the airport felt like a long journey she thought would never end. She felt the urge to tell the driver to stop the car so that she could run home and hug her son one more time. The trip to America was a combination of joy and pain for Dania, who couldn't stop thinking about the son she left behind.

"I hope you had a nice trip," Don said as he shook Dania's hand.

"Yes, I did. Thank you, sir."

"Your cousin has done a great job getting you here. You should be proud of him."

"I am. Thank you!" Dania said.

"So, what we have done for you is that we have reserved a job for you as a housekeeper at a hotel here in DC, where you will be working until your paperwork is ready. Then you can go your way and do whatever you want." Don turned to Lazo and asked, "Do you know the Coal Master Hotel downtown?"

"Yes," Lazo said.

"That's where she will be working. She will be paid in cash for now, then when her papers are out, she will have the legal documents that will allow her to do many things. However, if you find something better for her right now, that's fine, but she will be on her own for her asylum application; we don't want anything traced back to us."

"We understand everything. Thank you very much for your kindness, sir! My cousin and I are very grateful to you," Lazo said.

"No worries," Don said. Turning to Dania, he said, "You will get a chance to meet your benefactor—you know, the person who did all of this for you—you will meet him soon, and you can thank him yourself, OK?"

"OK, thank you," Dania said. Lazo and Dania got up, shook Don's hand, and left. Don put the packet that Dania brought for her asylum application on top of a pile of folders on his desk. The cold drizzle of February got Dania wet and shivering as they walked back to the car. She held the collar of her coat tight, almost choking herself. She wished she had waited until summer to come to America. She jumped into the car just as Lazo unlocked it. He turned on the heat, laughing at her.

"You wanted to come to the United States, right? You're here now." They both laughed. Dania blew into her hands.

"It's so cold."

"Kamao and Ayefumi have organized a small party for you this evening," Lazo said. When they arrived at Kamao's and Ayefumi's apartment after some grocery shopping, the smell of baked chicken mingled with some hot mac 'n' cheese welcomed them.

Ayefumi opened the door with a smile. "Welcome to the United States, Dania!"

"Thank you," Dania said. Lazo entered first and hung his jacket in the closet next to the front door, then helped his cousin hang hers.

"Here are my friends. You've already talked to them; now you're meeting them in person. Here is Ayefumi, and there is Kamao." Dania greeted them with a handshake and a kiss on the cheek.

"I hope you had a nice trip," Kamao said.

"It was delightful, thank you. Also, thank you for the money you lent me. You're very kind. I'll work to pay you back."

"No worries, there is no rush. Whenever you can."

"The food is delicious," Lazo said, tearing apart a chicken thigh. "You guys are great cooks."

"This is good; thank you," Dania said.

"You are welcome. And we are sorry for what happened to Manuel," Ayefumi said, pouring some sparkling grape juice into her cup.

Dania told her new friends about the situation back home and about her son. Kamao listened to her story. She seemed like a decent person with a poised attitude. She chose her words carefully, and Kamao began to admire her good manners. Her English wasn't bad, he thought. He found her beautiful, with her long dark hair nicely tucked into a ponytail. He was happy he could help her.

Dania had been working at the Coal Master Hotel for about a month, and she liked the job. Many of her coworkers liked her; they found her sweet, as she always helped anyone who needed help and never complained about a thing. She noticed that the guys looked at her with a particular attention, but she tried not to give anyone the wrong idea. She heard them whisper things about her sometimes when she walked by, like the day when James and Nathan, two maintenance boys, were moving a couch in the lobby, and James said, "This girl is so hot! Look at that body! Wow. Small and firm!"

"Shut up and pull, sex addict!" Nathan said.

"I can't help but appreciate the good stuff, unlike you."

Dania was making the bed on the fourth floor for a coworker who was on break when Kurt, the hotel manager, knocked on the door.

"Hey, Dania, when you finish here, go to room 213 in hall B, OK? I will ask Celine to continue on this floor." Hall B was one of Dania's regularly assigned halls on the second floor. That's where the VIP rooms were, and 213 was one of them. Celine was a girl from Haiti who didn't talk much. She helped whoever needed help but only gave short answers whenever a coworker wanted to engage in a conversation with her. She was an elementary school teacher in Port-au-Prince before coming to the US. She'd been working at the Coal Master for a while.

"OK," Dania replied. She finished making the bed and went to hall B and knocked on the door.

"Come in," a voice said inside the room. Dania opened the door and saw a man sitting on the bed, a severe look on his face. He was reading a message on his phone. She stood next to the door, wondering what she was there for.

"Can I help you with something, mister?" she asked. The man looked at her and smiled. He stood up, walked to her, and shook her hand; he had a firm grip. He looked like an important person in his dark blue suit with a lapel pin on the collar of his jacket.

"I am Steve Bradford." Dania recognized the face; she'd googled the name when Lazo told her that the person helping her was Bradford, a man who worked with the president. "Does that ring a bell?"

"Yes," Dania said.

"Can I see your phone for a second?" Dania gave him her phone. He turned it off and put it on the dresser.

"You had a nice trip, I believe."

"Yes, I did," Dania said.

"Now, you can't tell anyone about me, about what I am doing for you. I am going to help you with your paperwork. You want to become a legal resident, right?"

"Yes . . . sir," Dania said, starting to get nervous as the man looked around the room, scrutinizing everything.

"I can help you with that; that's not a problem for me. But we are going to have an agreement; are you OK with that?"

"Y . . . es, sir," Dania said, trembling. The man stood in front of her. He was tall with thick dark hair and some gray spots. He must be approaching his sixties, Dania thought. He looked at her for a moment, grabbed his briefcase on the bed, opened it, and took out a brown folder.

"Open it and see," he said and handed her the envelope. She took it and opened it. Her picture was on top of a form that read I-589, Application for Asylum and for Withholding of Removal.

"Thank you, sir," she said with controlled excitement. Bradford gently took the file back from her.

"We just need to send this form to the proper agency, and you won't need to worry about anything else. I would take care of the rest."

"Thank you very much, sir, thank you!"

"You're welcome. Do you wonder why I am doing this for you?" Bradford said and walked toward her.

"No . . . sir," Dania said, shaking, beginning to suspect where things were heading.

"Well, you are lovely. I don't usually do this for everybody. I just help them with the visa, and I don't worry about anything else; I let somebody else do the rest. But you, when I saw your picture . . . I couldn't help it. I wanted to do more for you." Dania stepped back and hit the dresser behind her. She wanted to scream but couldn't. It would mean the end of her dream. She had dreamed of a safe life in America where her son could have a good education, away from M18. She had dreamed about going to school in America and getting a nursing degree. A scream would put all of that in jeopardy.

"Please, sir . . . can I do something else to thank you? Please!"

"Come on, don't do that! I don't want to hurt you; I want us to have an understanding, an agreement." He put his arms under her beige uniform and started rubbing her shoulders. "Do we have an agreement? Come on; answer me!" His breathing began to accelerate as he pressed her against his chest. Dania folded her arms to protect her breasts. He was becoming impatient, unable to wait for an answer. He started kissing her on her head and her cheeks. He turned her around and pulled her toward him. Dania was stuck between the dresser and the muscular man. She remained quiet, hoping that he would come back to his senses and let her go.

When she got back to the apartment, she ran into the shower, hoping to clean any remaining sticky liquid between her legs. A pregnancy would ruin her dreams, she thought. She stayed in the shower for an hour, crying and in pain. She didn't eat dinner that night; she crawled into her bed into a fetal position and cried all night. The next day, she didn't go to work; she didn't call in either. Kurt called her phone, and she didn't pick it up even when she recognized the hotel's number. She wondered about what her next move should be. She didn't imagine anything like this happening to her. She had been in the country for barely two months, and she already needed to decide to either stay or go back to her gang-infested country where she would face certain death if the word got out that she came back from America. Aunty Graciela had left San Salvador with Junior to go live with her sister Maribel in Santa Ana, one of the safest cities in the country, in the western coastal region. Since Dania was no longer working at the hospital, there was no need to stay in the capital. Dania was mad at herself and at the world. She should have fought back—why didn't she fight back? She should have done something: scream, scratch him. She wondered if what happened was the plan from the beginning and if Lazo was part of it. She quickly dropped the last assumption. She felt ashamed for even thinking that Lazo could have set her up like that. She trusted him with her life. Lazo had sacrificed a lot and had gone through a lot for her; he would never do something like that to her. But she wanted to blame someone. Yes, she blamed herself for not fighting back, but there must be someone else. She got out of the bed and took a shower, but still felt the large, filthy hands on her skin. She went into the kitchen. Her roommate had left early, as usual. She took a large kitchen knife, looked at it, contemplated it, and turned it around. Her pain had turned into bitterness, but with that knife in her hand, she felt her weakness going away and a strange power taking over her. She thought about how the blade could stop her pain right there, in that kitchen. She suddenly threw the knife away and began panting heavily. "Oh my God! Oh my God! Junior, I am sorry, I am sorry, baby." She dropped to the kitchen floor, in tears.

She stayed in her room for the rest of the day. At 8:00 p.m., she poured herself some apple juice and ate two muffins. Her phone rang; it was Lazo. She picked it up but wouldn't say a word.

"Hello, *prima. ¿Qué pasa?*" Lazo said.

"Hi, Lazo," she replied, in a quiet voice.

"Sorry, I haven't called you today. I was busy, but I will see you tomorrow, OK?"

"I will be doing a double shift tomorrow," she lied.

"OK, I will see you on your day off."

"OK, that's fine." When Lazo went to see her two days later, it didn't take him a long time to realize that there was something wrong. Her face was swollen, her hair scattered, and she avoided eye contact with him.

"What is wrong, cuz?" Lazo asked.

"*Nada*," she said.

"What do you mean, '*nada*'? I've never seen you like this; you're freaking me out right now."

"If I had known this was what was waiting for me here, I wouldn't have come to this country," she finally said in a bitter voice.

"What is the matter? Dania, just talk to me, please!" Lazo said, concerned.

"Did you have anything to do with this, Lazo? Tell me the truth." She couldn't contain her tears.

"You know I would never do anything to hurt you! What is it, Danita?" Lazo held her in his arms; she was inconsolable.

"*Hijo de puta*," Lazo said. "I can't believe this! I thought they just wanted money. Ramon told me there was nothing to worry about. *¡Puta mierda!*" Lazo got up and started pacing in circles, breathing heavily.

"Lazo, please calm down!" Dania said, worried about what was going through her cousin's mind. She had never seen him like that before either. She knew him to be a calm, reasonable guy. Lazo left the apartment, slamming the door.

When Lazo arrived at the Live Sense Security System, LLC, Ramon was in his office, talking to some employees. Lazo patiently waited for him to finish and rushed in as the two guys came out. Ramon was heading toward the door when Lazo rushed in and stood in front of him.

"Hey, Amigo, *¿qué pas*—?" Lazo sent a strong punch that landed on Ramon's upper lip, busting it open. Ramon tumbled and fell behind his desk, knocking his chair out of the way. He got up, grabbed a tissue, and started to wipe the blood off his lip. "What was that for?" he said. "You know I can shoot you right here, right now, right? You came to my office and assaulted me."

His secretary, a frail middle-aged woman, alerted by the commotion, rushed in. Seeing the boss bleeding, she said, "Do you want me to call the police, Ramon?"

"No, don't call anyone," Ramon said. "Please close the door behind you."

"What fishy business do you have going on? What did you get my cousin into?" Lazo said.

"What the fuck are you talking about, man?"

"Don't play dumb with me. That Bradford son of a bitch raped my cousin in that hotel she is working at."

"What does that have to do with me?"

"Are you going to tell me you didn't know about this? You guys have some kind of network to exploit and abuse women you help come to this country, don't you?"

"I have no idea what they do to the women. I just help out and get my money. No one told me anything like this before. If he raped her, why didn't she go to the police or something?" He paused and grimaced as he patted his split lip with a clean tissue. "I need to go to the hospital. Don't ever set foot in my office again, or I will shoot you right on the spot, and don't ever call me again, ever! Even if I'm desperate, you'll be the last person I will call to help me with my crew. You can go find someone else to punch in the face." Ramon walked out of the office, leaving Lazo wondering about what to do next. He would have no problem finding another contractor to work with until he could start his own company. But what to do about Dania's situation?

Chapter 14

Dania didn't go to work for almost a week. Her phone had stopped ringing; Kurt had stopped calling. She started to feel better; she began to recover. The thought of her son and the good that her being in America—her becoming a legal citizen in America—could do for him helped her get better and stronger. Lazo came over at five thirty as he said. Dania made him some *pupusas* the way he liked them.

"Mmm, this is delicious, just like back home," he said. After gobbling down three *pupusas*, he put the plate on the kitchen counter and said, "What are we going to do now?"

"I had some time to think, and I don't believe I have a choice but to go back to work. I will go back tomorrow. I can't go back to El Salvador; what would become of Junior and me? And you gave Kamao your word that we're going to pay him back. I must go back to work. There's a lot at stake if I don't go."

"What if Bradford comes back?"

"I don't know, and I don't want to think about that."

"We can go to the police, but would they take your word against that of a powerful man like that son of a bitch? Besides, they may want to check your status, and your visa is expiring soon."

"I understand all of that," Dania said. "That's why I don't want to think about it and just get back to work and see what comes next."

"You don't have to go back to that hotel, *prima*," Lazo said. "I can find something else for you to do. There are plenty of jobs you can do without papers."

"Yeah, but would I have the same opportunity to get my asylum application approved? You heard what Don Ashford said. If I go somewhere else, I am on my own." Lazo sighed, feeling sorry for his cousin, wondering what else he could do to help her. He started to feel desperate.

"I don't even know if they'll take you back at the hotel," he said. "You haven't been to work for almost a week."

"I know; I will go and hear what they have to say."

"You're very strong, *prima*! You are." Lazo said to his cousin, looking at her with admiration. "I am so sorry; I wish I could do more." He hugged her and held her tight.

When Dania went back to work the next day, everybody was looking at her as if she were a ghost coming back from the kingdom of the dead. She expected Kurt to call her to his office to admonish her. She thought he would threaten to fire her, but that didn't happen. Kurt avoided eye contact with her the whole day.

"Your assignment sheet is on your locker in the break room," he said, looking earnestly at something on the screen at the reception desk. Dania thought he was delaying the meeting with her on purpose, but nothing happened during the entire shift, and in the middle of it she had a strange feeling after talking with Celine: Kurt knew what Bradford did to her. He had arranged it; he knew the right time. She saw herself as a fly caught in an immense spider web needing to find its way out. She was making the bed in room 211 in hallway B on the second floor when Celine walked in.

"Hi, can I come in?" she asked.

"Yes, of course."

"I was worried about you when I didn't see you the past few days. I don't have your number to call to check on you. Are you doing OK?"

"I am fine. Thank you!" Dania said, wondering what Celine's deal was. She came in, closed the door, walked to the other side of the bed, and started to tuck the sheet in. "I usually don't get into people's business, and I don't like small talk, which often turns into gossip, but I noticed something different about you. I like you. I am not saying I am better than everyone else. I just think that talking to people with no real purpose is not for me. Those kinds of talks get you into trouble, you know? But I think that things will be different with you. I feel like we can understand each other." She paused to let Dania respond, or at least nod, but Dania did neither, waiting to see where Celine's palaver was heading.

"Well," Celine continued, determined to get her point across regardless of Dania's silence or pretended indifference, "I suspected what happened to you, and when you stayed home all those days after Bradford was here, I knew I was right. Look," she said, holding Dania's hand. "Please stop for a second." Dania put the pillowcase she had in her hand on the bed and stood, looking at Celine, her arms crossed.

"What do you think happened to me?" Dania asked.

"He forced himself on you, didn't he?"

"Why did you say that?"

"Did he not?" Dania ignored the question, looking down. "Never mind. Forget I said anything," Celine said and headed to the door.

"Wait!" Dania said. "If you know what happened to me, then would you serve as a witness if I press charges? Would you help me report it to the police?"

"Don't be a fool, girl!" Celine said. "What kind of proof do I have? Was I in the room with you?"

"So how could you know if anything happened?"

"This is not my first day here."

"So he did it to other people too? Did he do it to you?"

"Don't ask me stupid questions like that. You will not get the answer you want. All I can tell you is that you must think about what is important to you. You have to choose between losing the fight against a powerful man in Washington and getting sent back where you came from or working your way through this and getting what you came here for. Because if you lose the fight, or if they find out that you are trying to get them into trouble, they will send you back to your country before you realize what has happened to you. Some people came into this country and became legal residents and citizens without too much trouble; you and I are not that lucky. Now, you have three options here: One, you can pack up your things and go back to your country; two, you can leave this job but stay in America and run every time you see a cop car pulling into a parking lot; or three, you can find a way to manage through your ordeal and survive it to see your asylum approved and see yourself on your way to becoming a US citizen. Other people did it; it's up to you. Bradford and his friends do keep their word, you know! You will get your papers if you play this right."

"So he did it to other people!"

"Well, I can promise you: you are not the first one."

"How do you know all of this and you're still here?

"Now, if you want me to help you, don't ask me too many questions about myself, I don't like spilling my beans, but I will tell you one thing. I got my papers; I'm just keeping this job a little longer to . . . you know, save a little bit. But I will be leaving soon. I have my plans. You know a little about me now, so you better keep that to yourself." Celine said those last words looking around like there were other people in the room she didn't want to hear their conversation.

"Thank you for telling me all of this, Celine," Dania said. "What do I do now?"

"You have to make your own decisions. I gave you your options. Now, let me tell you one more thing: if he doesn't like you, he will not come back, but looking at you, I am pretty sure he will come back."

"What? No!" Dania said.

"What are you so afraid of? It's not like it was your first time, was it? Do you have a husband, a boyfriend?" Dania shook her head to both questions, arms crossed over her breasts, pulling back as to protect herself against an invisible Bradford. "Don't even think there would be any sign of him coming in and out of here. Every time he's gone, the surveillance footage is wiped clean of his presence. Now, you can still get some proof of him touching you, like finger-prints and other things, but he won't be stupid enough to leave a used condom behind." The thought of telling Celine that Bradford didn't use a condom the first time zoomed through Dania's mind, but she resolved not to mention it. She thought Celine would ask if he came inside her, and she would have to explain that it happened just as he pulled out, and she'd felt like her legs were stained for days regardless of the number of showers she took. "So, you have all the pieces of the puzzle; you can try to get him in trouble if you want, and you might succeed. But trying that will be to your peril," Celine said.

"Thank you!" Dania said as Celine opened the door.

Dania sat on the bed, perplexed. She knew that she had a decision to make and that that decision would define her future, in DC or in San Salvador.

After her conversation with Celine, she came up with an idea. She would make her way through her ordeal to get her papers, but she would also formu-late a plan to make Bradford pay for abusing her and undoubtedly other poor women. She called Lazo on her way home after her shift.

"Hi, cuz! What's up!" Lazo said.

"What are you doing this evening? I'm making some *empanadas* for dinner. Do you want to come over?"

"That sounds cool!" he said. Dania knew how to get Lazo's attention: cook his favorite foods.

"These *empanadas*, oh my gosh!" he said, after chomping down a couple of Dania's specialty. "So, how are things now at the hotel?" he asked.

"A girl who also works there told me some things today that I couldn't believe, but that made me realize that every problem has more than one solution; you just need to pick the one that works better for you."

"What are you talking about?" Lazo said.

"Bradford and his friends have, indeed, a secret evil network. They help girls get here, and they help them become legal residents and then citizens. They don't only charge money for their service, they also sexually abuse them."

"And no one is reporting them?" Lazo put his last *empanada* on the plate, his good mood fading.

"Unless we have a video recording or a sperm sample, nobody is going to believe an illegal alien over a senior US government official. I don't think he's going to leave anything around willingly. What he did to me, I don't think he planned it; I don't think he'll make that mistake again."

"What are you talking about, Dania? I don't like what you're saying."

"He'll be coming back, Lazo! Bradford is not done with me; he's coming back. And I can't let him get away with this. The other girls may have let him get away, but I won't."

"What do you mean he's coming back? And you're going to stay there and wait for him? I can find another job for you. Other people have gotten their papers and didn't have to go through that!"

"This guy hurt people; he hurts girls! And he hurt me; I want him to pay. He has to pay! I will get my papers, but I still want him to pay."

"So the girl who told you about this has been through it too?"

"I'm pretty sure she did, although she won't tell me."

"Something's got to be done about this!"

"Exactly! That's why I need your help, Lazo!"

"What do you mean?"

"I need you to place cameras in rooms 213 and 215."

"Are you out of your mind?" he said. "Dania! I can't believe you're talking like this."

"Some circumstances make people do things you won't believe, Lazo! I'm determined to make this guy pay. And I won't back down now." Lazo looked at his cousin with disdain, appalled by her suggestion.

"Are you telling me you want to let that son of a bitch do the same thing to you over and over again? Are you enjoying this?"

"Of course not! How can you say that?"

"What do you want me to say? The guy raped you, and you want to invite him for more."

"Who said anything about inviting? I told you he's going to come back because of what Celine told me, and I want to find a way to make him pay for what he's doing if he comes back. If he doesn't come back, good for me. I'll be safe, and I will get my papers. I want to be proactive, and I want to hurt him back; I want him to pay for what he's doing to other girls like me, whose only fault was to come to this country seeking a better life. I didn't ask for this, and I didn't deserve it; and I don't want to just forget about it. He has to be stopped." Lazo's disgust turned into empathy toward his cousin as she started sobbing. He hugged her, giving her gentle taps on the back.

"I am sorry! I understand what you are going through now. Please don't think I don't feel your pain. I just don't want you to get hurt anymore!"

"I may get lucky and things may not go as far as they did the first time. I will try to stall him, but I want him to pay no matter what. I want him to get caught doing something fishy, and I will wait till my papers are out, then I will bring everything out."

"OK! But how are we going to do this?"

"I'll find a way to get you to the two VIP rooms so you can place the cameras."

"And why those two rooms?"

"Because they are the only rooms with noise cancellation walls and other features a lot of people don't know about. Those are the only rooms people like Bradford use for their evil business. After the cameras are in place, I can only cross my fingers and hope for the best. Can you do it?"

"It might take me a couple of days, but I can do it."

"OK, a couple of days won't be a problem. Would the cameras fit anywhere in the room where no one can see them?"

"Nowadays, there are cameras of any size that can fit anywhere. If they have an opening in the ceiling, like a ceiling fan or a vent, that'll make things a lot easier. If you can take a picture of the bottom of the hotel's router, that'll give me all the information I need for a wireless connection. You can just download the app, and you will get the feed directly to your phone. We'll use motion-activated cameras; that'll be more effective, and they won't be recording twenty-four-seven."

"So that should work, right?"

"Yeah, it should." Lazo kissed her on the forehead. "I wish I could do more to help you, cuz," he said, fighting off his tears.

"You have done more than I can imagine, and I can never thank you enough."

Dania and Celine became work buddies, helping one another with their room assignments. It had been a week since Lazo installed the cameras, and Dania had been struggling to fight back the urge to tell Celine about them. Every time she came close to mentioning them, she remembered Lazo's warning: "Remember that what we're doing is illegal; if a word gets out, we are both finished." Celine was kind to Dania. She helped her, and now they shared little secrets.

"I told you Bradford will come back for you, didn't I? I saw him yesterday; how did it go?" Celine asked.

"You're so nosy!" They both laughed. "I finished him off with my hands before he went any further."

"You sneaky little . . ." Celine cleared her throat to avoid saying the words she thought might have offended her new friend.

"I know this will help me with my papers, but I still want to get him. I'll be keeping record of our encounter without him knowing," Dania said. Celine changed the topic as if the information her friend dropped was insignificant to her. But two days later, Bradford came back and called Dania to room 213.

"Can I see your phone for a second?" he asked, trying to hide his anger. Dania hesitated then gave it to him. He smashed it on the floor. Dania stood there with haggard eyes as the pieces flew in every direction. Bradford picked them up one by one, broke them all in half, and left the room. Dania, gasping, looked around for Celine to tell her about the incident, but she couldn't find her anywhere.

"She went home, she got sick," Kurt said.

Dania went home still in shock, unable to figure out what triggered Bradford's behavior. She wondered if he had found out about the cameras. But how would he have found out? she thought. Maybe he thought she had been recording their conversations on her phone, but how would he suspect that?

She kept trying to put the pieces together when Celine's sudden sickness hit her. The day before, Celine didn't seem too interested when Dania mentioned her plan to trap Bradford, but she was the only person she confided in about her project to expose him besides Lazo. The next morning, Dania was brushing her teeth when she heard the knock on the apartment's door. Her roommate opened it, and she heard a man call her name.

"Here I am!" she said, closing the bathroom door behind her. There were three people, two men and a woman in dark uniforms with Police ICE written on the left side of their vests.

"You are to come with us, ma'am," one of the male officers said. "We will wait for you to put something decent on. Cindy, would you please go in with her?" The female officer followed Dania to her room and waited by the door as she got dressed. Dania realized what was happening.

"May I please call my cousin?" she said in a pleading voice as tears started falling down her cheeks and her nose started running. "I need to call my cousin to say goodbye, please!"

"Please turn around and put your hands behind your back," the officer said, ignoring her plea. Dania was handcuffed and escorted out of the apartment. Her roommate stood by the door, speechless. "Please tell Lazo I am being deported!" Dania said to her.

Kamao was at work, stocking the chip shelves when he heard Beethoven's *Für Elise* in the front pocket of his jeans and reached for his phone. It was Lazo.

"Hi, Kamao, how are you?" he said.

"Not too bad," Kamao answered. "What about yourself? It's been a while."

"Yes, I know," Lazo said. "Would you be home tomorrow? I would like to come over and talk to you and Ayefumi."

"Yeah, that would be fine," Kamao said. "Tomorrow is my day off; that would be perfect."

"OK, see you then," Lazo replied.

"I am very sorry to bring this bad news, but Dania has been deported and can't pay the rest of your money. But as I said before, that becomes my debt now, and I will honor it. It's just going to take me some time, and I would appreciate your patience one more time." Kamao noticed how painful it was for Lazo to bring him the news about his cousin's misfortune. He looked at him, sighed, and gently tapped the back of his hand.

"Be strong, Lazo! I am sorry for what happened to Dania."

"How did that happen?" Ayefumi asked. "She came here when . . . in February, right? How could she be deported so fast?"

"She has only been here for a couple of months! What did she do that was so serious that they deported her so fast?" Kamao added.

Lazo sighed and looked at his friends, managing to fight back his tears. He took a deep breath. "The guy who helped her get the visa, the national security adviser, was sexually abusing her, and she threatened to report him, so he used his power to get rid of her. I'll never forgive myself for what happened to her. If I hadn't brought her here using that evil network, none of this would have happened."

"You didn't know, Lazo. You can't blame yourself," Ayefumi said. "All you did was try your best to help your cousin. I'm sure she knows that."

Kamao looked at Lazo with compassion and admiration for doing the best he could for his cousin. His loyalty and willingness to be grateful for what his aunt did for him was impressive, Kamao thought. He thought about Dania too and wondered what would happen to her now that she was sent back to the same insecurity she was running from. They had all dreamed about America but for different reasons. Unlike Kamao, Dania was seeking a haven, and she believed in America's ability to offer it. She thought she would be safe in the country she believed in, and she would have been if she hadn't come through Bradford's network.

Kamao had spent some time with her; not only did he find her attractive, but he was also seduced by her gentleness, her fine, polite, and thoughtful attitude. He remembered the few times they had a chance to talk, like when Dania got off work late one night during her first week at the hotel and there was no bus, and Lazo was doing a job in Connecticut. Lazo called Kamao and asked him if he could pick her up.

"Are you hungry?" Kamao asked when Dania got in the car.

"I am starving," she said. "I don't even know what I'm going to eat when I get home."

"Have you had a chance to visit DC since you've arrived?" he asked.

"No, not really."

"What do you say that we go eat something then visit one of the capital's breathtaking sites? The Washington Monument is closed at night, but most of the others are open twenty-four hours. However, if you are tired, we can do it another time."

"No; that's a great idea," she said. "This is going to be my weekend off anyway. I just don't know if I need to go home and change first . . ."

"Why? You look great like this."

Dania liked to keep her housekeeping uniform in her locker at work and change there instead of dragging it around town like other coworkers liked to do. Her blue jeans, rose-colored shirt, and gray sweater would do just fine for the late-night outing that Kamao planned for her. There were a few customers at Lincoln's Waffle Shop, one of the late-night restaurants in DC. The employees were fast and friendly, and Dania's ribeye, accompanied with some hash browns and iced tea, was delicious. For Kamao, an omelet and grilled cheese sandwich with some apple juice was a good choice for the night. He then took her to the Lincoln Memorial, and after taking a moment to contemplate and admire the iconic president, they sat down on the top step of the monument.

"I've always dreamed of moments like this: feeling like I am sitting on top of the world," Kamao said. Dania looked at him and smiled. "Can I ask you a question?" he asked.

"Yeah, sure!" she said.

"When you were thinking about a life in America, what were you hoping for that life? What was in your dream of America?"

"Wow," she said, and cleared her throat. "Do you really want to know?" He nodded.

"Well, I love my country, El Salvador, very much. And the life that I had, besides the . . . you know, the gang, the insecurity, was not bad. But with the recklessness and the corruption within the government that spread to the people, the incertitude of the future, every plan I made seemed uncertain. I've always worked hard in school; I was at the top of my class since third grade. I used to believe that I could accomplish anything. I wanted to become a doctor or a scientist to help people. As I was growing up, my fear of not getting where I wanted to be started to grow as well. When you see your loved ones taken away from you, just like that, and no one tries to know what happened and stop whoever did that, it's scary, you know?" She stopped for a moment to rest her trembling voice. Kamao tried not to interrupt her. After fighting back her tears, she continued, "When my mother was killed, I was devastated. I wanted to do something to change how things were going, but I was powerless, so I just wanted to get out. I wanted to go somewhere else, where people don't just do things without worrying about the consequences, you know?"

Kamao nodded and said, "Yes, I do."

"I know there's violence and gangs in America too, but there's also the chance, the opportunity for a better life. As time passed, I came to realize that many young people who join gangs back home believe it is the only life they can have, and sometimes that's true because they get severe punishment when they get caught and there's usually no chance for them to regain a normal life in society. But in America, there's always a second chance, you know? Look at Lazo."

"Right," Kamao said. "He came a long way. What fascinates you about America?"

"It's a country that offers hope, you know. When you believe that you can do something and you work hard for it, it's possible—not a guarantee, but possible for you to get there. And for me, that possibility, that chance, is all I need; it's all I want."

"And you seem to know a lot about America too."

"Oh yeah, when you want something, knowing or learning about it is not that hard."

"Lazo said you were a nurse or someone in the medical field back home?"

"Phlebotomist. I wanted to become a doctor. I knew I could get there, but things have changed. And later, after I had Junior, a life in America became my only dream, my only hope. Even if I don't become a doctor here, I can still get a good education and a good job. And I believe in the security that this country offers. People think twice before acting crazy because they know that the risk of getting in trouble is high. I wanted a safe place for my family, for Manuel and Junior." She stopped and wiped her tears with the back of her sleeve. He gently rubbed her back with one hand to comfort her.

"I admire your courage and your resiliency. I also admire your strong belief in what the United States can offer."

"Thank you," she said. "What about you? What can you tell me about yourself and your dream of America?"

"Hm, well, I will say that fate has been less harsh on me than you, and I am sorry for all the things that you've been through. In my country, things are different. Our problems are a bit different from yours. We don't have gang activities like in your country. Our problems mostly surround social welfare. A lot of people don't have clean water or a healthy sanitation system, especially in remote areas. Now, Ghana is doing better and continues to grow economically compared to other countries on the continent. My father has recently been appointed Health Secretary, and my mother is in wholesale business."

"Wow, congratulations on your father's appointment," Dania said.

"Thank you! Now, about America. I've always loved this country since I was a little kid, let's say in middle school. I received a nickname when I got to high school because of how obsessed I was with anything that concerned the United States. During geography and history lessons about the US, my teacher and my classmates turned to me for comments as if I knew about everything the lessons were about."

"Well, you gave them that impression, right?"

"I did! I just love how this country offers people so many options. You have a lot to choose from. You don't see that in many countries, even developed countries. I wanted to come here, live here, and have a family here."

"And how is that coming along?"

"What?"

"Family here."

"Oh, I'm far from starting a family, but I have a girlfriend."

"OK," she said with a smile. By the time Kamao dropped her off at her apartment that night, it was almost two o'clock in the morning. She took a shower and went to bed. She planned to sleep late.

Kamao enjoyed Dania's company and was saddened by her misfortune.

"What's going to happen to her now?" he asked Lazo. "She went back to the same place she was running from."

"They have moved to a different city, a little safer than where they were in San Salvador, but the bad guys will find out eventually."

"Hm. This is unfortunate. And that Bradford guy will get away with this and will keep doing the same thing to other girls," Ayefumi said.

"Well, if it would be a comfort, Lazo, I want you to forget about paying the rest of the money," Kamao said.

"No, no, no," Lazo retorted. "I gave you my word that I would pay you if anything happened, and now something happened, so I will pay you. You just need to give me some time."

"Lazo," Kamao said calmly, "I want you to know how proud I am of you right now; what you have done for your cousin is honorable. You are an honest and loyal person, and I am glad to be your friend. Your cousin had done a good job paying most of the money in the short period she had. What are friends for if I can't do my part to ease some of your pain in this moment of difficulty?" He paused and looked at Lazo, waiting for a response, but Lazo remained silent, struggling to hold in his tears. "You are going through a lot right now," Kamao continued, "so I want you to forget about the remaining . . . twelve hundred, right?"

"Yes, twelve hundred," Lazo said, and added, "Are you sure?"

"Of course," Kamao said. "I will prepare a loan forgiveness contract for us to sign tomorrow."

"Thank you!"

"You're welcome," Kamao said.

"Are you sure, Kamao?" Ayefumi asked in turn.

"Yes, don't worry about it, seriously. I will be fine without twelve hundred."

The flight back to San Salvador was a different experience for Dania. The handcuffs felt too tight under the gray blanket, and she could hardly move her hands to scratch her legs. Every movement she made drew the attention of the US marshal sitting next to her. She wondered what the other five deportees were thinking at the moment. She wondered if they were feeling as nauseous as she was. An area of the plane was reserved for them, and Dania couldn't escape the judgmental glance of the other passengers. To some, she was undoubtedly one of the pretty girls that criminal networks employed to do their dirty work, caught during a drug deal by an undercover DEA agent. To others, she was probably one of the millions of undocumented immigrants who had lowered her guard and landed in ICE's bucket. But for Dania, it was a broken dream, a dream full of hope for herself and her son, a dream now vanished, and those strangers on the plane would never know her story.

The lyrics of "America the Beautiful" ran on her lips as she quietly sang it, one of her favorite American melodies. She had memorized it by heart after watching celebrities sing it on TV during NFL games. She refused to believe that America had failed her. Many immigrants were successful in their attempt to gain asylum in the United States, and several of them now enjoyed the privileges that American citizenship granted them. She could have been one of them if it wasn't for the unexpectedly crooked network her cousin had used to get her into the country. Her application was probably not even submitted, she thought. "If her application for asylum was submitted or approved, she wouldn't have been deported," a friend of Lazo's, who was one of the lucky ones, had said when he learned about her misfortune. She still had faith in America and believed she could have had a good life with Junior. She had enjoyed her short time in the country. She missed sitting in the back of the city bus, contemplating the beauty of DC when going to work or going shopping. She liked the orderly fashion in which the items in the stores were organized; she got her shopping done in five or ten minutes when she was in a rush, as she knew exactly where every item was in her neighborhood supermarket. She was sure of one thing: it would be tough for her to go back to America. She had heard that once you get deported, it was almost a guarantee that you would never go back. She would miss America forever, she thought.

Her son and Aunty Graciela were waiting in the arrival hall. The marshal agreed to remove her cuffs before she met her son.

"I understand," the marshal said. "It is unnecessary to let your son see you in these handcuffs."

"Thank you," Dania said,

"No problem," the marshal replied. "I am sorry that this happened to you."

Dania held her son tightly for a long time when she arrived in the hall and cried on his shoulders. "I am sorry, my baby; I am so sorry I failed you!" She knew she had to start a new life in Santa Ana. Her mother's family was from there, but she grew up in San Salvador and felt like a stranger in her mother's hometown. Her aunties, Graciela and Maribel, were nice to her and her son, but something was missing; the city seemed like a ghost town. There were not many kids around for Junior to play with. However, it was safe for him and for her as well, far from M18. She was grateful to her aunts and her cousins, who surrounded Junior with love.

Dania spent her first week sleeping all day, and in the afternoon she went to El Tunco Beach to watch the sunset with her son. She had sent a few hundred dollars home every month for the care of Junior and for her savings account, and she was glad she did that. Her savings would help keep her going for a couple of months, and Lazo had offered to continue to send her and her son some money like he used to, at least until she found a job.

"No, Lazo, you have done enough for me. I can't ask you to do more," she'd said.

"At least until you can get a job or find something to do that can bring you some money, OK?" he said. She applied for a phlebotomist job at the local hospital, and the director told her that her experience in San Salvador would be an asset to his institution. The compliment put a smile on Dania's face—a chance for a new beginning. She called Lazo the next day to remind him to send her belongings soon.

"OK, I will send them next month," he said. "I'll finish cleaning up your room by the end of the month, then I will return the key and send you some stuff that you'll need."

PART IV

A VISIT TO THE MOTHERLAND

Chapter 15

Lindsey was overwhelmed by the hospitality everyone she'd met had shown her since she arrived in Accra a week earlier. She knew that it wasn't due to her whiteness, although she sometimes felt full of guilt that it might partly be the reason. She learned from the many conversations they'd had that Kamao's people were hospitable and genuine about how they felt about other people.

"The majority of the people that I know back home don't pretend to like someone. If they don't like you, it won't take you too long to notice," he told her. "I know that many of us who have traveled abroad have learned Western manners, especially in America where everybody smiles at everybody, even people they can't stand. Back home, people don't do that. If they like you, you will know it and you will notice their sincerity, and if they hate you, they will hate you with passion. It will be so obvious, you will understand why they couldn't pretend otherwise." So Lindsey knew that she would be well received in Accra. Still, she didn't expect it to the extent that her breakfast would be ready in the morning before she got up, that traditional Ghanaian outfits would be artistically made for her, or that every acquaintance of Mama Agatha's would call her *lonho-yovi*, or "daughter-in-law."

"But we are not married! Right?" she said to Kamao.

"What do you mean, 'right'?" They both laughed. "But don't even bother trying to change their minds. It won't work. They have made up their minds that we are going to get married. Just don't let that bother you too much."

"Are you kidding? I find it exciting. I can't wait." Kamao pretended he didn't hear her last sentence.

They had been together for almost two years, and they were both going to be seniors in college. For Lindsey, traveling to Accra with Kamao was a dream come true: it was an experience she had dreamed of since their conversation at Kaitlyn's engagement party. She knew her father wouldn't take the news of her trip to Ghana very well, and she knew there would be no perfect opportunity to tell him, like in movies where people patiently wait for the right time to drop the bomb.

As they were having dinner at their residence one evening in April, Lindsey drank a full glass of the Château Margaux, burped, and said, "Excuse me!"

"Honey, are you OK?" her father asked.

"Yeah, I am fine. Dad, I am going to tell you something, and you have to promise not to get mad because this is going to make me very happy and I want you to be happy for me."

"You know I can't promise anything, Lin, especially when I don't know what is coming at me. It depends on what you're going to say, and you know I don't like surprises."

"I am going to Ghana this summer with Kamao," she said, clearing her throat, as if the information didn't need much attention. The senator removed his glasses slowly, just like he usually did when he was about to say something important.

"Why are you so obsessed with this guy? Now you want to follow him to his country! Do you know how it is over there? You know what, you think you are grown and you can do whatever you want. So go ahead—do whatever you want." The senator got up and started to clear the table. "Did you think about what people might want to do when they find out who you are? Did you think about that?"

"Dad, I am not going to allow myself to be engulfed in negativity like that."

"Didn't you think about the fact that you could be kidnapped or raped?"

"No, Dad, I didn't think about that, and I don't want to think about that. Kamao will be with me; he won't let anything happen to me."

"Oh, yeah, because you trust him so much!" the senator said, rubbing his forehead, bothered by a sudden headache. His daughter was planning to travel to a foreign country, a country unknown to him, but a country whose name brought a distant annoyance, an amalgam of desolation and pestilence, an area of the world where people lacked the essential dignity of humankind. "What can I do to change your mind? What can I do to help you see reason?"

"Nothing, Dad. Absolutely nothing."

"Honey! Have you thought about me?" he asked in a friendly tone.

"What do you mean?"

"You are the only person I have in this world, and you want to leave me."

"Dad, it is just a vacation. It is just one month, and I will be back before you know it."

"One month! You will be gone for one month! Honey, the elections are only a few months away. I need you by my side." He paused. "You don't care about my reelection, do you?"

"Of course, I do, Dad. If being a senator makes you happy, I will do anything I can, anything reasonable to keep you happy. I will go anywhere you need me to go when I come back." The senator shook his head.

"I have a bad feeling about this. My opponent and people who despise me could use this trip against me; they could find anything to stain my campaign, any little scandal over there would become breaking news here, and you know it."

"Dad," Lindsey said, calmly, "this isn't about you; this is about me, OK? Stop looking for a connection between my trip and your campaign. Besides, what chances does McGill have against McAdams?"

"Oh, honey, he is doing very well. He is raising a lot of money and is gaining more supporters every day. You don't see how troubling this is for me!" The senator walked into the living room and crashed onto the couch.

Lindsey followed him and put a hand on his shoulder.

"Dad, I am truly sorry that I caused you so much pain with this news, but you have to understand that even if I wasn't going on this trip, we are not going to live together forever, and the time will come when you have to let me go, let me do what I want, go where I want. You just have to trust me." The senator didn't respond.

Lindsey grew up in America, her knowledge of Africa shaped by TV ads and movies like *The Gods Must Be Crazy*. In middle school, whenever there was a mention of Africa, the first thing that came to her mind was a miserable place covered with deserts and drought, where children ran around naked, malnourished; where people lived in huts and cohabited with wild animals. Africa, for her, was a land of despair and chaos. With her relationship with Kamao came a new image of the Dark Continent. She discovered other aspects of Africa she didn't think existed before, like how poverty isn't caused by a lack of resources but lack of goodwill.

The white Toyota Sequoia pulled into a large, gated compound with a beige three-story house majestically standing in the middle of a paved yard.

"Ah, my *Babamu* is back! Thank you, Jesus! You brought my son back safely." Mama Agatha's clamor drew her neighbors' attention. Some rushed outside to see what caused her overwhelming joy. Others who had received echo of Kamao's arrival informed the neighborhood.

"Her son is back from America. He brought a white girl. I heard that she is pretty and nice."

"Hello, Mama Agatha," Lindsey said as she got out of the car. "It's so nice to finally meet you," she said politely, reaching out her hand to greet her boyfriend's mother.

"Come here, my darling," Mama Agatha said, pressing her firmly against her massive body. "Look at you, my girl; you look prettier in person."

"Thank you," Lindsey said, unable to move her head, smashed against Mama Agatha's breasts.

"You are adorable, my sweet girl." Mama Agatha released her grip and looked at her with admiration.

"Thank you," Lindsey said, feeling uncomfortable with the eyes of all the people in the compound on her. She would gladly jump back into the car and hide until everyone was gone, but that would reveal a lack of social skills. After all, she was used to the cameras of reporters interviewing her father when they traveled to different places. She smiled at the cameras, sometimes posing as a star on the red carpet. She had exceptional diplomatic abilities. She wasn't shy, but this was different. She was in a foreign country, without her father, in the middle of strangers, the only person she knew and depended on being her boyfriend of almost two years.

Kamao patiently waited for his mother to notice him.

"Look at you!" Mama Agatha said, taking a few steps back to contemplate her son.

"America has changed you so much; look at your skin, shining like a shell on the beach." She touched his arm. "Ah! Your skin is so soft, and you have gained so much weight. It must be all those hamburgers. It is your fault, Lindsey."

"What! I didn't tell him to eat hamburgers," Lindsey teased back, adapting to Mama Agatha's good humor.

"You have to learn how to cook African food for him." They all laughed.

"Stop embarrassing us, Mama," Kamao said.

"Come, come," Mama Agatha said, and led Lindsey to the house. In the living room, decorated for the occasion, there were a variety of foods lined up on a table like at a banquet. Everybody Lindsey greeted wanted to hug. She graciously let herself go, overwhelmed by the welcome. Many people arrived in their cars to welcome the couple. Later, as they were snuggling in their room, Lindsey felt some guilt and became pensive.

"What is wrong, baby?" Kamao asked.

"I feel so ashamed—unworthy of you."

"What are you talking about?"

"Look at how everybody welcomed me here like I was one of them, like I was family. My father didn't even want you to come to his house, and when you came, he invited the most vicious people to taunt you."

"Don't be silly, honey! Your father did that because he doesn't approve of our relationship. He doesn't like me. Otherwise, I am certain things would have been different. Trust me, these people reserved a warm welcome for you because of what my mother told them about you. She told them you are a nice, down-to-earth, respectful person who quickly adapts to differences. If she had told them something bad about you, you would have come to an empty house where there would be only you and me."

"So it wasn't because I am white."

"Not entirely. Some people were curious to see my white girlfriend, but for the most part they were here to meet you and greet you. Some people don't necessarily like white people because they don't think they can be trusted, and that includes my mother, but they made an exception for you. Also, I know many Americans to be very hospitable. So it cannot be one-size-fits-all. I would judge every case separately."

She smiled and laid her head on his shoulder; he embraced her tenderly.

"Lindsey, it's time to pound the *fufu*." Ayoko's tender, prepubescent voice resonated outside Kamao's bedroom door.

"I am coming," Lindsey said. Ayoko was the new young girl Mama Agatha had taken under her wing to nourish, polish, and turn into an emancipated and independent woman. She was the girl from the traffic light who had been staring at Kamao's mother with the Pure Water basket on her head. After her mother visited Mama Agatha, the latter offered to take care of the girl with her mother's approval and trained her mother to manage one of her stores.

Ayoko had proven to be an intelligent and reliable girl that Mama Agatha admired and loved like her own child. She spoiled her occasionally. Ayoko earned good grades at school and started to master the different aspects of the wholesale business. Since they arrived, Ayoko had become Lindsey's companion and local guide. She showed her around the neighborhood, and Lindsey greeted everyone she saw with her pretty smile and friendly gestures. They greeted her back with compliments about her traditional Ghanaian clothes. Kamao's younger sister and Ayoko took her to a hair salon to braid her hair; it was the first time she ever attempted to do anything like that, and to her own surprise, she loved it when she looked in the mirror. Adjoa, the other young girl that Mama Agatha had raised, had become a boss on her own with a couple of retail stores. She visited Mama Agatha sometimes during Kamao's stay and greeted him like a stranger, probably because she was mad at him that he didn't come back for her and instead got himself a white girl.

"Is that Adjoa?" Kamao asked his mother the first time he saw her since they arrived.

"Yes, that's Adjoa. What is it? Don't you recognize her?"

"I didn't at first. She has changed a lot. It has barely been two years, and I couldn't even recognize her." Adjoa was no longer the young, innocent girl that Kamao knew had a crush on him. She had become a great admirer of cosmetic products and was no longer indifferent to men. She chose who she wanted to date and refused to settle down to become "a man's slave."

"I am still young and have all the time I need. Besides, men cannot be trusted. How do I know they are not just coming after my money?" She wore excessive makeup, had gained weight, and her dark, beautiful skin was shinier than before. Any time Kamao tried to talk to her, she responded with just a word or two and would turn away to someone else to start a conversation. It didn't take him too long to realize her grudge against him, and he decided to leave her alone. However, Adjoa managed to be nice to Lindsey and show respect, for fear of disappointing Mama Agatha and finding herself in the claws of her former protector.

"Is that *Deku dessi*?" Lindsey asked, pointing at the boiling sauce on the stove.

"Yes, my darling." Mama Agatha said, mocking Lindsey's accent. "That was a good guess. How did you figure that out?"

"Kamao has taught me a lot about your foods. I like *fufu* with *Deku dessi*; it's delicious."

"But what you guys have in America came in packages and cans, right?"

"Yes, Mama."

"Ah! Now you are going to taste the real thing. We have some large fish from Akosombo Dam. You can try it and tell me what you think. Do you eat fish?"

"I can try it."

Two muscular guys were pounding the *fufu* in a tall wooden mortar in the middle of the kitchen. "Is that how you cook the *fufu*?" Lindsey asked. "Is that how you pound it? Kamao told me about it and showed me some videos; I thought it was cool."

"You want to try it?"

"Baby, you don't have to do that," Kamao intervened.

"It's OK, baby. I just want to try it."

"It's OK, Kamao, she is not going to break," Mama Agatha reassured.

Lindsey took the long wooden pestle from one of the guys and started to pound the yam in the mortar. After a couple of strikes, she started panting, and everyone burst into laughter.

"You have to go through all of this to eat one meal?" she complained, returning the pestle to the owner. "This is a serious workout."

"That's where all the fun is," Kamao said, taking his shirt off and borrowing the pestle again from the guy. He started pounding with full force like an expert at work.

"Wow, you are a champion at this, babe!" Lindsey said.

After they finished the meal and were getting ready to visit the central market, Kamao went to Lindsey in the room and said, "You are really exceptional, Lindsey."

"Why am I exceptional?"

"My mother has been cooking for you since we arrived."

"And that's not normal?"

"Oh no, that's not normal. Many people call my mother a great cook, but she doesn't cook for us. She made us cook our food. She didn't even let the maids cook for us. She really likes you."

"Wow, I am fortunate then."

"Yes, you are. You are dear to my mother. Oh, don't forget: we are going to a reception tomorrow at my father's residence. If you need anything for the occasion, we should get it today."

"OK, thanks," Lindsey said.

Accra's central market was crowded, as usual.

"Wow, this is amazing, baby! I've never been in a place like this before; so many people in one place," Lindsey said. "So what kind of market is this?"

"This is an open market, where everybody can freely attempt to sell whatever they have, and once you buy it, a return is unlikely. So you can easily notice the difference between this market and the supermarkets we went to a couple of days ago."

"Fresh ice cream! Miss, do you want some?" a guy with a broad smile asked Lindsey, pressing the horn in his hand to invite potential buyers to his wheeled ice cream cooler.

"Sure," Lindsey said, reaching for her purse.

"No, thank you! She is fine," Kamao said, and gave the ice cream man twenty cedis. "Honey, it's OK to say 'no, thank you'; it will not be considered rude. You don't have to reach for your purse every time someone asks you to buy something, otherwise you're going to get robbed or get fat before we leave."

"But I don't want to be rude."

"It won't be rude if you say 'no, thank you' just like you do back home."

"Got it," Lindsey said, nodding with a smile.

As they stopped by a bracelet stand to allow Lindsey to explore the exquisite work of Ghanaian artists, Kamao noticed something familiar about the person in front of them who was talking to the merchant. The dark-skinned, svelte lady with a curly wig—a white blouse firmly secured at the waist by a vivid red belt that matched the red shoes—was none other than his former girlfriend. The dark leather pants added a glowing look to her outfit.

"Ceci, is that you?" The woman turned around.

"Hey, Kamao . . . when did you get back?"

"About a week ago." Cecilia looked at the couple, not surprised that a white girl had replaced her.

"This is Lindsey," Kamao said. "My girlfriend."

"Hello," Lindsey said, stretching her hand to greet Cecilia, who responded to her smile with a timid, "Hi, how are you?"

"This is Cecilia."

"Oh, Cecilia! It is very nice to meet you. Kamao told me about you."

"He did, did he?" Cecilia replied.

It didn't take Kamao too long to notice the toddler whose hand Cecilia held firmly. He had curly brown hair with fair skin and a pointed nose that suggested his father's race. He looked tired, his skin burned by the summer heat.

"Who is this little guy here with you?" Kamao asked, bending over to shake the boy's hand.

"This is Luke, my son," Cecilia said, ready to repel any attack or accusation from her ex-boyfriend.

"It's very nice to meet you, Luke," Kamao said. "OK, Ceci, I'll see you later."

"Yeah, see you guys later," Cecilia replied.

As they were leaving the market, Kamao noticed a Black guy not too far from them, wearing a pair of dark sunglasses with a baseball hat and khaki shorts under a gray shirt. He had seen him a couple of times as they moved around in the market. He didn't look familiar. Kamao felt something strange, but decided to keep it to himself.

Kamao knew Cecilia had changed her phone number after he left; he had called her several times from the US and she was inaccessible. But he didn't know that she had moved out of her apartment.

"Do you know where she moved to?" he asked one of Cecilia's neighbors.

"No, I don't. Sorry, sir."

"It's OK, thank you," Kamao said.

He knew who could give him any information about Cecilia. He got back into his car and drove in the pouring rain to Tema, about twenty miles from Accra, to Dansu's newly built villa. Kamao kept a few smartphones and cameras in his car to give out to old acquaintances, who he knew might blame him for visiting them empty-handed. Dansu liked the Samsung Galaxy Kamao brought him.

"Thank you, man," he said. "I was dying to get one of these, you know, straight from the USA."

"I like your house," Kamao said.

"Yeah, got it finished two months ago."

"Yep, everything smells fresh."

"Look, man," Dansu said, after they made themselves comfortable in the living room, a bottle of vodka on the table, "I didn't want to be the one to spill the beans, but you are my friend. Now, I have to confess: I didn't tell you anything because I found out after you left and you guys weren't together anymore, so I didn't think it would change anything. And besides, I didn't want to spoil things for you over there."

"So who is the kid's father?"

"George Morsel."

"George . . . the guy from Total Export?"

"Yeah, that's him."

"That guy is old enough to be her father."

"Well, that didn't seem to matter! She works as a manager in one of his warehouses now. I think it is the one where they sell cocoa beans, by Sankara Circle." Dansu paused and took a sip of his vodka. "I am sorry, man. But at least the kid is not fully Black. If he were, we would all be thinking he is yours. I would certainly have called you about that," Dansu said, feeling guilty for keeping his friend in the dark about his ex-girlfriend's dealings.

The residence of Ghana's Health Secretary was crowded with dignitaries, local and foreign, who came to congratulate Nana Ofando for his accomplishments. In his year and a half as Health Secretary, several areas of the country's healthcare system had significantly improved. The mortality rate of women in labor in rural areas due to a lack of medical assistance had significantly decreased. More children had been vaccinated against polio and meningitis. Two new hospitals had been built in Tamale and Takoradi in Northern Ghana. During a World Health Organization conference in Geneva, the Ghanaian government was congratulated, and the Ghanaian delegation received a standing ovation from the other delegates for the country's accomplishments and its continued effort to improve its healthcare system. Lindsey was not new to soirées packed with dignitaries, but she was excited to meet all those VIPs from various countries around the world. The reception was held in the large compound of the residence under the tall palm trees on an agreeable starry night.

"Hello, Lindsey! How are you doing?" Nana Ofando said as he shook Lindsey's hand.

"I am doing well, sir! Thank you, and congratulations on your accomplishments," Lindsey said, intimidated by the charisma of her boyfriend's father.

"It is great to see you again, and I hope you're enjoying yourself in Accra."

"Yes, I am!" Lindsey said, nervously rubbing her hands like a teenage girl before her first kiss.

"I see that you like our traditional outfits," Nana Ofando said, pointing at her colorful *kente* dress.

"I find them lovely," she said.

"You look nice." He looked at her with admiration.

"Thank you! You too."

"Did Kamao tell you that I would like you guys to stay here tonight? I'm hoping that we can spend some time tomorrow before I leave."

"Yes, he told me. That'll be nice. Thank you."

"OK, I will see you around."

"Yes, see you."

Kamao waved at Lindsey after she finished talking to his father, and she headed toward him when someone called her. She turned around.

"How are you?"

"Hi," she said. A chubby man with a sunburned face approached her and shook her hand.

"I am Don Shirley."

"Oh! Good evening, Mr. Ambassador," she said.

"I am a friend of your dad's. Please know that we are your family here. If anything or anyone is bothering you, here is my direct number. All you have to do is call, and we'll find you wherever you are." He lowered his voice as he spoke to her, getting so close that she felt his spit on her face. He took a blue card out of his coat and slid it into her hand.

"OK, thank you, Mr. Ambassador," Lindsey said, thinking what a strange man Don Shirley was.

Lindsey kissed Kamao on the neck; he opened his eyes and stretched. "Good morning, baby," he said and kissed her on the cheek. "How was your night?"

"It was wonderful," she said. "I went downstairs; I saw your dad. He is reading the newspaper. I think he is waiting for us."

"What time is it?" Kamao asked.

"Seven thirty."

"You are already dressed?"

"Yeah. Baby, come on. Your dad is waiting."

"OK! I am getting up. Geez! Why are you in such a rush?"

"Your father is waiting for us. He's all dressed up already."

"Let him wait. He's the one who wants to talk to us."

Lindsey waited for Kamao to get ready, and they both went down to the living room. Nana Ofando was sitting on the couch. On the glass table in front of him was a nicely decorated ceramic coffee mug with its lid on and three matching coffee cups.

"Good morning," he said. He got up and filled up two cups of coffee for them.

Kamao wondered what his father wanted to talk to them about. It didn't seem to him like a mere breakfast invitation. Nana was smiling but seemed to have a severe look on his face at the same time.

"How was your night?" Nana Ofando asked.

"It was great," Kamao said.

"I slept like a baby. Everything is so amazing. Thank you for the amazing hospitality," Lindsey said, holding onto Kamao's hand.

Nana Ofando smiled, revealing his well-aligned white teeth. "I hope you are enjoying yourself here, Lindsey," he said.

"Oh yes. I didn't expect the amazing experience I am having. I am grateful."

Nana Ofando nodded. "I am glad you are having a good time. Well, I wanted to talk to you guys just to shed some light on a few things. Lindsey, Kamao, I know that you both are adults, and I have no intention to get into your business. However, I wanted to make sure everything is OK. Lindsey, you are not just anybody. I know who your father is. I was there in your country when he became a US senator. I know that most of his positions are not in favor of people like Kamao and myself. I would like to know what your father thinks about your relationship with my son. Is he OK with it?"

Lindsey looked at her boyfriend, wondering what he had told his father.

"Hm . . . I am not sure what you've heard, but I am sure he will come around."

Nana Ofando smiled and said, "Would you believe me if I tell you I haven't heard anything? Kamao didn't tell me anything. I never asked him who his girlfriend was, simply because it didn't matter, at least until I met you. So is he OK with you guys dating?"

After Kamao had introduced his girlfriend to his father, a day after they arrived in Accra, he called him into his home office when Lindsey was getting acquainted with the other siblings.

"I never suspected that your girlfriend was Lindsey McAdams," Nana Ofando said. "How did you end up with her?"

"We were in the same class in college."

"Is her father OK with this?" Kamao sighed, trying to find the right words. "Don't answer that question," his father said. "I want to hear it from her."

"Oh! Don't do that, Papa, please."

"Relax. I won't say anything to embarrass you. I want the two of you to spend the night here after the reception on Sunday because I want to talk to both of you on Monday morning. Does anybody else know who she is, your mother, or . . . anybody?"

"No, I don't think so," Kamao said, a little worried about his father's inquiry.

Lindsey cleared her throat, wondering how to respond to Nana Ofando's question about how her father felt about their relationship. "He is not thrilled about it," she said, "but he will come around. I am happy with Kamao, and he's starting to see that." She squeezed the hot coffee cup with both hands, hoping it would break and burn her, which would put an end to the unexpected interrogation she was being subjected to.

"What do you mean, he is starting to see that?"

"When I told him about the trip here with Kamao, he wasn't delighted, but he wasn't as angry as I thought he would be. He didn't threaten to take anything away from me like he usually does."

"OK. I am sorry I made you uncomfortable. I hope you guys enjoy your day." Nana Ofando said. He got up and took his briefcase.

"Thank you," Kamao and Lindsey said simultaneously.

"Did you take her to Labadi Beach yet, Kamao?"

"No, not yet!" Kamao said, scratching his cheek, not looking at his father.

"You will love the view," Nana Ofando said to Lindsey.

"I look forward to it."

Lindsey stayed on the couch, wondering why Nana Ofando asked her those questions about her father's position on her relationship with Kamao. Did it matter what anybody thought? Kamao got up, sensing that it would be best to let her be, as she didn't utter a word when he asked her if she wanted a toast. She was upset; he knew it. He went back upstairs and thought it would be better to give her time to collect herself.

Lindsey had hoped that her father would come around and would let her and Kamao be together. She didn't expect that he would accept Kamao with open arms and give them his blessings, but she had hoped that he would stop seeing her boyfriend as a threat, as a danger to the United States. She never found justification for her father's hatred toward immigrants. She knew it wasn't a Republican thing to hate immigrants because she knew many Republican congressmen and women who opposed the administration's policies. These officials denounced the way asylum seekers were treated, like Senator Andrew Blair from Arizona, who was known as a fierce defender of "the voices that are not always heard," a phrase he used in one of his speeches. A former marine lieutenant, Senator Blair had been stationed in countries in South America, Asia, and Europe. "My opinion of refugees, immigrants, and asylum seekers," he said during a debate on the issue of immigration, "is that they are like us; the only difference is that they are less fortunate. They were born in countries where they don't have opportunities like we do here. They were born in countries where they don't always enjoy freedom like we do here. We all agree that we don't want to make it easy for thugs, thieves, and other bad guys to come to our country. That's why we have a sophisticated vetting system in place to help us have an idea of who those people are who want to come here. One thing I can tell you is that most of the people who do come are hard workers and honest, decent human beings." Many Republican senators shared Blair's view, but not McAdams.

"Would your father have been OK if your boyfriend was from an Asian or South American country or a race other than Black?" Kamao asked Lindsey one day, as they were discussing the senator's opposition to their relationship.

"It would have been the same," Lindsey said. "He simply hates immigrants from 'third world countries,' as they call them."

"But he hates US-born Black people too, right?"

"He denies it, but I know he does. I know how he treats the few Black people he deals with."

"So if I were a European, let's say Norwegian or British, he would have been OK with it?"

"I think so. It wouldn't be as big a deal as it is with you."

"And you? What about you? What made you want to date a Black guy? Why are you so different from your father?"

"I would say my mother played a big part in how my personality developed. She was more tolerant of people in general and was very generous. She had done a lot of volunteer work as a nurse practitioner in Myanmar and Cambodia during some dark times in those countries' history. She helped Doctors Without Borders when she was there, and she also did some volunteer work in some hospitals in Nicaragua with the US Peace Corps."

"Wow, that is quite an accomplishment."

"Yeah! She kept a good relationship with many people in those countries and sponsored many children, especially from some remote areas in Nicaragua. That experience had shaped who she was, and she passed that sympathy on to me, I guess. What I regret is that I wasn't curious enough to learn more about countries like Cambodia and Nicaragua, countries that are not like the United States. My mother didn't tell me a lot about them either. She taught me to be tolerant, open-minded, and not full of myself, though. So maybe all of that helped."

"Hearing these things about your mother helps me understand why you're so different from your father."

Lindsey finally got up and went to the room. Kamao was in bed, eyes closed, but she knew he wasn't sleeping.

"Do you know why your dad asked me all those questions about how my father feels about our relationship?"

"To be honest with you, I am angry at my dad for questioning you like that, but I didn't think it was a good thing to confront him directly in front of you. I will bring the subject to him later and tell him how I felt. He will understand. But as I am thinking more about it, I believe there are a lot of politics in this situation. I am sure your father has contacted your embassy, and my father might have received a hint about something. Everybody has an informant everywhere."

"Why do you say that?" Lindsey asked, stunned by Kamao's comment.

He sat up in bed and said, "I don't know what the ambassador told you yesterday, but I saw him giving you something; I didn't want to ask you anything because I didn't think it was essential and it was none of my business. But I am sure other people saw that too and might be wondering."

"He gave me a card with a number on—"

"Stop, stop, stop! . . . You see? This is what I don't want, feeling like I am making you say things or justify yourself to me." Kamao got up and went to Lindsey, who was standing stoically. He hugged her, and she couldn't hold back her tears. "I am sorry about all of this; I truly am. I don't doubt that if there is anything that I need to know, you'll tell me. You trust me, right?"

"Yes," she said, sobbing and wiping her tears.

"I can trust you, too, right?" Kamao said.

"Yes," she said.

"Now that we are talking about trust, there's something I must tell you that could corroborate my theory that there might be more to all of this than we think." He paused. He held her hand and asked her to sit on the bed with him. "You remember the day we were in the central market and met my ex-girlfriend?"

"Yes."

"I noticed a guy, a Black guy, not too far from us. He looked away quickly when I looked at him. He didn't seem like a regular guy. He was with the ambassador yesterday during the reception."

"The same guy?" Lindsey asked, incredulous.

"The same guy. I am pretty good with details, you know that. He could be one of the soldiers from the embassy, probably a marine."

"Are you saying my father has someone following us?"

"I can't confirm it, and I don't want to believe it, but it seems that way. However, I don't see the guy everywhere we go, so it's hard to say."

"I don't know what to say," Lindsey said, looking down.

"There's nothing to say; we just have to wait and see what happens."

Chapter 16

Kamao arrived at Sankara Circle looking for the cocoa bean export warehouse. The area looked different than the last time he was there. Many businesses had opened. The economy must be booming, he thought. He barely recognized his old tailor's shop. Papa Jondoh was in his shop, his sight fading. The round bifocal glasses were not helping, as he didn't recognize his *boss*—as he used to call Kamao—when he entered the shop.

"Good morning, *Ofa*," Kamao said.

"Sorry, I am 'bout to close. I am closing early today," Papa Jondoh said without looking at the customer. He was busy looking for his phone.

"How are you, *Ofa*? It's me, Kamao, *Apeto*." Kamao wondered if the older man had forgotten about him. Papa Jondoh turned around, slowly leaning on his walker.

"Eh! *Apeto gne*, wow! I didn't know it was you. Ah! Look at you! You have changed a lot. Look at you! Is it the hamburgers or what? You are so fat now. Eh! America! It's truly a blessed country. Aren't you a lucky one, my son? Some of us are still here about to die soon, eating *Akamu* and *Kenkey* every day."

"Ah, *Ofa*, will you ever stop talking like that? God has blessed all of us in many ways."

"Yes, you're right! I have too many blessings to be grateful for." After a moment of reflection, he asked him, "Like what?"

"Ah, you're blessed, *Ofa*!" Kamao said. "By the way, this plaza looks different now with all these new businesses; I barely recognized the place."

"Things are changing every day."

"I am looking for a place," Kamao said. "It is a cocoa bean export warehouse."

"You mean the White Donkey's place?"

"What? Who?"

"The White Donkey, that's what we call him; the white guy with the burned, dirty skin who stole your girlfriend. He wanted to buy all the shops on this block, you know! We had to go to the mayor's office to complain before he dropped his plan. He thought he could just come to our country and kick us out of our huts like that. Stupid white guy! He's so arrogant. Thank God they are not all like that. I love my sweet Stephen."

"Who's that?"

"My niece Cynthia's husband."

"Oh yeah, the guy from England. Yeah, he has always been nice to you, giving you all those pounds. They are still together?"

"Oh yes! They are married now. They have two kids."

"Wow! That's fantastic. That's true love," Kamao said.

"Anyway, the warehouse is right there. Just turn right at that red light, and you will see it on the right," Papa Jondoh said, pointing his walker to the front door. Kamao was anguished to see his old friend getting older and more desperate. It seemed like his clients had abandoned him, not even bothering to come and collect their finished outfits, already paid for, that were hanging from the dusty ceiling covered by spider webs. Kamao took his wallet out and handed Papa Jondoh five hundred cedis and two hundred-dollar bills.

"What is this?" Papa Jondoh said, waving the dollar bills in the air.

"Some money to help you." Papa Jondoh started tuning in a circle, singing and dancing, waving his walker and almost hitting Kamao on the head. The last time Kamao saw his old friend so happy was when Ghana won its third game in a FIFA World Cup.

"Thank you, my son. God bless you. Ah! What am I saying? You are already blessed. With that beautiful white girl of yours."

"How did you know I have a white girlfriend?"

"Ah! Don't worry about it; I am happy for you."

"OK, I will come back to see you again before I leave, OK?" Kamao left the shop and went to the cocoa bean warehouse. Cecilia was sitting at a desk in the back of the large warehouse where hundreds of sacks of cocoa beans were piled up, waiting to be shipped abroad. Some employees were loading the sacks that had already been purchased onto trucks. Cecilia was talking to a client, and Kamao sat on a chair in an area arranged as the waiting room. Cecilia shook the hand of the customer and walked with her to her car outside the warehouse. She came back inside and walked to Kamao, who couldn't keep his eyes off her. She looked elegant in her multicolored, tie-neck striped blouse and blue jeans. The straight, long brown hair fell on her shoulder like it was her own. She walked with assurance, giving orders to her employees. She had the look of an accomplished businesswoman proud of her prowess.

Since Cecilia took over the management of the cocoa beans department of George Morsel's Total Export, the revenue of that section of the company had doubled, and Morsel had stopped overseeing the activities of the warehouse, as he knew things were in good hands. He gave Cecilia total freedom to run the warehouse as she wished, and she turned it into a success. She was friendly with the suppliers, and would go to the villages herself and see how she could help to hasten the harvest when things were slowing down. She would bring the farmers small gifts, perfumes for some, chocolate bars for others, and the farmers loved her and wanted to do anything to please her. From word-of-mouth, she became the favorite client for several cocoa bean farmers across the country. "I was born a businesswoman," she once said to one of her former university buddies. "I don't know what I was doing in the political science department. No offense, but that was boring."

"Mr. America, welcome," she said, smiling at Kamao.

They shook hands, and Kamao said, "Thank you. Can we go somewhere? I can get you a beer, and we can talk a little."

"Oh! I am working. I can't go anywhere. I have two more appointments in the next two hours, so I am stranded."

"You are very busy, then?"

"Yeah, as you can see."

"I do, and you look nice. Things are going very well for you."

"You can say that again!" Cecilia paused and bowed her head, her hands crossed, feeling awkward suddenly, not knowing what to say next. They were both standing in the middle of the warehouse. The employees kept themselves busy, pretending to be unaware of the unease that was obvious between their boss and the stranger.

"How is Luke?" Kamao asked.

"He's OK, thanks," Cecilia said, looking at Kamao with intensity as she prepared for a fierce confrontation.

"He looks like he is a year and a half. Is he?"

"Something like that," Cecilia said, gnashing her teeth, her hands still crossed.

"Were you pregnant when we were still together? Because that's what it seems like."

"You came back with an American woman, just like I predicted, and you're asking me questions? You wanted me to wait for you? For what? So I can be heartbroken?" Sensing how agitated Cecilia was becoming and willing to de-escalate the situation, Kamao remained calm.

"Ceci, you broke up with me. I wanted our relationship to work; I wanted a future with you."

"How would that have happened when you were leaving?"

"We would not have been the only couple to have a long-distance relationship! People do that all the time, and they are fine."

"Well, that wouldn't have worked for me."

"Is that why you went and got pregnant by someone else while we were still together? Why did you do that? You knew you were pregnant, that's why you broke up with me, right?" Cecilia couldn't utter a word; Kamao's calm voice disarmed her. "Ceci, please look me in the eyes and tell me the truth. We are no longer together. You have accomplished great things for yourself, and I am happy for you. I just want to know the truth. I want to know that you didn't break up with me because I was leaving, but because you were carrying someone else's baby. I felt miserable for months when I arrived in America because I felt like you were right, that I abandoned you. I still feel guilty and I want that to go away; only you can make that happen." Cecilia remained quiet. "I will be honest with you," Kamao continued, "I am not happy that you cheated on me; I am angry about that, I won't lie to you. But there is nothing to do about that now. I just want to know and hear it from you that my trip wasn't the cause of our breakup." Kamao paused to give Cecilia a chance to answer, but she still wouldn't say a word.

"Did you break up with me because you were pregnant with George Morsel's child?" Kamao said at last.

"Yes," Cecilia said, finally, still looking down.

"Well, thank you for telling the truth. There is no need for flashbacks or a fight. I wish you well. Take care of yourself." Kamao left the warehouse, got into his car, and drove away. He decided not to say anything to Lindsey about his encounter with Cecilia and the revelation, although he was confident that she had already figured things out on her own.

When Kamao got home, it was 2:30 p.m. Lindsey was just waking up from her nap, and Mama Agatha was going through some paperwork in the living room.

"Hey, Mama, how are you? Did Lindsey enjoy the errands with you this morning?"

"I think she loved it. What kind of man leaves their woman when they bring them to visit their family?"

"Oh, no, it's fine, Mama," Lindsey said as she walked into the living room. "Kamao told me he was going to run some errands on his own since you and I had also planned our little adventure." Mama Agatha smiled. Kamao said a soundless "Thank you" to Lindsey, and she replied, "You're welcome."

"If you are rested enough, are you in the mood to go to Labadi Beach this afternoon? The weather is perfect for an afternoon at the beach," Kamao said.

"Yeah! Absolutely. I've been looking forward to the occasion. Are we going to swim?"

"Yeah, if you want to."

"Yes, I want to," Lindsey said. "I'll grab my swimsuit."

There were a few people at the beach when Kamao and Lindsey arrived. "I can't believe this place is empty at a time like this. I wonder what's going on with the people," Kamao said as they settled down.

"It's not empty," Lindsey said.

"This is nothing compared to the crowd that usually gathers here this time of the year."

The beach looked clean. A cool breeze from the Atlantic Ocean was whistling through the coconut trees, sounding like a sweet melody to ears of the beach lovers. A beach bar in the distance was playing music from some local artists. There, some lovers sitting at a white plastic table were sipping coconut juice with straws. Lindsey looked around the area, contemplating.

"This is all beautiful, baby! Wow, I love it," Lindsey said.

"I am glad you do," Kamao said.

"Yeah, this is nice." Lindsey took off her jeans and T-shirt and ran into the water; Kamao followed her. They splashed each other like children. Some teenagers playing soccer in the sand looked at them and laughed. Lindsey was amused to know that they were the object of such admiration. After almost half an hour in the water, they got out and lay on a towel.

"I wish we could stay here like this forever. I am so happy, baby!" Lindsey said.

"It's stunning, isn't it? This is the Atlantic Ocean. You see that over there?" Kamao said, pointing at an old beaten white building with a lot of stairs. "That's one of the slave forts. That was where they stocked the kidnapped men, women, and children like merchandise before shipping them off across the ocean to the New World."

"So it's just like the one we went to last time. I hated that place. It looked like it was still haunted by the memory of innocent people being sent off to a land unknown to them, never to see their loved ones again. I can't believe how people can be so cruel. Treating other human beings like that; I feel so ashamed."

"About what? You did nothing wrong. You weren't even born. As far as I am concerned, I blame those who sold their sons, daughters, brothers, and sisters to strangers to be taken to a land they had never heard of themselves. That's the part I've never understood. I blame them most."

Lindsey had been right about the Cape Coast Castle. The place gave visitors the sense of a presence that wasn't there. Every corridor of the castle filled Lindsey's head with the image of slaves in chains sitting on the hard floor naked next to one another, unable to escape the dreadful fate that awaited them. She felt the chilling touch of the past mingled with the thick air. Every word of the tour guide sounded in her ears like a gruesome recount of the untold story: the story of men and women who embarked on a journey against their will, and who had encountered unimaginable suffering, both mental and physical. She ran out of the dark labyrinth of Cape Coast, gasping for air, and refused to go back inside when Kamao invited her to.

"Can I ask you a question?" Lindsey asked after a moment of silence.

"Yes, of course."

"I was wondering . . . is your mother married to your father? If she was, then who was the other woman we saw the other day when we were at your father's house?"

"OK!" Kamao cleared his throat. "My father has three women. They are not his wives; he cannot legally marry more than one. So he didn't marry any of them. Now, don't ask me how things are arranged between him and the women; that, I don't know. But I know that there are many other families like mine where the women take turns being with the man weekly, which means one of the ladies will be the man's 'favorite' for the week and will do everything for him like cooking, doing his laundry, and, of course, sharing his bed. In return, she can ask for favors." Kamao gave the example of one of his elementary school friends, Osofo, whose father lived on a military base, sharing a four-bedroom house with three of his women and their children. Osofo's father had his own room and the women joined him, taking turns weekly. Every woman shared a room with her children. Sometimes, Osofo came to school in the morning tired and sleepy because his mother and the other two women had a melee throughout the night when his father was gone on a mission. Osofo told Kamao about how his father abused the women, slapping them and beating them with a belt.

"I hate my father for beating women like that," he told Kamao one day during PE. "I will never do that to my wife, and I am only marrying one. Why does he live with them if he doesn't like them?" he said. The abuse continued until the new commander of the camp locked Osofo's father up for two weeks after Osofo's mother told the commander's wife about the mistreatment. A few months later, the youngest of the women, who was fifteen years younger than Osofo's father, left with her two children. "I liked her," Osofo said. "She was so beautiful. I don't know what she was doing with my father. I've heard her say to one of her friends that my father was a liar; that he told her that she would be the only woman in his life and that he was going to treat her like a princess. It was all lies. She said after she got pregnant with her second child, he wouldn't even look at her anymore," Osofo confided in Kamao.

Kamao told Osofo a little about his own family. He told him that, although things were a lot different with his father, who treated his women better, he wasn't proud of him either for having so many women at the same time. He kept his family secrets to himself.

"There were many families like that when I was growing up," Kamao told Lindsey, "where one man had children with several women who lived together in the same house or separate compounds. You'd think it happened because the men had money, like my father, but Osofo's father had nothing. He was just a corporal or something. But things are changing now. Our generation is a little different, and girls nowadays don't let themselves be dragged into situations like that. They will leave if there is someone else involved, or they will make sure everyone stays away from one another. But they wouldn't stay with a man in the same house if there were other women living there already.

I don't know why our society tolerates such things. It's insane, but it is what it is, I guess."

"But your family is different, right? Your father doesn't mistreat his women."

"Yes, that is true. The women all seem to like one another, and they all treat everybody like their own children. My mother traveled to Lagos with one of my half-sisters one time, and everybody thought she was her daughter. They even stayed in the same hotel room."

"Wow, that's amazing!" Lindsey said.

"I think, unlike Osofo's dad, my father was the one who visited the women and stayed with each one for a while."

"Then who is that woman who was in your father's house when we spent the night there?"

"That is his first woman—I have a hard time saying that—she came to stay with him as the lady of the house, and everyone is OK with that. As a government official, he thought it would be a good thing to have someone with him like his wife to show around. He takes her to official gatherings and celebrations. It seems like there was some agreement between him and the other women because my mother never complains about that; she knows that she will get anything she wants from him. But I still don't understand how they do that."

"Your mother is an amazing woman," Lindsey said. "When we went out today, everyone we met was excited to see her. She was so friendly and kind to everybody, even her employees. I liked the places we visited. She is running a big business too. She said she had opened a few stores in your name."

"Yes, she did. And my father transferred a couple of his businesses into my name too, like he did for his other children. I have an accountant who takes care of all of that for me. He is an old friend."

"And you call me rich?" Lindsey said. "Why are you wasting your time in the US working in a gas station when you could be running your little business kingdom here?"

"Well, first, if I hadn't gone to the United States, I wouldn't have met you. Second, I've always wanted to go to the US; I just love your country. But you are right about me working at a gas station, a person living a life of a king in another country can easily become a nobody in America, and a lot of people find themselves starting from the bottom when they get to the US. Unless you are a celebrity or someone well-known, no one cares who you are or what diploma you have. There are many doctors and lawyers from around the world who work as store clerks and laborers in the US. Some of them give up trying to get back on their feet and resolve to keep those jobs; others go back to school and work their way up."

"I am so sorry," Lindsey said, shaking her head. "I don't understand why it's like that."

"It is a different standard, that's all."

Chapter 17

The days went by fast, and Kamao and Lindsey only had a week and a half left to spend in Ghana. Mama Agatha and one of her maids set up the breakfast table. Kamao was the first to join them just as they were finishing up.

"Good morning, Mama," he said.

"Good morning. Where is Lindsey?"

"She's in the bathroom getting ready; you know how you women are, taking your time."

Kamao grabbed an apple on the fruit basket on the breakfast table, but Mama Agatha slapped the back of his hand. "Be a gentleman; I taught you better. Don't you know how to be a gentleman and wait for your woman?" Kamao rubbed the back of his hand and quietly sat down, ashamed of himself.

"Why do you like Lindsey so much, Mama?" he asked after a moment of silence.

"She's nice," Mama Agatha said, still busy setting up the table.

"Her mother died when she was little. She had taught her well, from what she told me. But she was raised by her father after her mother passed away."

"Then her father had taught her well too," Mama Agatha said. "I would love to meet him too. It's good to know there are some good Christians who know how to raise their kids to fear God. Do you know him?" Mama Agatha didn't usually ask questions about people's families. As a good African mother, she could quickly tell if a child came from a good home or not, only by observing their behavior.

"I know him a little," Kamao said. "He loves his daughter; he would do anything for her. I like him, and I respect him."

"It's been a while now since you came down and Lindsey is still not here. She's usually here by now. Are you sure everything is OK with her?"

"I'll go check on her." Kamao went upstairs and knocked on the bathroom door. "Baby, is everything ok?" He could barely hear Lindsey's voice.

"I . . . I . . ." Then he heard her throwing up. He opened the door and saw her on the floor, holding the toilet seat, sweating and panting, "I can't . . . I can't breathe, I—"

"Don't say anything, baby, don't say anything, I got you," Kamao said, holding her in his arms. "Mama! Come quick!" he screamed. Mama Agatha rushed upstairs and ran into the bathroom.

"Holy Jesus! Lindsey!"

"Mama, please stay with her; I'll go get the keys and pull the car around."

"What are you talking about, taking the car! You should call an ambulance."

"Mama, an ambulance will take forever to get here, and we don't want to alarm the entire neighborhood, do we?"

"You are talking like you forgot who your father is." Mama Agatha rushed back downstairs, picked up the house phone, and dialed Nana Ofando's number.

"It's Lindsey, Nana! She's not doing well. Please, send an ambulance."

"OK, right away!" Nana Ofando said and hung up. He called back two minutes later. "An ambulance and a police car should be there in about three minutes," he said. "What happened?"

"We just found her on the bathroom floor; she is vomiting and has trouble breathing."

"OK, when the ambulance arrives, tell the driver to take her to the regional hospital; I will meet you guys there."

Kamao came back with his car key. "Let's go, Mama, the car is ready." Just as he finished speaking, an ambulance pulled into the driveway, announced by a loud siren. A police car followed behind with four armed police officers jumping out of the vehicle and taking position at the front gate to keep curious neighbors away.

The Greater Accra Regional Hospital, located in the northern part of the city, was one of the fanciest buildings in the area. His diplomatic approach to issues and his proactive character had prepared Nana Ofanda to address the situation that arose with Lindsey's sickness effectively. It seemed like he had predicted or foresaw something like this happening: He knew how quickly a minor incident could turn into a diplomatic nightmare between two countries, especially when one of them was the United States of America. Nana Ofando had made the necessary arrangements at the hospital so that Lindsey would be treated with all the attention a VIP could get. A couple of old friends who were doctors at the hospital were informed of Lindsey's arrival. Two hours later, Nana Ofando met Mama Agatha and Kamao in the family area after receiving an update from his good friend Dr. Mensah.

"She had a perforated bowel," the doctor said as he met them in a family room on the ICU floor.

"What is that? Is it dangerous?" Mama Agatha asked.

"It is a serious condition but treatable with dedicated care. She will be fine," he said. Kamao was praying that nothing worse happened to Lindsey.

"Can we see her?" he asked.

"Not yet," his father said. "She is still in intensive care. She will be having surgery soon. You should go home; I will update you guys as soon as I hear something."

"I am not going anywhere, Papa," Kamao said.

"Neither am I," his mother added.

"OK, suit yourself," Nana Ofando said. "I'll see you guys later." He went back to his office and just as he sat in his chair, his phone rang; it was his secretary. "Yes, Yemi?" he said.

"Pardon me, sir, but the Minister of Foreign Affairs is on the phone for you; he said it is urgent."

"OK, I'll take it. Thank you, Yemi."

"You're welcome," Yemi said.

"Hi, Olateh, how are you?" he asked.

"Quite well, thank you. I was informed that Lindsey McAdams has been admitted to the regional hospital. Thank you for informing the embassy and my office promptly. I just got off the phone with the US ambassador; he has requested to meet with me. What do you know about her situation?"

"You know who she is, right?"

"Of course I do! What do we know?"

"Well, she was admitted for a perforated bowel. She is in good hands; she will be fine. I am monitoring the situation. I just got back from the hospital. I am sure the ambassador is going to request an emergency evacuation. I have no doubt you will handle him, but I would like to ask you a favor. Please tell him that I will give him an update of the situation in person—tomorrow, if his schedule allows."

"Will do, thank you," the Minister of Foreign Affairs said, and hung up.

Nana Ofando leaned back in his chair with a smile on his face, "I knew this would happen." He called Yemi—a svelte, dark-skinned, and pleasant girl—who opened the door. "Please, call the US Embassy and ask if the ambassador will be free for a meeting tomorrow."

"OK, sir!" Yemi said and went back to her desk. She knocked back at Nana Ofando's door five minutes later. "The ambassador's schedule is full tomorrow, but he can talk to you on the phone between 2:00 and 2:30 p.m."

"OK, thank you, Yemi!"

Yemi called the embassy at 2:13 p.m. the next day and passed the call to Nana Ofando.

"Mr. Ambassador! How are you doing today?"

"Quite well, thank you! What about yourself?"

"I am just fine. Thank you! I believe you are aware that Lindsey McAdams has been admitted to the regional hospital."

"Yes, I am. Please understand that my country has a protocol in place for a situation like this. We will take care of it. You don't have to worry about anything."

"I would like to make you aware, Mr. Ambassador, that the situation is under control, and Lindsey doesn't have a life-threatening condition. We are capable of efficiently addressing the situation. We have all the equipment needed to take good care of her. So there is no need for the alarming move of an emergency evacuation."

"I appreciate your reassurance, Mr. Secretary, but as I said, we have our way of addressing situations like this. Thank you."

"Mr. Ambassador . . ."

"I have to go, Mr. Secretary. Please forgive me!"

The ambassador hung up. Nana Ofando held the phone to his temple for two minutes, staring at a picture of him at the inauguration of a hospital in Takoradi.

Kamao and Mama Agatha were with Lindsey in her recovery room when the ambassador arrived at the hospital. The Marine that Kamao thought was following them was not with him. Lindsey was in a single-patient room with a large TV on the wall and a fridge. She couldn't eat yet. A nasogastric tube was placed in her nose down to her stomach for liquid-nutrient intake and to keep her system empty when needed.

"My father talked to the ambassador earlier today. It seems like they're going to evacuate you," Kamao said.

"My father called me too, just before you came. He told me the same thing. I am waiting for the ambassador to give him my answer."

"What are you going to tell him? You're not going?"

"Of course not. I am not going anywhere! I am not leaving you, and I'm in good hands here. They'll have to sedate me to get me out of here; I am not going anywhere, not like this!"

Kamao smiled, proud of his girlfriend for her bravery, but he was at the same time terrified at the thought that the senator might blame him for his daughter's defiance. And God forbid if anything worse happened to Lindsey as a result of her refusal to be evacuated. Kamao thought he would just stay in Ghana and forget about his precious green card if that happened. His phone rang.

"Excuse me," he said and went out.

"I thought you were pregnant, Lindsey! You scared me, girl!" Mama Agatha said when she was alone with Lindsey.

Lindsey laughed. "Sorry, Mama! I didn't mean to scare you like that. Pregnant! You thought I was pregnant, huh?"

"Yeah! When you were vomiting and weak and all . . ."

"No, I don't want to be pregnant, not yet. I want to be pregnant only as a wife, not as a girlfriend." The ambassador came in just as Mama Agatha headed to the door to join Kamao.

"Hi, Lindsey, how are you doing?

"I am feeling better. Thank you! And before you say anything, I talked to my father; I am not going anywhere. I am staying here until the end of our vacation."

"Lindsey," the ambassador said, installing himself in the recliner next to Lindsey's bed, "what we are doing is in your interest, and you are not the first person this has happened to. We've always had people who become sick suddenly, and we want to do our best to make sure they are well taken care of back home."

"So are you saying they can't take a good care of me here?" The ambassador didn't answer her question and managed not to show his anger toward her, whom he thought a spoiled little brat. "That's exactly the reason why I don't want to leave," Lindsey continued. "This is not a jungle where nothing can be accomplished. This hospital has all that it needs to take care of me. Nana Ofando would never allow anything to happen to me, I am sure of it."

The ambassador had nothing else to say. He got up and said, "Well, suit yourself; I will go and send my report and recommendations."

"Thank you, ambassador, for coming."

Nano Ofando was pleased when he learned from Kamao that Lindsey had refused to be evacuated. "That's quite a girl you've got there, son! You better take good care of her if, of course, she decides to stay with you. I like her, you know! I'm sorry for the interrogation the other day. I am simply trying to be cautious and proactive, knowing who her father is. You need to be careful with someone like that." Kamao smiled at his father and nodded, preferring not to say anything.

PART V

BACK TO DC

Chapter 18

Lindsey was admitted to Saint Matthew Hospital upon her return from Accra. Her wound had almost healed, and Dr. Thomson checked on her during his morning rounds.

"Good morning, Ms. McAdams," he said.

"Good morning, doctor. I can go home, right? I feel great." The doctor pulled her chart. He pulled her gown and examined her wound.

"You should be able to resume your regular activities in a couple of days. Any plans?"

"I don't have anything particular in mind. I just want to get out of here."

"I understand!" the doctor said with a smile. "You can go home tomorrow."

"OK, doc! Thank you."

"You're welcome."

Lindsey had made new friends and had learned a lot during her trip to Ghana. She had the chance to visit a few villages and was impressed by how happy the people were with the very little they had. Many lived in huts with no TV, no electricity, and no running water, and yet they seemed happy. In a village near Ho, where she spent a couple of days with Kamao, she was impressed by a group of young girls, buckets on their heads, coming back from the nearby river, singing. The next day, she asked one of the girls, Amadeh, a seven-year-old, if she could join them. They gave her a bucket that was halfway full and she couldn't keep it steady on her head; the water poured out with every step she took, and she got herself wet. The children around laughed. "I can't do this; it's too hard," she'd said, chuckling. "How do you guys do this? And you all are so good at it!"

"It's practice; it's habit. We do this every day," Amadeh said. She and her friends showed Lindsey how to walk and keep the bucket of water steady on her head.

Lindsey thought she now had something to compare her life to. She thought she could have been one of those girls, living with little, but appreciative of what she had. She thought there might be a different definition of poverty. Those little girls in that remote village of Ghana may be materially poor, but they were rich inside; they were glowing, their happiness unquestionable. They didn't have running water in their homes but going to the river to fetch water was an adventure that in itself brought them joy. They went to the river by themselves and were not worried about kidnappers. Parents left their house for the local market or the farm with peace of mind, knowing that their kids were in good hands with the neighbors. The sense of community was powerful. Lindsey was buried deep in her thoughts when Kamao knocked on the door.

"Come in," she said. Kamao opened the door, a bouquet of freshly cut daisies in his hand.

"How are you feeling, baby?"

"Great! I'm feeling great. The doctor said I could go home tomorrow. I've been here for almost a week. I hate it."

"It's OK, everybody needs to rest sometimes." He kissed her and gave her the daisies.

She smelled them. "Thank you!" Lindsey put the flowers on the table and held Kamao's hands, inviting him to sit on the chair next to her bed. "I want to thank you for the trip," she said. "It was wonderful. It will remain one of the best experiences in my life. It has changed me and my view of life forever. I am more appreciative of what I have, and I can understand others better now that I've seen something different from what I am used to." Kamao kissed the back of her hand with a smile.

"I will be happy to do anything that would bring you joy." He stared at her. She felt uncomfortable, wondering if he was going to say something grave, something worrisome. "Lindsey," he said, looking serious, "I love you with all my heart. I came into this relationship with caution, and I already told you why. But after discovering your inner beauty and after realizing how far you are willing to go with me, I want to tell you that I, in turn, am willing and ready to go on the long ride with you." Lindsey felt her cheeks itch a little; she wiped the two streams of tears with the back of her hand. She stretched out her arms, leaning over to embrace him.

"What you said was beautiful, thank you."

"I meant every word of what I said," he said, still looking severe.

"I know you do, and I love you too. You mean so much to me. I pray every day that my father sees what we have and give us his blessing."

"Yeah . . . we can hope for that, can't we?"

"Some strange things have been happening since we got back," Lindsey said.

"Really? Like what?"

"He had been acting nice, and he asked me if I love you, and when I said yes, he said 'OK' and nodded. I found that weird because my father has never been interested in knowing my feelings for you."

"Wow! That's interesting. Can we see that as a good sign?"

"I would; I definitely would. I see that as the beginning of something good."

"OK," Kamao said, nodding thoughtfully.

"Megan and Trish visited me yesterday."

"I haven't heard from them in a while. How are they doing?"

"Good . . . Megan has a new boyfriend, and Trish is still single. Megan's new boyfriend is a jerk, but she likes him. From what she said, he seems kind of aggressive and overbearing, but she likes him, so I guess I will have to tolerate him." Lindsey paused, took the bottle of water on her bedside table, and drank it. She quietly stared at the bottle for an extended period of time, which seemed awkward to Kamao.

"What is it?" he said.

"I want to ask you something that I am sure you don't want to hear, but I want you to think about it, because it will make me very happy if you can do it for me." Kamao didn't say anything, preferring to hear what it was before giving any answer.

"He—Megan's new boyfriend—wants to take her to a nightclub somewhere downtown this Saturday. He said one of his favorite rising artists is coming to town and will be performing at Cosmos nightclub. Megan wants me to go with her, and I don't want to go alone—I can't go alone. I won't feel safe. So she said if you agree to come, that will be even better. She said Trish would also be coming with someone that's not a real date, but with you and I, she would have peace of mind and . . ."

"I don't like nightclubs," Kamao said. "I don't go to those places, and I told you that before. There are fights; people get drunk and crack each others' heads open with bottles. There is all kinds of stuff. That's not a place for me . . ."

"I know, baby, I know," Lindsey said, holding his hands. "I know. I don't like nightclubs either. The music is too loud and all the other stuff you said. I wouldn't have talked to you about this if it weren't for Megan. I know you; I know that's not a place you will be happy to go to. But I am begging you to do it for me, please. Megan means a lot to me." Kamao liked to make his girlfriend happy. He was planning to take her to a particular place once she was discharged from the hospital. He had something in mind. But going to a nightclub was not in his plan. His hatred for nightclubs didn't start in the United States.

When he was a freshman in high school, one of his older half-brothers, Kuameh, was killed by a drunk driver who was pulling out of a nightclub's parking lot. Kuameh died the next day at the military hospital in Accra. He was a student at the military academy and was scheduled to fly to London in two weeks to continue his training. He went to the nightclub with his girlfriend to celebrate his promotion. After that, Kamao swore never to set foot in a nightclub, or even in a bar, unless it was not crowded and had soft music. What Lindsey was asking him to do was beyond his tolerance threshold. He loved her and knew he would do many things for her, but having to go to a nightclub to make her happy—that was pushing the limit for him. The anxiety that always accompanied his thoughts of nightclubs did not allow him to compromise.

"I can't go, baby. I am sorry to disappoint you, but I don't want to go. It is not my thing, honestly."

"OK," Lindsey said, letting go of his hands. "It's no biggie." She smiled, but he knew that it was a smile of disappointment. He hated to disappoint her. Only a few weeks ago, she refused to be evacuated from Ghana. She was sick, but she chose to stay to show how much she loved being with him and to show her father and anyone else who saw her boyfriend's country as a shithole that it was a decent place where everyone could receive quality care in hospitals. Kamao felt guilty for Lindsey's sudden sadness and was ashamed of himself. It was possible to overcome his disdain for nightclubs just once, for the sake of his love for her. He looked at Lindsey; she managed to keep a smiling face while avoiding eye contact.

"Is it that important for you?" he asked.

"Baby, let it go, it's OK," she said. "I told you why I wanted to go, and I understand why you don't want to. Let's just leave it there, OK? I will call Megan later and tell her that we can't come."

"I don't want to see you like this," Kamao said. "I am sorry that I made you sad. I am sure I can manage my dislike of the place if going will make you happy. I want you to be happy, baby, I do. If going to that club with you to support Megan will make you happy, I will be glad to do it. Your happiness brings me joy."

"I don't want to go anymore," Lindsey said, freeing herself from his tender grip.

"Come on, baby, don't do that, please," he said, "I will do anything for you. I am sorry for my reaction earlier. I didn't know how important this was for you. I'll go anywhere with you, and I will do anything for you. I am sorry!"

"OK," Lindsey said; she picked up her phone on the nightstand. "I will call Megan and let her know that we're coming." Her phone rang as she was about to call Megan. "Oh! It's my father," she said. "Hi, Dad!" She listened to her father quietly, and without hesitation gave the phone to Kamao, who looked at her, bewildered. "It's for you," she said. "My father wants to talk to you."

"What?" he said quietly and took the phone.

"Hi, *Kamoo*! How are you doing?" the senator said.

"I . . . I am doing well, sir. Thank you. How . . . about you?"

"OK; I would like to meet with you and learn a little more about you. Would you give me your number, please?"

"Of course, sir!" Kamao recited his ten-digit phone number in a trembling voice, clearing his throat after every set of three digits.

"Thank you!" the senator said and hung up.

"What did he want with you?" Lindsey asked.

"He asked for my number; he wanted to know me a little more," he said, still confused.

"You see? More signs of his good faith. I knew he would come around."

Kamao remained quiet. The senator's sudden interest in him didn't make sense. Lindsey thought it was about time she told her boyfriend some things about her father.

"My father is not an awful person deep inside, you know! He is a good man; you may find it hard to believe, but he cares about people, a lot. There are some things I didn't tell you about him because I was angry at him for how he deals with certain things, like our relationship."

"I don't believe people can be totally bad, just like no one can be perfect. There is a little bit of good and bad in all of us. And I told you many times that I like your father. I don't like to focus on the bad side of people anyway. But I am interested to know some of his good attributes."

"Well, I can tell you that he donates a lot of money to many charities that operate overseas, particularly in third-world countries. He solely funded the construction of an orphanage and a clinic in Brazil run by one of his child-hood friends who is a priest. From what I know, he is the only donor of those two facilities, and he had a bank account opened just for the orphanage and the clinic."

"Wow! He has a big heart," Kamao said, nodding thoughtfully.

"Yeah! And he doesn't talk about it because he fears that some of his opponents might use it against him."

"How?"

"They might say it is political propaganda and that he has a fishy business behind it. Others might say it is a strategy to keep struggling people in their country by giving them just enough to survive."

"That's absurd," Kamao said. "By opening the orphanage and the clinic, he created jobs for many locals, and yes, if they are happy with their jobs, they won't need to consider coming to America. What is wrong with that? I think that can be a great foreign policy strategy anyway: encourage and support foreign governments to attract investors and create jobs and opportunities for people so they won't need to think too much about coming to America."

"Yup, my father and I go there almost every year to see how things are going. The people in Teresina love him. Every time we go, crowds gather to take pictures with him."

"Wow! He must be very popular there!"

"Oh yeah! He would easily become president if that place were a country." They both laughed. Kamao was grateful that Lindsey had shared another image of her father with him. He was now willing to believe in the senator's good faith regarding their relationship.

Kamao went to work that Monday afternoon wondering what the deal with the senator was. He had been dating Lindsey for almost two years, and the senator had only shown hatred toward him, then, suddenly, he asked for his number because he wanted to learn more about him. Lindsey exulted at her father's sudden interest in her boyfriend, but not Kamao. As he liked to do in challenging situations, he resolved to be cautious. With someone like Senator

McAdams, he knew that he needed to be prepared for anything. His phone rang—speak of the devil.

"Hello! Is this *Kamoo*?" the senator asked.

"Yes, this is him," Kamao said.

"This is Senator McAdams."

"Hello again, sir," Kamao said, nervous as always when he was talking to the senator.

"If you are free tomorrow around noon, I would like you to come to my office at the Capitol. We'll have lunch and talk. Would that be OK?"

"Yes, sir; that would be fine. I will be there."

"OK, great! This is my cell number in case you change your mind or you can't make it. And please don't tell Lindsey anything about this. Can you do that?"

"Yes, I can do that."

"OK, see you then. Bye."

Kamao hung up, and his heart was pounding. What did the senator want with him now? he wondered. The last time they were together, the senator had invited a squad of annoying and condescending members of American high society to patronize and intimidate him. He wanted to stay positive, but he believed that there was something fishy about his girlfriend's father's sudden interest.

The senator was in his office when Kamao arrived at the Capitol.

"Hello, welcome. The senator will see you now; he is in his office," the secretary said.

"You are right on time, *Kamoo*; welcome. Please have a seat," the senator said, as Kamao entered his office.

"Thank you, sir," Kamao said and sat down.

"I need to finish something quickly, and we will go out to eat something. Is that OK?" the senator asked, looking at Kamao over his glasses.

"Yes, that's fine." Kamao used the few minutes he was given to explore the room. Most pictures on the walls depicted the senator and his family. Some showed him and Lindsey and some places they had visited. One picture drew his attention. The senator was standing in front of a building in the middle of a crowd of adults and children. Next to him was a man in a cassock holding a large black book with a long rosary that was hanging from the side. Kamao thought he was the childhood friend turned priest that Lindsey talked about and that the building was the orphanage, with the orphans spread around the senator and the adults being some curious supporters or employees. He considered asking the senator about the pictures to start a conversation that could consolidate their relationship, but gave up the idea after some thought.

"OK, I am all done for now. I will finish the rest later. Are you ready?"

"Yes, sir!" Kamao said.

"Then let's go."

Le Petit Coin, a chic French restaurant two blocks from Pennsylvania Avenue, was one of Senator McAdams's favorite places to go on special occasions. When he called to reserve a table, an area was set up for him and his guest, away from the eyes of curious customers and passersby.

"This is a nice place, sir!" Kamao said, keeping up with his American good manners.

"Yeah, it's nice, isn't it?" the senator said as they sat down and the two bodyguards who accompanied them positioned themselves a few feet away. "You have great table manners," the senator said, after observing Kamao's every move, from how he held the spoons and forks to how he dashingly spat the fish bones in his colorful, aromatized napkin and folded it back. He smiled and didn't say a word, knowing well that the lunch invitation was a test. The senator was more relaxed than usual, acting like he'd known Kamao for decades and was used to his company. His poised and courteous attitude caused Kamao to relax a little. Maybe Lindsey was right: the senator might be finally coming to his senses.

"Tell me about your family," the senator asked.

Kamao nervously cleared his throat and told the senator that his father had a dozen children from a handful of women and that his family, regardless, lived in perfect harmony. He told him about his father's prosperous career as a scientist before joining the government to become the Health Secretary. He told him about his mother and her successful wholesale and retail business that was expanding beyond the country's borders into the neighboring countries of Togo and Côte d'Ivoire. The senator listened to Kamao with a blank stare, not too impressed with his family's success.

"Would you walk with me for a while in the national park? I have something to show you," the senator said. Kamao wondered why the senator cut him short. He knew then that the senator didn't care about him or his family. One thing was evident: Brad McAdams was up to something, and Kamao decided at that moment he was going to stand up for himself and his love for Lindsey and fight back against the senator.

"Why are you so strongly against me dating your daughter, Senator? For what reason do you dislike me so much?" he asked.

The senator smiled; he gently tapped Kamao on the shoulder and said, "I don't hate you. On the contrary: I like your perseverance. My daughter seems to be very fond of you, and that is why I decided to see things differently and take a different approach than before." Kamao couldn't picture what the senator was getting at. He wondered if it wouldn't be better to bid the senator good day and leave, but for Lindsey's sake he resolved to carry on with the sunny afternoon adventure with Mr. McAdams.

There were a few people at Lincoln Park when Kamao and the senator arrived. The latter headed straight toward an imposing bronze statue that depicted a Black woman holding something in her hand that Kamao couldn't see, and two children reaching to get it.

"This, my friend, is a statue that I find very inspirational." Kamao looked down on the pedestal and read, Mary McLeod Bethune, 1875–1955. "People find it surprising when I tell them that one of my favorite historical figures is Mary McLeod Bethune, particularly people who call me racist," the senator said. "I admire this woman because not only did she contribute greatly to this country, but she knew the right place to start her journey to the top. According to historians, she was the first person born free in her family and the first to get a formal education. She always knew her place. She focused on the limit of her reach and managed to develop her corner of the large garden that this country represents. She became popular among her people first and later caught the eye of the nation because she focused on what she could manage and who she could have influence amongst. And as her preeminence grew, her fame reached a national scale, and her image is forever engraved in the nation's memory. She became an important member of Roosevelt's administration." The senator spoke passionately about the woman that Kamao knew nothing about, but whom he already intended to research.

"Why are you telling me all of this, Senator?" Kamao asked, resolved to stop wondering about the senator's motives.

"What are your intentions regarding my daughter?" Mr. McAdams said, turning to his interlocutor.

Kamao was a bit perplexed but understood that the occasion was probably his only chance to convince the senator he was a good fit for his daughter.

"I love her. I love her very much. I see a future with her, and I want to be with her. I had hoped to have this moment with you, Senator. I have the intention to propose to her soon and was hoping that I would have your permission—"

"What are you bringing into this relationship?" the senator asked abruptly.

"She has my love and protection."

"Your protection? From what? How will you protect her?"

"I won't let anything happen to her. I am sure about that."

The senator laughed, shaking his head as though he were thinking how funny Kamao's baby talk was.

"Lindsey is the only person I have left in this world. After my wife and my son died, she became my world. Everything I do, I do for her. I worked hard to make sure she won't need anything when I am gone. I work hard to make sure she is well taken care of when I am not around. You have no clue what it means to keep her safe." Kamao began to sense a rage in the senator's voice and wondered if he should simply leave and avoid the drama that was likely to result from the encounter. He knew, however, that walking away would mean the end of his relationship with Lindsey—the only thing he was now sure the senator wanted. If he couldn't fight off her father's attacks, then he wasn't worthy of Lindsey's love, he thought.

"What do you expect from me, Senator? What can I do to prove to you that I am serious about your daughter and that she is and will be happy with me?" he asked, facing his girlfriend's father.

"I can't expect anything from you because you have nothing to offer her: no safety, no protection, only the pleasure of the moment. What do you bring into this relationship compared to what she already has?"

"If you worry that I am with your daughter for her money, you can ask her if I have ever taken a penny from her."

"She's already started wasting her time and assets traveling with you."

"I paid for both our tickets for our trip to Ghana. I was taking her there, so I told her to let me pay for the trip. I can take good care of your daughter if only you stop seeing me as an opportunist."

"Lindsey is a sweet girl—naïve and too trusting sometimes," the senator said, with a calm voice, looking away. "My job is to protect her the best I can."

"You don't need to protect her from me. I've always had her best interests in mind and always will." Kamao paused and sighed as the senator remained silent. "I wouldn't mind signing a prenup if my taking advantage of your fortune is what you are worried about."

"Ha ha! Lindsey would never agree to that," the senator said, amused.

"You know that she loves me then, but you refused to accept that. Why? I have the feeling that money is not your only worry. What is it that makes me so unworthy of your daughter? Is it because I am an immigrant? An African?" Kamao was shocked by his own audacity, standing before a prominent United States senator and questioning him vehemently. It wasn't something he would typically do, but his future with Lindsey was at stake, and he saw himself ready to brave the storm that was coming his way. McAdams' two bodyguards were watching the two men from a distance, far enough to be strangers to the exchange but close enough to rescue the senator if there was a need to do so. The senator smiled.

"I like you, and I admire your tenacity. You care about Lindsey. I tried not to care about who she wanted to date. I wanted to be a liberal parent. But I figured that could not always work, especially considering the situation that we are in . . ."

"What situation—?"

"I will tell you what: you and I are going to have an agreement. If you slowly let things go with Lindsey, I will help you with a lot of things, starting with this." The senator took a checkbook and a pen out of his jacket pocket, wrote a check, and signed it. "This will only be a start; I will help you get whatever you need—job connections—you can start leaving your mark wherever you want. But of course, no one could know about this arrangement, especially Lindsey." He handed the check to Kamao.

"You want to buy away my love for your daughter with thirty thousand dollars and some favors?" Kamao said, smiling and shaking his head. He folded the check and handed it back to the senator. "I don't want to lose respect for you, Senator. So I will politely return this check to you, but please, don't ever do this again. You clearly don't understand that certain things are far beyond your control, no matter how powerful you are. I have one thing to ask of you: if you're not going to give us your blessing, can you at least leave us alone?" Kamao left the senator in front of Bethune's statue and called for a taxi.

"What about fifty thousand dollars?" the senator yelled, his voice echoing behind Kamao, who didn't turn back.

Chapter 19

KC Mile's promotional night had turned out to be an important event. Fans and the nightclub regulars responded in a significant number to the advertisement of the performance at Cosmos. The club was crowded when Lindsey and Kamao arrived.

"Oh, man! This place is jam-packed," Kamao said. They went to the bar and waited for their friends there. Megan texted Lindsey that they were a few minutes away.

"You are going to show your dancing skills tonight," Lindsey said.

"I am not going on that floor," he quickly retorted, as if he knew precisely what she was going to say. After his feud with the senator, Kamao had been conflicted with his decision to propose to Lindsey. He had ordered an engagement ring that came on the same day Mr. McAdams invited him. He left the ring in the bag in his closet and couldn't decide when the right time would be for a wedding proposal, especially now that the senator had made it clear to him that he would be a consistent obstacle to his happiness with Lindsey.

"So, what are we drinking?" Lindsey continued to tease him.

"I don't want any alcohol, but I can get you whatever you want," he said, looking at her with surprise.

"I was just joking; relax, baby," she said, pinching him on the forearm. "Don't be so tense. I won't ask you to do this again, I promise." Kamao nodded. He was wearing a blue polo shirt under a dark suit jacket with a pair of blue jeans that landed on top of two leather moccasins. Lindsey had on one of her favorite blue dresses for special occasions. As they started getting bored, Megan, Trish, and two guys walked in. Lindsey waved at them.

"You look stunning as always, Lin," Trish said, hugging her friend tightly.

"You look stunning yourself," Lindsey said.

Megan's left hand was locked in her boyfriend's as she approached Lindsey and Kamao and said, "This is Marvin; Marvin, these are my friends Lindsey and Kamao." It was Trish's turn to introduce her "date" that wasn't a real date: it was her annoying nerdy neighbor, Kris, a newly graduated computer engineer who worked part-time at the neighborhood college and wouldn't leave her alone. Trish knew from the start he wasn't her type: too pale and too frail for her with his curled ginger hair that always looked like it needed a new application of gel or conditioner. The round bifocal glasses that allowed him to see his surroundings appeared to fit his panicky and agitated personality. He was kind to her, and she didn't want to break his heart, so she kept him around and let him spoil her on occasion. He'd surprised her with a 75-inch TV when she told him that she accidentally cracked hers when she tried to kill a fly. The new TV took almost an entire wall of her apartment, but she kept it to keep him happy. His parents were both corporate executives, so he could afford to spend money on a girl he liked, especially since Trish didn't mind.

Megan's new boyfriend Marvin looked fearsome, like a giant assassin or a villain in a Hollywood action movie. His athletic body was accentuated by a tight burgundy V-neck T-shirt neatly tucked inside his blue jeans, revealing his stout biceps. He was an inch or two taller than Kamao, with some freckles on his face and arms. His scattered red hair made Kamao wonder if he had forgotten to brush it or if that was part of his style. His handshake was firm, making Lindsey bounce in pain.

"Sorry, bad habit," he said. Kamao looked at him with fury but maintained his cool. "Let me make it up to all of you," Marvin said, as he sensed that he was making his new friends uncomfortable. "Bartender," he called, "bring something strong for everybody, will you?" Kamao politely declined, followed by Lindsey, who looked at Megan with a distressed smile.

It had been almost an hour and a half, and the party was at its peak. KC Mile's performance raised applause and cheering from the crowd. Megan, Marvin, Trish, and Kris hit the floor and showed their dance moves. Lindsey joined them for a while, but came back to stay with Kamao, who was still standing by the bar, attempting to enjoy the party without getting on the dance floor. He wanted to please his girlfriend, but he wouldn't violate his principle: he wasn't a nightclub guy, and he wasn't going to become one, not even to please Lindsey. When the pack joined Kamao later, there was a new couple with them.

"This is my friend Jim," Marvin said to Kamao, who shook his hand with a "How are you doing, Jim?"

"I think it's getting kind of late now. Are you ready to go, baby?" Lindsey asked Kamao.

"What? The party is just getting started," Marvin said. He got behind Megan and put his arms across her chest while rubbing himself against her.

"What the fuck is your problem, Marvin?" Megan yelled angrily, freeing herself, disgusted by his behavior. "I am not your bitch, so stop treating me like one."

"Wow! Pretty mama," Marvin said, "calm down, all right? You don't have to be all aggressive and shit. We all know how things are going to end tonight, so why don't we just start heating it up a little?" He walked back to her, his arms opened.

"Get away from me; you're drunk," Megan said, attempting to push him away. He firmly grabbed her wrist and pulled her. Megan tripped and almost fell. He pressed her against his chest with both arms, almost strangling her.

"Isn't that fun, hm? You feel the muscle, right? It's going to be all yours tonight."

"Stop, please! You're hurting me," Megan pleaded, on the verge of crying. Lindsey looked at Kamao, silently begging for his intervention. The latter gently patted Marvin on the shoulder.

"Come on, man, just let her go, all right?"

"Man, don't touch me!" Marvin growled, throwing a backhand that Kamao dodged.

Megan used the distraction to free herself for a few seconds before Marvin rushed and grabbed her again from behind. This time, he reached inside her blouse and grabbed her breast with one hand and pulled her waist toward him with the other.

"Why don't you let me feel what I will be working with tonight, huh?" he said, petting her.

"OK, that's enough," Kamao said, pushing him back while holding on to Megan to free her from his grip. Marvin tumbled and rolled on the floor. He got back up, fuming with rage.

"You piece of shit! Trying to play the hero, huh? To please the ladies? I am gonna teach you a lesson." He charged at Kamao and threw a punch. Kamao swiftly averted it with an inside block and delivered a backhand, full speed, that landed on Marvin's right cheek. The blow threw him back on the ground with a groaning sound. Jim jumped behind Kamao and grabbed him, locking both of his arms.

"What do you think you're doing, punk? You think you're tough, huh?" Jim said. Seeing Kamao's torso exposed, Marvin rushed back to his feet and charged the second time but received a front kick to his solar plexus and fell on his back, struggling to breathe. Kamao headbutted Jim with full force, and the latter hopped in pain, holding his bloody nose, freeing his opponent.

"He broke my nose! Oh, shit!" he said. Kamao was shocked by his work; he tried to comfort his victim and apologize, when he heard "Watch out, baby!" and turned around only to receive a firm fist that split his upper lip and threw him on the ground. Two security guards, alerted by the fight, rushed to the scene as Kamao got back up and started to clean his bloody lip with the back of his hand, panting.

Kamao's nightclub fight was a subject of discussion between Lindsey and her friends, who saw in her boyfriend a real gentleman, a true hero, who fought and risked his safety to protect a woman's dignity. But Lindsey was engulfed by guilt because of Kamao's two-day incarceration and thousand-dollar fine. It was her fault that Kamao got into a fight in that nightclub, she thought. If she hadn't begged him, nothing would have happened. He hated nightclubs, and he'd told her. She wondered why she didn't let it go for real. She wasn't happy that Kamao went to jail.

"I am sorry, baby! It was all my fault," she said when she went to pick him up after he was released. "If I hadn't convinced you to go, none of this would have happened."

"It's OK! Let's put it behind us," he said, patting his swollen stitched lip. He didn't feel like talking or hearing Lindsey's apologies. He just wanted to go home, take a hot shower, and lay down. "You don't mind dropping me off at my place and letting me recuperate for a while, do you? We can talk tomorrow if that's OK!"

"Yeah, sure!" she said, regretting that she couldn't even spend the evening with him with the possibility of apology sex. She drove home after dropping him off, thinking about how she was going to face her father, who called her earlier about the matter. For Senator McAdams, Kamao's brawl at the nightclub was a perfect opportunity to push his agenda to distance him from his daughter. As he was weighing his options, Lindsey pulled into the driveway. He came out of the study to meet her in the living room.

"Are you OK, honey? Come here," he said. He hugged her tightly.

"Thanks, Dad, I needed that."

"How are you feeling?" he asked, freeing her.

"I am not OK! I think Kamao is mad at me because I made him go to that club. He didn't want to go. I am so disappointed in myself," she said, crashing on the couch.

"Come on now, honey! How could you be mad at yourself? It isn't your fault that the guy is violent and impulsive."

"You weren't there, Dad. I was. He didn't fight because he was provoked; he put himself in harm's way to defend Megan. How much more unselfish can a person be than that?"

"Did you know this wasn't the first time he beat someone up so badly and had to appear before a judge? He busted his roommate's lip over a small argument."

"Where did you hear that from? Have you been digging up dirt on him?" Lindsey got off the couch and walked to the window, upset with her father's persistent disapproval of Kamao.

"I am rather well informed."

"Well, you weren't there either. He told me what happened. The guy stole his money, all he had when he first came here."

"And you believe him?"

"Of course I believe him!" Linsdey paused and took a deep breath, regretting yelling at her father, but resolved to confront him and to ask him to back off from Kamao.

"Why do you hate him so much, Dad?" she continued. "What has he done to you? Don't you see that I love him, truly? Everything you are doing to hurt him is hurting me." Lindsey couldn't hold back her tears anymore.

"This guy is trying to take advantage of you, and you don't see that. You say you love him. He just wants to take advantage of you. My job is to protect you against anything and anyone. You are blinded by whatever he is tricking you with. I don't trust these people."

"Who do you mean by 'these people'? Do you mean immigrants? Africans? How many of these people do you personally know to judge them like you are doing right now? You just function on assumptions and prejudice. I've seen Kamao's family; I've lived with his people; they are decent, kind, lovely, and fun to be around. You don't know these people—I do."

The senator shook his head, smiling, amused by his daughter's naivety. He went back to his study, and Lindsey went to her room and called Trish, in tears.

Kamao lay in bed gazing at the ceiling, lost in his thoughts. Things had started going downhill for him again, and this time faster than he thought. He was no longer angry at Lindsey as he was a few days earlier. It wasn't her fault after all that he got into a fight at the nightclub. He simply couldn't stand by and watch Megan be defiled by the immature, perverted Marvin. He fought against the thought that Lindsey was partially to blame for making him go. He knew he would forgive her soon; he just needed that evening for himself to figure a few things out. It was his second time getting into a fight in America—he knew it wouldn't be suitable for his record—and he wished he had done things differently. In the situation with Adeomi, he could have avoided the physical altercation. But how could he have done things differently at the nightclub other than not having gone at all? There was another problem: Senator McAdams, who wanted him to end things with his daughter.

Kamao knew that by defying the senator, he had created for himself a dreadful enemy and would have to watch his back as well as every one of his moves if he wanted to carry on with Lindsey. His phone rang. It was Ali. What does he want this late at night? Kamao thought. He picked it up.

"Kamao!" Ali said. "Something terrible happened. Peter is dead; he got shot. The police cars are everywhere. I need you to come and help me close the store. Please!"

"OK!" Kamao said before looking at the clock. It was 2:13 a.m.

Kamao arrived at the gas station half an hour later and couldn't find a spot on the illuminated cement parking lot. There were half a dozen police cars with crime scene barricade tape stretched across the lot. Several nearby residents, excited to be the first witnesses of the police response to the crime scene, resolved to stay and watch everything. Their smartphones kept flashing and they told newcomers stories that didn't match reality.

"Excuse me, officer," Kamao said to one of the police officers, after parking his car a block away. "My name is Kamao. I work here; my boss just called me to come and help him."

"Can I see some ID, please?" the officer said. Kamao handed him his driver's license.

"I will be right back," the officer said and entered the store. A few minutes later, he came back with two plastic bags and handed Kamao his ID. "Here, cover your shoes with these; you can go in."

A resident, one of the regular customers, approached Kamao. "What happened, Kamao? They said Peter got killed. What happened?" he asked.

"I don't know," Kamao replied. "I just got here." The officer raised the yellow tape for Kamao to go in. He entered the store and saw white linen covering a body on the floor. He felt a chill run through his body; he almost fainted. There was Peter, the refugee, the resilient guy from Asia, his friend, whose stories he loved to hear regardless of the heartbreaking images they created in his mind. Peter, who was happy to be in America with his family, was lying motionless in the middle of the cold cement floor. Kamao thought about his family. He had met some of them: his wife Prashu and two of his daughters, Sangita and Dina. Peter certainly had no life insurance, Kamao thought.

Ali waved for Kamao to come inside the cabin. "These motherfuckers!" he said, as Kamao entered. "They have issues with everybody. They have issues with rednecks, with whites, with Indians, everybody." Kamao wondered who he was talking about until he realized that he meant African Americans, after discovering who the suspect was. "They complain about everything, they say everybody is against them," Ali continued, "and all they do is smoke every day, sell drugs, and rap, that's it."

But you sell them what they smoke, Kamao thought. Ali's hands were shaking as he counted the money.

"They are going to close the store," he said. "I don't know if it will open again." He put the money on the counter, unable to hold his emotion. "We come to this country for a better life after they messed up ours and look at what they are doing to us!" He started sobbing. Kamao wondered who he meant by "us."

"What happened?" Kamao finally asked. "Do they know who did this?"

"It was John," Ali said. "He didn't even hide his face, he didn't even run. Everything is on camera. The police said they found him in his house, and they took him to the station already."

"John, the Solo Guy?" Kamao asked, incredulous. Ali nodded. John was an army veteran who was dishonorably discharged for substance abuse while on duty. He had a long gray beard and thick dreads. He didn't talk to anyone besides the store employees and Ali. He always had a cigarette in his mouth and was never seen with anyone, which granted him the nickname "Solo Guy." "Why would he do something like this?" Kamao asked. "He and Peter are friends."

"You should know not to trust these people," Ali said. "I am sure he killed him over something stupid. These people don't settle issues with fistfights like we do in other countries; they just shoot for every little thing because it's easy for them to buy guns like candy."

Kamao couldn't keep his eyes away from the body on the floor even as he helped Ali count the money and arrange the cash register area for an indefinite closure. It could have been him lying there, he thought. He worked the night shift sometimes when Peter was off or couldn't come in for some reason. He and John never argued but who knew? John liked to come in late at night and play on the gambling machines till dawn sometimes. He preferred to come in when there were not a lot of people around. He helped Peter sometimes, volunteering to serve as a second hand or bodyguard when Peter needed to make coffee and it was too quiet outside. Ali and all the employees knew he carried a gun. He showed it to Peter and told him he always had it on him; that's why Peter liked having him around at night. Kamao never bothered Solo Guy nor asked him for a favor when he was covering for Peter. He never rejected John's offer to help either, and he would thank him with a cup of coffee or a bag of chips. John seemed like an honest guy who never took advantage of kindness. He would pay for the second bag of chips when he liked the first one that he got for free. Something might have been going on with him the night he killed Peter, Kamao thought.

Ali told Kamao how, based on the camera footage, Peter and John were the only people in the store that night before the incident. John was the last person in the game room, playing after the last couple left, smoking one cigarette after another. Every time he won some money, a ticket would print under the cash register with the amount, and Peter would hand him the corresponding cash when he came to claim it, or he would go to the game room and give it to him. John had already lost a good amount of money after playing for two hours on the gambling machine.

He came to the cabin door and knocked after playing for another hour with no ticket printed.

"I won twenty dollars," he said when Peter opened the door.

"I didn't see any ticket printed," Peter said, "Let me go check." Peter checked the ticket printer, but there was nothing. "The ticket didn't print. Go try to print it again," Peter said.

"Just give me my fucking money, man! I ain't got time for no bullshit," John said, starting to get agitated. He wouldn't let Peter say a word as he carried on with ranting and cursing. As Peter opened the cabin door to tell him one more time that the ticket still didn't print, John pulled him out of the cabin and pointed his gun at him.

"OK, calm down, man," Peter said, his hands raised. "I will go get you the twenty dollars."

"Oh, now that you see the fucking gun, you gon' give me my money, huh?" Peter didn't finish shaking his head in a full cycle before John pulled the trigger. Peter fell, gasping, as the bullet lodged in his abdomen. John walked out of the store like nothing happened, leaving his victim in a pool of blood. A customer walked in thirty minutes later and saw a stream of blood under the door that led to the hallway with no sign of Peter behind the cash register. She alerted the police, and the officers who responded first saw Peter's body when they opened the door to the hallway. John was arrested with no resistance, but would not say a word to anyone during his interrogation.

"You can go to the store on Covington if you still want a job," Ali said.

"Isn't Covington a ghetto too?" Kamao asked.

"Yes, but there are bars and a nightclub next door with security guards, and I have a gun in that store. You know how to use a gun, right? I didn't know how to use it before I came here, but now I do." Kamao didn't find it necessary to answer that question. He wondered if it was worth it continuing that gas station job. He resolved to start looking for another job, a flexible job that would allow him to finish his last year in college. He would go to Covington while looking for something safer, he thought.

He left the store around 4:30 a.m. and noticed a car following him, turning every direction he headed. His heart started pounding as he wondered what he should do. He pulled into an empty plaza, and the black SUV didn't follow him. He sighed in relief and waited for a few minutes before getting back on the road and noticed the car behind him again less than a minute later. He moved to the left lane on the two-lane road and pressed the accelerator. The other driver accelerated as well and stayed in the right lane to reach Kamao's side and raised a piece of cardboard. Kamao read: You need to know your place, nigger, or you will end up badly. The car drove off, and Kamao's heart started pounding again as he was certain the message was meant for him. That driver couldn't be mistaken; he must have known who Kamao was. He wondered who might be coming after him and thought about Marvin, who was probably taunting him through one of his acolytes while in prison for sexual assault. He couldn't stop thinking about the incident when he arrived home and remembered something the senator said when they stood in front of Lady Bethune's statue, about staying in one's place. He rejected the idea that the senator would want to hurt him.

Glass House's mid-July poll in Senator McAdams's home state found him six points behind the Democratic candidate, the successful businessman and former mayor of San Antonio, Kenneth McGill. The senator's support for a "cavalier immigration policy," as many of his constituents called it, began to pose a threat to his plan to reclaim his seat in November, and his opponent never missed the opportunity to use the slightest mishap in the handling of the migrants' situation at the southern border to criticize the senator and to present himself as a better alternative to Brad McAdams in the coming elections. A high-tech business mogul, Kenneth McGill transferred his business skills into politics, where he used every opportunity to sell his image as a valuable candidate. He was in his late forties, with some gray hair growing on each side of his head. A great orator, he drove crowds to his rallies and raised long-lasting applause with his enchanting rhetoric. Millennials and Dreamers who thirsted for politicians with a new vision saw him as their champion. For them, there was a necessity for change in the country's politics, from immigration to healthcare and education.

"I hear your cry, graduates with heavy student loans," he said at a rally in El Paso. "Brad McAdams has been a senator for over three decades and has no clue what his constituents' issues are; he should ask himself what he has done to make them want to keep him in the Senate. Look at what is happening at our border: children are being separated from their parents and piled up in holding facilities like sardines. That has to stop. We have to find a new way, a more humane way, to address immigration issues. If I am elected senator, I will work with my colleagues from both parties to find solutions that are acceptable for all, that guarantee the preservation of intrinsic human rights for all, for illegal parents and the innocent children they bring with them to this beautiful country of ours, the United States of America."

"Scumbag!" the senator said, throwing his glass of wine that shattered against the wall. "He just loves to vilify me; son of a bitch!" he said, rubbing his head and grinding his teeth. His campaign advisers looked at each other, perplexed, wondering about the proper course of action to take. They were viewing a recording of the opponent's rally to plan their next move. But with the senator's continued outbursts, they found their job much more difficult each time.

"I've been thinking about something, and I wonder if you would consider this option, Senator," Andrew Zora, the newest addition to the campaign team, said.

"Go ahead, Andrew," the senator said, turning to him.

"I wanted to say . . ." He cleared his throat, suddenly feeling a tightness grip him. "That guy who is dating your daughter—we all know how much you disapprove of the relationship, but what if you let him get closer to you and let them be together to show your detractors a totally different side of you that contradicts some voters' perception of you?"

"That's not such a bad idea," one of the older advisers added. "You could play it cool, at least until the elections are over and you win your seat back. In the meantime, you could let him travel with you and Lindsey and let him appear as one of your closest advisors."

"That's out of the question!" the senator said. "That little vermin wants to propose to my daughter; allowing him to get closer to me would only get his hopes up, and things will get more complicated later if I let that happen."

Chapter 20

Kamao sat behind the bulletproof glass at the gas station on Covington where Ali sent him after Peter was killed and the store was closed. He gazed at the store floor through the glass, his eyes zooming from one shelf to the other. It was 4:00 p.m.; people would be leaving work soon, and it would be a busy time. But for the time being, all he needed to do was wait, abandoned to his thoughts. He had had enough of the gas station job. Not only had it become more dangerous, but he wanted to try something different; it didn't matter if it would be more exciting or boring. Something different than selling cigarillos and White Owls to customers who smoked weed all day. After his graduation next year, he would look for something more suitable, a professional job. As a political science major, there would be a wide range of options lined up for him to choose from. He looked at the counter and stared at the 9mm Glock that Ali kept in the store. "I like to leave it on the counter so they can see it and know what would be waiting for them if they wanted to try something," Ali said.

Kamao wondered if he would have the guts to pull the trigger if his time came, looking at his victim hitting the ground as life departed him. He thought he should quit. He could quit the job and still survive, relying on the money his mother would send him from his business back home. But he didn't think that would be ideal, to rely on an outside resource while living in America. And besides, he liked working; he found it rewarding, and that was the essence of the American pride: men and women doing their part to contribute to the country's economy and enjoying the freedom and protection guaranteed and owed to them by their government. He had a bright future in America, he thought. He was on the path to graduate from college without the burden of a student loan; that, he thought, was an accomplishment. Many people would envy his good fortune. Having an outside resource was valuable, but he wouldn't rely on it to live in America. He would continue to work hard and build wealth here in America, apart from his family's accomplishments.

Le Petit Coin had become Kamao's favorite restaurant in DC after Senator McAdams took him there. That was the place he chose to make up with Lindsey.

"I like this place. It is very nice," Lindsey said. "My dad brought me here a couple of times. How did you know about it?"

"DC is not that big, you know!" he said, smiling. He wondered if she would guess that it was her father who showed him the place. She never asked him about that call from her father at the hospital. He didn't think she had forgotten about that; she was probably waiting for the right moment to ask him about it, he thought. He had told her about the night he was followed, the same night Peter was killed, and what the sign that the driver was holding had said.

"Did you ever find out who it was that was following you?" Lindsey asked.

"No, I didn't, but I am still thinking about it." They both remained silent for a while, each one wondering what the other person was thinking.

"Do you think it could be my father trying to scare you with one of his dogs?"

"Why would you suggest that?"

"We had a fight the other day after you got out of . . ."

"Jail, you can say it," Kamao said, holding her hand and smiling at her. "That's OK! I am over it."

"I can't understand his hostility toward you; it's been growing since the incident at the nightclub. He gave me so much hope when we got back from Accra, and suddenly he changed course again. You remember at the hospital when he wanted to talk to you?" Kamao nodded, nervously. She remembered.

"Did he ever call you back?"

"No," he said, almost choking on his word, ashamed to have to lie to her so audaciously, like a skilled conman.

Lindsey shook her head. "Unbelievable! He was just playing me all along," she said. "I am going to ask him if he sent his dog on you that night. I need an answer. He'd better back off of you. He needs to stop acting like the world belongs to him. I feel like I don't know him sometimes." Two streams of tears started running down her cheeks. Kamao reached for a napkin and gave it to her.

"Thank you," she said. "I am so sorry you are going through all of this and still stand by my side."

He smiled, opting to swallow his next words: I still stand by you because I love you.

When Lindsey got home, her father was in a meeting in his study. Some cars were parked in the driveway. His campaign advisers needed to polish his speech before his next rally in two days. Working late in the evening and into the night became their new routine as the senator vowed to reclaim his seat come November. Lindsey waited patiently for her father's guests to leave then caught him as he headed upstairs. "How are you, Dad?" she said.

"Oh, honey! I didn't know you were home," the senator said, letting go of the handrail.

"Do you need anything from me for the rally on Thursday?" Lindsey asked, getting off the couch.

"I will be happy to have you with me there. People seem to like you, and that might boost my chances to snatch my seat from that maggot McGill, who thinks he can sideline me."

"I don't think he's got any chance against you. The lead he has right now is just a bump in the road, I think. Anyway, we will see what happens, right?"

"You're damn right, my girl!" Lindsey poured herself a glass of water and looked at the clock; it was almost 9:00 p.m. She couldn't wait till the next morning with her burning need to know her father's involvement with the incident on the road.

"Good night, honey," the senator said, heading back to the stairs.

"I do have a question for you, Dad!"

"Yes, go ahead," the senator said, turning back for the second time, his glasses in his hand, looking exhausted.

"Did you send someone to scare Kamao off a couple of days ago?" The senator smiled, shaking his head.

"Does that guy have to appear in every one of our conversations now?"

"That guy's name is Kamao, and I love him. Why is it so hard for you to see that?"

"You keep giving him ideas to the point that he talked about proposing. I'm not in the mood to talk about him tonight; I am going to bed."

"What? What did you just say, Dad? He talked about proposing?"

"Oh, damn! I don't want to do this tonight. Yes, he talked about proposing when I met with him. How is he going to take care of you with a damn gas station job? Don't you see the picture here? Are you so blind that you can't see what this guy is doing?"

"I don't understand you, Dad! Tell me this: you were willing to let me date and possibly marry people like Travis, an immature and ignorant brat, or Johnathan, who was living a double life, but you can't stand it when I find someone that I love, a guy who respects himself and who respects women. I thought you didn't want to be in my way as to whom I wanted to be with? You didn't dig any dirt up on the other guys I dated before, but you won't leave Kamao alone." She paused to catch her breath. The senator was silent, looking at his daughter unabashed by her complaint. "It is because the other guys were white and he is Black. You can't deny it anymore, huh? You are pathetic. I am not going anywhere with you on Thursday." She picked up her jacket that she had laid on the couch and went to her room. The senator stood in the middle of the living room.

Lindsey went to Kamao's apartment the next morning and caught him right as he was getting ready to run some errands before going to work. "You had a meeting with my father, and you told me he didn't call you? I can't believe you lied to me," she said, pushing the door as he opened it, almost hitting him with it. Kamao knew that the time would eventually come when he would face the reality of telling Lindsey the truth, but he was unaware that it would come so soon.

"I . . . I . . ." he uttered, taking a few steps back from the fearful lioness Lindsey had suddenly become. He never thought she would come out so bold; the peaceful, innocent, almost naïve Lindsey, as most people thought of her, had mutated into a belligerent, fearsome being that made Kamao feel like running through the walls to escape her rage.

"And you were going to propose, he said?"

"Baby, if you can only calm down, I can explain," he finally said. She grabbed onto the couch as if she was afraid she would faint. Kamao gently grabbed her arm, inviting her to sit down.

"Let go of me," she said, pushing him away. The commotion would have awakened Ayefumi if he and Kamao were still roommates. After Ayefumi's wife and son had joined him three weeks earlier, Kamao had moved to a single bedroom apartment in the same complex.

"I am sorry I didn't tell you I met your father."

"You lied to me. I've asked you; you said no. You lied to me."

"Yes, I lied to you. I am sorry."

"Why? I thought we trust each other?"

"Of course we do! Your father asked me not to tell you anything."

"And you listened to him? Why?"

"I don't know. I thought gaining his confidence would bring out something good."

"And why haven't you proposed as you told him you wanted to? Did you mean it?"

"Of course I meant it."

"Then why didn't you do it?" Lindsey's insistence made Kamao uncomfortable. He didn't want to spill everything out.

"I . . . I needed to think."

"Think!" Lindsey got up and walked toward him. "What do you need to think about? Are you having second thoughts, or don't you love me anymore? First, you lied to me, and now you need to think? Were you even serious about proposing, or did you lie to my father about that too?"

Kamao couldn't find the right words to respond to Lindsey. He stood there, his eyes fixed on her, his mouth open, with no sound to utter; he appeared for a moment like a soldier taken by surprise by a flying bullet that landed inside his chest. Lindsey took a few steps toward the window.

"I feel like I don't know you anymore; the lie, the doubt . . . the uncertainty. Is there something you are not telling me?"

"Your father offered to give me fifty thousand dollars if I broke up with you."

"What! He really did that?" Lindsey asked.

"Yes! And of course, I refused and walked away."

"So nothing has changed between us! Then why didn't you propose like you wanted to?"

"After the incident on the road, I thought . . . if it was your father, he might have other plans, so it would probably be better to wait a little bit and see."

"It was him," Lindsey said. "I asked him; he didn't deny it." She held Kamao's hands. "The fact that you refused that money is proof that you care about me and that your values are stronger than money and power, and I admire that about you. I am sorry that I doubted you and that I was angry at you." Kamao nodded and smiled as she hugged him and kissed him on the cheek. Lindsey took leave of Kamao in the parking lot with a long, tender kiss. He noticed a sticky note on his dashboard when he got to his car. He picked it up and threw it on the passenger seat. He started the car and attempted to back up but felt resistance. He got out and inspected the vehicle; all four tires were deflated. He thought about the sticky note and rushed to read it. This is your second warning, it said.

He called Lindsey. "How far are you? Can you come back? There is something I want to show you."

"It must be him," Lindsey said after reading the note and seeing the slashed tires. "It's my father's doing, I am certain of it."

Lindsey called Megan after she left Kamao; she needed to talk to someone. On Spencer Street, she was talking to Megan with such intensity that she didn't notice the yield sign and almost cut in front of a turning car, provoking a trail of profanity from the other driver. Half a mile farther, she swerved to avoid a head-on collision, and the phone landed under the gas pedal. She slowed down and picked it up. Megan could hear her sobbing.

"Pull over, Lindsey!" Megan said. "You need to stop driving. Pull over to the shoulder, please! I will call you back in a few minutes." Lindsey turned off the engine and rolled the windows down. Would her father go as far as hurting Kamao to put an end to their relationship? She felt sad that her father's pride was more important to him than her happiness. He wanted her happy, she recalled, and she was happy, but he wasn't. Megan called back, and Lindsey asked if she would let her stay with her in her apartment.

"Of course," Megan said. "You can stay with me for as long as you want."

"Thank you," Lindsey said. She went home, packed up a few things, and called her father; it went straight to his voicemail. "Dad," she said, "I am disappointed in you for what you are doing to Kamao. I won't be staying at home for the next few days, and if you do anything to hurt him, you will never see me again."

After listening to her message, the senator called Agent Murdock from his office at the Capitol and said, "Stand down on that boy for a little while, will you? Tell your guys to stand down for now."

Kamao sat on a bench in the small park across the street from Joseph Elk's Auto Repair. His car would be ready soon, but he was tired of the waiting room. In the park, he saw some children playing in the sand under the shadow of the trees, their mothers chatting and laughing while keeping an eye on them. One of the kids, a boy, probably four years old, drew Kamao's attention. The child's light skin suggested the race of one of the parents, and Kamao thought he could be the father to a mixed-race child in a few years if he stayed with Lindsey. He would love it. He had pictured a future with Lindsey, but things were becoming more complicated. He knew he had no real power to confront the influential US senator. He remembered his father's words—warnings, rather—the eve of their departure from Accra: "You are a man with your mindset, facing your own life choices," Nana Ofando said. "You probably think I no longer have anything to teach you, which is true, but just remember to trust your gut when it tells you at some point to retreat. A mackerel who swims with sharks and sees them as friends is only preparing his funeral. Remember, you don't have a family there until you create one on your own." Kamao wondered if his father knew what was coming; he also wondered if his love for Lindsey was strong enough to surmount the senator's hatred toward him. He reached for his phone and dialed Lindsey's number.

"Hi, baby," Lindsey said. "Is everything OK?"

"Yeah, everything is fine. I am waiting for the car to be fixed. Ali sent someone to cover for me until I get to the store. Hey, listen, what would you say about going fishing this Saturday? I heard the Potomac River is a nice getaway place to clear our heads; what do you say?"

"Yeah, that's a good idea," she said.

The spot that Kamao chose for his fishing outing with Lindsey was a quiet area hidden under some trees that allowed a few places of sunlight, adding a delight to the early-August, Saturday-afternoon romantic escape. Lindsey got out and opened the trunk to pick up the picnic basket, but Kamao rushed to snatch it.

"Hey, what did you do that for?"

"You will be tempted to open it!"

"What do you have in there? It smells delicious."

"It's a secret, baby! Just follow me."

"OK! Whatever you say," Lindsey said. She picked up the blanket Kamao left for her. He locked the car and held her hand as they walked. Kamao thought Lindsey was happy. He liked seeing her happy. For Lindsey, Kamao had an advanced sense of gallantry; his plan for a picnic was more proof. She liked it when he spoiled her, when he made her feel special, not with extravagant gifts, but with simple gestures that put her at the center of his attention. The spot Kamao found was on level ground, covered with short grass. "I am famished," Lindsey said. "I have to eat to get the strength to go fishing."

"Of course, my love," Kamao said. "Anything you want." She laid the blanket down, and they sat down. Some kayakers could be spotted on the horizon, and a few other people could be seen in the distance, some fishing and others walking. Kamao opened the basket and handed Lindsey a foil-wrapped minced-beef Wellington cooked in a puff pastry.

"Mmm," she said, after the first bite. "This, this is . . ." She was unable to finish her sentence.

"What did I tell you about talking with your mouth full, huh?" Kamao said in his paternal voice.

"Sorry, Dad!" she said, managing to swallow a portion. They both laughed.

"Let's not go there," Kamao said.

"Right, right," she said. "But what is this, though? It is delicious. Where did you get this?

"You ask too many questions; just eat your food."

"You're so mean!" she said, amused, and resumed chewing her food like a starving eagle who caught a baby fox in the falling night and began enjoying himself on the spot. A serving of fruit salad followed the meal, with some Château Latour to accompany it. "Mmm, I love French wine! It's nice being here with you today after the crazy week with all my father's . . ." She stopped, seeing the firm look on Kamao's face.

"I love being here with you today, and I want this to be a special moment for us," he said after a moment of silence. "I am so lucky to have you! You can't imagine how happy you make me. If only . . . never mind."

She leaned over and kissed him. "Oh, my phone—I left it in the car," she said, struggling to get up.

"What are you going to do with your phone? I left mine too, on purpose."

"I understand, baby, but I have to capture this moment for future generations."

"For future what?" he yelled behind her as she rushed toward the car. She got her phone and headed back, and as she got closer to him, Kamao got on one knee and opened a black box.

"Lindsey McAdams," he said, "from the moment I set my eyes on you in that first class we took together, I hoped to have a chance to talk to you one day, and after our discussion at Kaitlyn's engagement party, I hoped for this very moment, and now it is here." Lindsey started shaking and covered her mouth in a surprised gaze. "We have been through some . . . things, but the fact that we are here together at this moment means that we have a lot to count on. We have our love, and we care for one another. Lindsey, I love you. I want you to be my wife. Will you marry me?"

She sighed, cleared her throat, and wiped her tears. "Yes, I will marry you." He put the bright diamond ring on her finger, got up, and kissed her. They heard some clapping with "Congratulations!" An older couple they hadn't noticed had watched the whole thing.

"Gosh, where do you get some privacy in this country?" Kamao said. They both laughed and asked the couple if they wouldn't mind taking some pictures of them.

Chapter 21

Carrie Reynolds's birthday was one of the rare occasions for the president to show his gratitude to his closest friends and political allies by inviting them to an exclusive soirée at the White House that usually ended with a movie in the family theater room. Senator McAdams hadn't talked to his daughter for an entire week, although he knew that she was staying with Megan. The First Lady had insisted that he bring his daughter to the party, so the senator called and left a message. For Lindsey, going to the party at the White House with her father could present an opportunity for reconciliation. It would be the perfect night to announce her engagement to Kamao to her father and talk him into burying his hatred for her fiancé. She came back home and put on a beige dress embroidered with blue sapphires for the occasion. She rode to the White House with her father, who didn't notice the ring, and she was relieved that he didn't, because the plan was to tell him when they returned home. She wished Kamao was with her. She missed Mama Agatha's parties that she organized in the middle of her compound under Accra's starry night, where a cool breeze from the Atlantic whistled in the palm trees. Young girls, men, and women shook their bodies, dancing around in a circle, waving colorful handkerchiefs to the sound of loud tam-tams, singing melodies known to all. Lindsey had joined them a couple of times and tried her best, moving at times in the direction opposite the crowd, leaving Kamao no choice but to burst out laughing. She found the classic American high society gatherings annoying and wished she didn't have to endure them.

It didn't take the First Lady a long time to notice the ring on Lindsey's finger. "Is that an engagement ring?" she said. "Congratulations, Lindsey! Do I know who the lucky guy is, Brad?" The senator looked at Lindsey's finger and smiled at the First Lady.

"No, I don't think you do, Carrie." For the remainder of the evening, Lindsey played in her head different scenarios of the fight she was going to have with her father at home. Senator McAdams, a veteran politician, didn't let his daughter's surprise engagement revelation ruin things for him. He came to the party to show the president his undying allegiance and to prove to other members of Reynolds's inner circle his role as an essential ally and one of the president's right-hand men. His great mood didn't fade for a second, to his daughter's surprise. She doubted that he had become indifferent to her choice and cared less about the engagement. She thought it better to prepare for a major showdown.

Lindsey thought about Kamao and felt a tightness in her chest; she wanted to call him to see if he was OK, but she couldn't; that would not be very polite, she thought. The First Lady tried to keep her in her company for the evening, and Lindsey found nothing more annoying than sitting in the middle of all these women, DC dignitaries' wives buzzing about their husbands' accomplishments and gossiping about who they thought the president would pick as his new VP in the coming elections, as his growing discontent with his second-in-command was no secret to anyone. Lindsey stole a glance at her father occasionally, only to find a man who seemed to have completely forgotten about her existence. On the ride home, he didn't exchange a word with her and simply bid her good night when they arrived and went to his room. Lindsey found her father's silent treatment unbearable; she would rather have him yell at her, express his anger and fury in words. But now she had no idea what he was thinking, what he was plotting, but she was certain he was planning something. She called Kamao; he was about to get off work. It was 11:30 p.m.; the night shift guy was running late. "Be careful going home," she told him. "My father has been acting all weird, and that scares me more than anything."

"What did he say?" Kamao asked.

"He said nothing, and that's the problem. He said nothing and he did nothing. Now I am terrified."

"So you told him we're engaged, and he just walked away?"

"I . . . I didn't tell him."

"So he doesn't know anything yet?"

"He does."

"OK, now I am confused."

"The First Lady saw the ring and congratulated me; that's how he found out." Kamao didn't know what to say, but he knew they both had a good reason to be scared, especially when the senator wasn't saying anything. There was a big storm ahead; of that, he was sure.

Her father was in the dining room, drinking some coffee with a bagel while reading the newspaper when Lindsey came downstairs the next morning. "Good morning," she said.

"Good morning," her father replied without taking his eyes off the paper. She thought it was the right time to talk about the night before; she owed her father an apology for not telling him the news herself. She poured herself some coffee and pulled out a chair.

"Dad, can I talk to you for a second?" He put the newspaper down and gazed at her, readjusting his glasses.

"I am deeply sorry about last night. I didn't mean for you to find out about the engagement that way. Can you forgive me?"

"OK," the senator said. He picked up the newspaper and continued reading. Lindsey finished her coffee and went outside; her car was not in the driveway. She came back in and saw her dad still at the dining table, reading his newspaper.

"Have you seen my car?"

"Last time I've checked, I purchased that car. I still have the receipt."

"It was a gift!"

"Well, not anymore. Since you want to prove to me that you don't need me anymore and don't have to listen to anything I say, then you shouldn't count on me for anything from now on. You're not going to take what I've worked hard for and give it to some wannabe who thinks he can come here and take whatever he wants, things that other people have worked for. I am also suspending the regular transfer to your account, so I suggest you use whatever you have in there wisely, because once it's all gone, you are on own. You might as well start looking for a job like your pathetic boyfriend, or fiancé, or whatever you want him to be." Lindsey knew her father wasn't joking; he was not agitated and wasn't yelling; he had thought this through. And she needed to find a different way to approach him rather than a head-on confrontation.

"I've already told you I am sorry."

"You're sorry!" the senator said, removing his glasses to face his daughter with no barrier between them. "Can you imagine how embarrassing it was to find out about my daughter's engagement from the First Lady? The First Lady! I've tolerated you long enough. If that's the life you choose, then don't count on me for anything. Let me warn you, and you better take my word for it: if you keep this up and end up marrying that scumbag, I will change my will, you will get nothing from me. I'll give it all to a charity and forget I ever had a daughter."

"Would it make you happier if we sign a prenup? I wouldn't mind doing that."

"Do you think me a fool?" the senator retorted. "What would that change? Would that prevent you from giving everything away? Huh? I never thought you would disappoint me to this point. And to think, all my life I've worked hard for you so you don't lack anything! Well, good luck with your life if this is the path you want to take. I am done. I don't want to see that guy in my house ever again." He went to his room, leaving Lindsey standing in the dining room, frightened. Her father was not bluffing; she realized that now. She could buy a new car, that was not a problem, but now she believed her father would cut her off if she went through with her plan for a future with Kamao. She never meant to hurt her father or cause him so much pain. Her dilemma, the one she had put off for a long time, became obvious: she no longer thought she could navigate between her father's world and Kamao's. She faced dire choices this time. She sat back down and cried. Her father had been present in every moment of her life.

Senator McAdams had cherished and protected his daughter with his love. She loathed his political views and how he viewed people like Kamao, but she loved him profoundly. But with Kamao, she found a new kind of happiness, a freedom from the traditional and undiscussed norms: the unbearable, extravagant, and condescending life of the American high society, hidden from the eyes of the public. The hypocritical idea that everyone was equal while those on top managed to keep the circle tight. With Kamao, she had a different view of the world, and she was not afraid to experience new things, but the cost would be a steep one, severing ties with her father. She needed to clear her head; she needed to think. It had crossed her mind to move in with Kamao, but she resolved to give it some thought first, as that might not be the right move now. She packed up more clothes and offered to pay for Megan's rent until she could figure things out.

"Let's keep our hope that he will come around," Megan said.

"I doubt that," Lindsey said. "I don't think he will ever come around. I used to think he might, but not anymore." She squeezed a pillow between her legs and pulled a blanket over her head, hoping to sink into the couch.

It was past midnight when Kamao parked his car in his regular spot. The neighborhood was asleep; some annoying barking dogs could be heard in the distance. He picked up a few shopping bags from the back seat and headed to his apartment. Lindsey told him about her ordeal with her father. He wanted to meet her and comfort her, but he thought she might need some time alone to think. He liked to take time to think about serious issues, and he assumed it was the same with other people. He knew that Lindsey was facing a grave decision. A union with him would cause a severe blow to her relationship with her father; it was obvious that the senator was not playing games. His recent reprisal showed that he was adamant in his decision to punish his daughter, and an attempt for reconciliation while they were still engaged would only make things worse.

Kamao reached the top of the stairs and was about to open the door to his apartment when he felt a cold wire rapidly circling around his neck. He dropped the key and grocery bags and tried to grab the wire in a frenzied movement as two strong gloved hands were pulling it tight. He felt the wire digging into his skin, his vision turning blurry as he became lightheaded. He attempted to push the metal out of his skin with one hand while grabbing the aggressor's arm with the other but realized it was a fruitless effort. Feeling that he only had a few seconds left, Kamao pushed back on his aggressor; both rolled down the stairs, and the wire loosened. Kamao rushed to get up, braving the bruises and the cut in his neck and didn't see the second aggressor come out of the dark, hitting him with a metal bar. He felt a sharp pain in his ribs. Both men continued to hit him with metal bars. The noise alerted a neighbor who opened her window.

"Hey! What are you guys doing down there?" she said. The two men rushed to their car and drove off. The woman came out and walked toward Kamao. "Are you OK, sir?" she said, and dialed 911. "Hello! A man is lying in the parking lot. He just got jumped by two guys; he's not moving."

Mrs. Sterling became Kamao's best friend after he was discharged from the hospital and was on bed rest for a week. His two broken ribs seemed to be healing faster than his swollen face. She did his shopping for him and cleaned his apartment. Had she been younger, Lindsey would have been jealous and would have thrown her out. In the hospital bed, Kamao had time to think. He couldn't stop thinking about his father's adage about the mackerel swimming with the sharks. Maybe he was a mackerel who didn't know his place after all. Lindsey came to visit him at the hospital and turned her face and wept the first time she saw him lying in the bed wrapped up from head to toe in white bandages. He was half conscious then. He reached his hand and greeted her with a smile. There wasn't much to be said. They both knew who was behind the attack and for what reason, but he couldn't say any of that to the police. "I didn't know who they were or what they wanted," he said when to the two police officers who came to his room asked him if he knew who his aggressors were.

"I am so sorry," Lindsey said as tears continued to run down her cheeks. She tried to hold his hands and comfort him, but every touch provoked an "ouch!" and she gave up. "I can't believe my father would be capable of ordering anyone's death, let alone my fiancé's," she told Megan. "He is going to pay for this. I am going to make him pay for this."

"You have no proof that he was behind this, Lin."

"Who else can it be? Who else would want Kamao dead? The woman who found him said the men who attacked him took off in a black SUV. My father's dogs, Corey and his guys, drive black SUVs."

One thing Kamao was concerned about after leaving the hospital was the bills. He would use his savings to pay it, and that would dig a hole in his finances. But he had resolved not to get into a habit of asking that money be sent to him from Ghana. That would not be a good economic strategy, he thought. After obtaining his green card, he requested that Ali pay him by check and withhold his taxes; he wanted to start practicing good citizenship. He had been enjoying the American way of life and didn't mind paying his fair share. He just wished he had health insurance—though he would still pay a lot of money out of pocket—but his gas station job didn't offer that.

"You wish this country would let go of its ego and embrace a little bit of progressivism, but they are so scared of anything that ends with 'ism' except for capitalism. What harm would it do to make sure every citizen and permanent resident has some type of guaranteed health coverage?" Mrs. Sterling said. Kamao looked at her and smiled.

A frail gossip, Mrs. Sterling was a retired United States Postal Services clerk who preferred to live in an apartment instead of a house. "You're surrounded by people when you live in an apartment complex," she said. "An old hag like me would die alone in a house and decompose before anyone noticed. Here, if you don't come out for a couple of days, people will start wondering." She owned two houses but preferred to rent them out rather than live in either of them. "Without my husband," she said, "I can't bear it. I'd rather stay here with my Burton." Burton was a black Labrador she'd adopted from a shelter. She had a daughter, a medical doctor who volunteered around the world with Doctors Without Borders. "She was heartbroken when her first love ran away with another girl in college. She vowed never to give her heart to any man or anyone again and chose to embrace saving lives around the world. My poor Cindy! She visits me every Christmas. I will invite you when she comes next time."

"Thank you," Kamao said. Mrs. Sterling knew more about Kamao than he thought.

"That fancy girlfriend of yours—she is a senator's daughter, isn't she? You must be careful; those people are powerful. If they like you, you can relax a bit, but if they don't, you better be careful and watch your back; stay away if you must." Kamao wondered what she was getting at and what she knew. She might have been listening to their conversations in the parking lot. He thought it would be better to leave that subject alone, although it got him thinking more about him and Lindsey, what would become of them considering the recent developments. Kamao never paid attention to Mrs. Sterling before his misfortune. She walked her dog more than he wanted to be walked, a cigarette hanging on the side of her lips, waving at him and Lindsey without ever saying a word to them. She must not be fond of rich people, but she'd saved his life and now they were friends, and that was what mattered the most.

"Lindsey called earlier; she will be spending the evening with me. She will be helping me put a few things into order."

"Hm, it's about time someone decides to take care of her man," Mrs. Sterling said, tying up the trash bag that she was about to take out.

"She has been here a lot . . ."

"Yes, but how much has she done to help you in your current state?"

"You know I am doing better now, and I can do most chores myself." Kamao paused and looked at the nice elderly lady with admiration. "You can't imagine how valuable your company and help has been to me the past week, Mrs. Sterling. I am forever in your debt," Kamao said, putting a jacket on.

"Well, I didn't do anything anyone with common sense and a bit of dignity wouldn't do," she replied as she opened the door with the trash bag in her hand.

"I can do that," Kamao said, gently taking the bag from her. "I'm going out."

"Well, I am gone then. I hope you enjoy your evening."

The engagement hadn't been too long for Kamao and Lindsey, but it sure had many bumps because of the events of late. Kamao thought that a serious conversation with Lindsey was overdue. He had put off the idea of marriage for too long, but now that he was feeling better, there was no need to wait any longer. The evening together would be the perfect opportunity to settle the matter once and for all. The occasion was too solemn to waste it in his tiny apartment. He had a brilliant idea: he would take her to a fancy restaurant, then they would spend the rest of the evening at the Washington Monument to contemplate the spectacular view it offered at nightfall. Lindsey was delighted by the idea of going out.

"It would do us both good," she said. She was pleased that Kamao knew so many excellent restaurants in DC and loved to share his exquisite tastes with her.

"Didn't I tell you the site is delightful at night?" Kamao said when they arrived at the National Mall, and assuming Lindsey was not too impressed due to her silence, he added, "Sorry, I forgot that you grew up here and have seen this a million times."

"No, that's not it," she said. "Yes, I've seen it before, but this time it's different. It feels different, standing here with you, looking at the reflection of this magnificent monument in the pool, with all these lights and the breeze . . . I am speechless. It's amazing." She locked her fingers in his as they walked along the reflecting pool.

"There is something I wanted to ask you," Kamao turned and held Lindsey's hands. "I know we got engaged not too long ago, but a lot of things have happened since then. And I've been thinking—what is the point of all this struggle if we keep putting off what we both want: a life together, to cherish and be there for one another. Why don't we get married? That's what I want. What about you?"

Lindsey pulled away in shock. "Get married? You mean now? In the middle of a crisis?"

"Why not? I love you, you love me! Why wait? What do we have to wait for?"

"But we are still in college!"

"Yes, and we are both seniors now. We only have one year left. I thought this is something you wanted," Kamao asked, surprised by her reaction.

"Yes, of course! But not now!" she said.

"Why not?"

"My dad just tried to kill you, and I'm not talking metaphorically."

"I know that! I was there."

"Well, what if he tries it again? I can't bear it to lose you."

"I don't believe that a father in full control of his senses would wish to make his own daughter a widow, no matter how much he hates her husband, especially when he knows that she will see his hand behind it. A fiancé is easy to get rid of, but not a husband."

"You have thought this through, I see!"

"Yes, I have. Your father would be a madman to make any move on me once we are married. He may push you away and deny you many things, but I don't think he will attempt what he did last time again." Lindsey's hands started shaking as if a vicious crab had chosen that very moment to pinch her finger.

"What is the matter, baby? I don't understand; what's going on?"

"We don't need to rush anything, baby! Do we?" she finally said, her hands still shaking and her breathing accelerating.

"We are not rushing anything; we have been dating for almost two years. Why not get married now?"

"My father can still come around. He might just need a little more time."

"A little more time for what? The man tried to kill me." Both felt the tension, but it was too late to back down; it would not be easy to leave the matter halfway discussed. Lindsey took a few steps away and turned back.

"I told you what he said. He will cut me off; he will change his will. I believe he meant it."

"So what?"

"What do you mean, so what? Where are we going to live? How are we going to live?"

"Like many other couples: in a house, with jobs." Lindsey smiled, shaking her head.

"Why is that funny?" Kamao asked. "Ah, I see! That's not the life you dreamed of with me. I am sorry if I've ever given you the impression that I'm after your money."

"I know you're not. But it is a good thing to have a decent life."

"I have a decent life."

"You know what I mean."

"No, I don't! Maybe I need some enlightening on this matter." He paused and caressed his chin. The intensity in their tones alerted some curious strollers who stared at them with a million questions. "I thought you didn't care too much about the high life," Kamao continued, "and now the thought of losing some privileges is freaking you out." He looked at her with attention, wondering if he was wrong about her. "I can assure you that we will not be poor, Lindsey. I may not be able to offer you the same life as the one you have right now, but we won't be poor; I will work hard to make sure that it doesn't happen, and you will too. I'm sorry to put you on the spot like this," Kamao continued. "I can't imagine how difficult it is for you. It appears to me as if you hoped that you could have both your father's world and mine; some people are indeed lucky and can have it all, but it seems you're not one of them." He walked to her, gently moved her hair away from her face, and dried her tears. "I will never ask you to choose between your father and me; that wouldn't be fair, but you have to make sure you know what you want because situations like this occur often where one has to make a choice, but I don't want you to make one in my favor if it's too difficult for you."

"I'll need some time to think," she said, wiping her tears.

"I know, I don't expect you to give me an answer tonight anyway, but how long will it take you to decide to live with me? I hope it doesn't take you too long, as your father's men may not be unlucky next time. I will drive you back." He opened the door for her when they arrived at Megan's apartment. She got out, kissed him on the cheek without a word, and headed to the stairs. He held her arm and gently pulled her back. "Lindsey, please say something to me."

"I need some time to figure things out," she said in a severe tone, looking away.

He sighed, looked down, and then back at her. "Maybe we both need some time to figure things out. What do you say?"

"Yes," she said as their eyes met under the dimmed streetlights. He squeezed her hand as she turned toward the stairs. He watched her reach the top and open the door to the apartment.

The breakup with her fiancé took a toll on Lindsey, who wondered who it was that caused their separation. Her father was the first to blame, of course, she thought, because if it weren't for his persistent hatred of Kamao, there would have been no need for them to take a break. She wore the same gray pajamas for days, her hair tangled, and she hadn't been outside since the night Kamao dropped her off after their conversation at the monument.

"What happened to your eyes?" Megan said when she returned and found Lindsey on the living room floor, gazing at the ceiling. "You're crying, still? When are you going to stop that, Lin?" Lindsey didn't respond.

"I am sorry I couldn't help you," Megan said. She joined her on the floor and put her head on her lap. "These matters are too serious and too complicated for a third party to get involved in. I am sorry. What are you going to do?"

"I don't know!"

Megan tried her best to stay out of her friend's drama. She loved Lindsey and had become fond of Kamao too when she came to know him better and experienced his gallantry and respect for women as well as his self-respect. She hoped that they could find a way to make up soon, but she knew too well about the matters of the heart to hold on to a naïve hope.

"Class starts next week. What are you going to do?"

"I am not going," Lindsey said.

"What do you mean you're not going? It's our last year. I know that what you're going through is tough; trust me, I do. But you need to get it together and find your strength, OK?" She helped her friend sit on the couch and sat next to her; she put her hand in her hair to straighten it up a little. "You're going to take a shower and look beautiful. You need to go out and get some fresh air. We can go to the mall and see what's new."

PART VI

CROSSROADS

Chapter 22

In the employees' break room of the Coal Master Hotel, Kamao and two coworkers sat at the table, eating their dinner while watching a golf tournament on the 32-inch TV. Kamao wished it was a soccer game; he would have watched it with such attention that he would have forgotten when his break ended. He knew nothing about golf and found it rather dull. He had enjoyed working at the hotel so far; his first two weeks weren't too bad. Kurt had him do some light maintenance jobs since he told him that he was quite handy, and the regular maintenance guy was out sick. Kamao didn't mind, especially when Kurt offered to reduce the number of rooms he needed to clean for his shift. Although the job was temporary, until he found something better or he finished his last year of college, it was a good regular job for Kamao: he had teammates to talk to and wasn't confined behind bulletproof glass, seeing most customers as potential criminals. As he grew tired of the gas station, Lazo encouraged him to apply for Dania's old position, and he got lucky. In that hotel, he found a community, people to exchange with, although it was mostly just small talk and people complaining about overworking, excessive taxes, and high-interest credit cards.

"This is a trap, you know?" Sergey, one of the other two employees in the break room, a guy from an Eastern European country, said. Kamao guessed his origin from his name and accent. "They say you need to get a credit card to build up your credit, then they charge you high interest rates and ask you only to pay a minimum, which makes your debt hard to pay off. Then after they take tax from your paycheck, they make you pay tax on everything you buy."

"Yep!" Armand, the other coworker in the room said, eating his ice cream like someone was about to walk in and yank it away if he didn't finish it quickly. He nodded to what Sergey was saying without taking his eyes off his cup. Kamao assumed Armand knew that Sergey was a complainer and wanted to just let him talk. Armand didn't seem like he wanted to talk to people anyway; Kamao heard him speak French sometimes and later learned that he was from the Central African Republic. He was one of the rich kids back home who didn't have to work but simply enjoyed a good life from his father's business empire, until he adventured in the US and realized that rich in his country didn't mean rich in America. Regardless of his new status as a commoner, he saw his coworkers as below him and didn't like to waste his energy talking to them.

"He thinks he is above everybody else," Beatrice, from Martinique, told Kamao once. "He is so full of himself."

"Everything you do, you have to be careful, or you are going to end up with no money, you know! You are going to be broke," Sergey continued. "It's a crooked system, you know? And by the time you find out you are being used, it is too late, you know! You will find yourself at the bottom." Kamao wondered where he got his information from. He seemed uneducated and a little strange, but Kamao was sorry for him. He usually couldn't stand people who complained a lot about life in America. He always felt the urge to ask them, "Why are you still here if you believe that a lot of things are unfair?" He hoped they just shoved it or returned to their country if life in America was so unbearable. But with Sergey, he felt different; he felt compassion, wanting to sit with him and correct his misconception of America, like how he didn't need to drown into debt to build his credit, or how he didn't have to make the minimum payment every month, but could pay more to cut the interest. He hoped he would get the chance one day to open Sergey's eyes.

He was still gauging his thoughts when Sergey asked him, after scrutinizing him, with a smile, as Armand wouldn't pay him any attention, "You're new, right? How do you like it so far?"

"It's OK; I like it."

"Yeah? It's not too hard?"

"No, not at all," Kamao said. Armand got up and left without looking at anyone.

Kamao looked at the time on his phone. "Oops, it's time to get back." He threw his leftovers in the trash and shook Sergey's hand. Sergey smiled, revealing two broken front teeth and some rotten ones in the back. Kamao hadn't talked to Lindsey in weeks; she knew that he was leaving the gas station job and that he had a couple of interviews for positions in a couple of hotels in DC. The last time they spoke, he called her hoping to hear some comforting news, but got nothing. So he thought it would be better to leave her alone.

He didn't tell her that he had a new job. He wondered what might be going through her head; how much their relationship meant to her.

Lindsey's phone no longer rang as much as it used to. She hadn't talked to her father or Kamao for weeks. She only went outside when Megan forced her. All she did was eat and watch TV; she had gone to the gym a couple of times.

"Who are you mad at," Megan asked her, "your father or Kamao?"

"I don't know! Maybe both."

"You don't know? How come? I know why you are mad at your dad, but what did Kamao do that upset you? I don't see why you're mad at him. The guy loves you; we all can see that, and he wants to marry you. What is wrong with that? Isn't that what you wanted?" Lindsey got off the couch, crossed her arms, and walked to the window. She looked outside with full attention as if she was expecting someone.

"You don't understand," she said.

"Well, help me understand, then!" Megan replied.

"I told you many times; he is rushing for no reason."

"What do you mean for no reason! He almost got killed because he didn't give up on you. He's still alive probably because someone knows that you guys broke up." Lindsey looked at Megan with a glare full of reproach but was unable to contradict her, as she knew it was the truth. "I wondered why your father hasn't called you since he got what he wanted," Megan continued, "or is he waiting for you to reach out first? I am sure he knows you're with me."

"I am not going to call him until I find a way to make him pay for the pain he has caused me." She sat back down on the couch and turned the volume up on the TV just as a live interview with her father's opponent was starting.

"What about college?" Megan asked.

"Taking a semester off never hurt anyone."

Lindsey watched the entire interview and exclaimed at the end, "This is it!"

"This is what?" Megan said, rushing out of the kitchen.

"McGill is coming to DC; I think I just got the perfect idea."

"The perfect idea for what?"

"I am going to help McGill defeat my father in November."

"What! Are you insane? Why?"

"What do you mean 'why'?" Lindsey got up, revigorated, feeling victorious suddenly. "You know what he did to me, to my fiancé . . ."

"Who you don't seem to care about lately."

"How could you say that? You have no idea what I'm going through. You have no idea how hard it is for me to be unable to give him the answer he's waiting for."

Megan sighed. "And why will McGill accept your help? Why would he believe you're sincere?"

"Oh! There are things that he will be happy to hear, and he can easily find the proof if he knows where to look, and I won't mind showing him the way."

"And that's just for payback to your father?"

"Yeah! He should retire from politics anyway. Maybe when he no longer has a Senate seat to worry about, he will come to his senses and relax on my man."

"You haven't talked to Kamao in weeks, and you still call him your man? And please, I don't want to have anything to do with what your 'plan' is."

"Don't worry; it would all be on me." Lindsey got up and went to the room to get ready for a shower, feeling an anticipated victory.

Lindsey arrived at the Coal Master Hotel at 4:05 p.m. Corey Murdock drove her there. She knew how to get him to do her favors as she knew how much he loved money. And Agent Murdock never asked the senator or his daughter questions; he simply got the job done and collected his reward. "I have a secret meeting with someone important, and I need you to accompany me," Lindsey told him. "I can count on your discretion, right?"

"Not a problem," he said. "When would it be?"

"This Thursday, I have to be there by four."

"You got it!"

When Kenneth McGill read the note sent to him with high importance, he sat down and thought about it for a long time. He then read the letter a second time, then a third, and a fourth. Who could this informant be who wanted to give him damaging information on Senator McAdams? he thought. He looked at the bottom of the paper again and read, No reward needed. The initials were suggestive, but he didn't want to believe it. He would have disregarded the note if he hadn't come across the mention of the senator's dealings in Venezuela. His team had tried to dig up that dirt on the senator but had hit a dead end. It might be the opportunity he was hoping for after all, and if this secret meeting was a success, it would undoubtedly be a considerable blow to McAdams's campaign. He had dismissed his security detail and had arranged for Lindsey to come in through the back door. He was a regular at the Coal Master Hotel, and he knew he could count on Kurt's discretion. "Make sure you only let her in when the lobby is clear." Kurt nodded and came back to the reception desk.

"Where is Kamao?" Kurt asked the receptionist.

"In the break room," the guy behind the counter said. He went to the break room; Kamao was still eating his food, chatting with the other coworkers on break.

"Kamao, room 215 needs another one of the bottles of wine you took in earlier." Kamao got up and went to Kurt.

"What is wrong with that guy?" Kamao said in a low voice. "He told me I was not holding the bottle properly and that I needed more training before serving VIPs. He was very rude. I don't want to go back in there; can you have somebody else do it?" Kurt looked at him with a grimacing face.

"That's your hall, Kamao; there is nobody else to do it but you."

Lindsey sat in the back of the lobby; she wore a black dress with sunglasses that made her look like a spy.

"Hi," McGill said, as he pulled a chair and sat down. Lindsey smiled and shook his hand, she still had her sunglasses on, holding her bag firmly against her chest. She kept looking around like someone was watching her, and she struggled to talk whenever someone walked in.

"I . . . I . . . this was a mistake!" She got up and wanted to leave.

"Wait," McGill said, holding her by the elbow. "I know a safe place where we can talk without worry. Follow me!" Lindsey followed him as he took the back stairs. His room was right next to the stairs on the second floor. Lindsey stood next to the door and opened her bag; she pulled out a blue folder and handed it to McGill. He sat in the recliner next to the window and looked through the file. He took his glasses off after a minute, disappointed.

"I've heard about this deal of McAdams's in Venezuela! My team tried to track it and it led them to nothing."

"Look on the last page," Lindsey said calmly. "There is a name that you will recognize at the bottom before the signatures."

McGill looked on the last page. "Omar Cazares!" He got up and rubbed his chin like a pirate who couldn't believe he had found a hidden treasure. "Your father is dealing with Omar Cazares! The guy finances rebel groups in Central and South America and sells weapons to terrorist organizations all over the world."

Lindsey gasped.

"I am sorry," McGill said. "I suspected it was you when I read the note. I just couldn't understand why you would want your father to lose the election."

"It's personal."

"I understand. It's none of my business to know why." He looked at Lindsey, a hand on his waist, the other holding the blue folder like a trophy. "You know who this guy is; you should know that bringing this out into the public will inflict serious damage to your father. It could trigger a congressional investigation implicating him deeply." McGill started to get agitated. He couldn't believe he was holding the jackpot, the clear path to the Senate.

"How do I know this is not a setup? How do I know you're not fooling me or plotting something? Maybe you and your father planned this to have me bring out some false information that could damage my credibility." Lindsey tried to remain steady and calm but couldn't stop shaking as McGill's agitation started to frighten her. She moved closer to the door, her hands behind her back.

"Are you wearing a wire?"

"What? No!"

"I just need to know that you're not setting me up. Why would the daughter of my opponent in a Senate race meet with me and hand me the key to my victory, with nothing in exchange?"

"I told you, it's personal. It's between my father and me. And you have to promise me you're not going to push for an investigation on him."

"Oh, you don't have to worry about that. All I want is his seat. I will leave him in peace, I promise. That's not what concerns me right now, though; how do I know that this is real, that you're for real?" He was talking, walking closer to her. Lindsey rushed to open the door, but McGill quickly pushed the door closed and threw her on the bed.

"I am not wearing a wire, I promise! Please let me go."

"It's too late now; I have to check it for myself." He sat on her and pulled the zipper down behind her back. Lindsey tried to free herself unsuccessfully. He pulled the top of her dress down her shoulders and struggled to stay focused on finding the wire as Lindsey's blue bra began troubling his mind. He no longer looked at her as a spy as a sudden desire gripped him. He began breathing heavily.

"If you're not wearing a wire, why don't we seal this moment to make it our secret?" He buried his face against her neck, holding her arms tightly on the bed.

"What are you doing? Let go of me!" Lindsey pivoted her hips with all her strength. McGill fell off the bed, still breathing heavily. Lindsey got up and reached for her bag on the floor.

McGill grabbed her by the hip and tried to get back up on his feet. The bottle of wine on the bedside table was the closest item she could grab. It landed on his head, and he instantly lost consciousness, tumbling like a branch from a tree. His head hit the bedframe on his way down, and he crashed on the floor, breathless, his skull opened. The wine from the shattered bottle mingled with McGill's blood and ran down the floor like a river without banks. Agent Murdock sat behind the wheel listening to the radio, his eyes closed, when Lindsey jumped into the back seat, shivering, sweating, and smelling like wine.

"I've just killed Kenneth McGill," she said.

Kamao didn't come out of his cloudy mind until the police car transporting him reached the DC Central Detention Facility. The last thing he remembered was that he was taking some clean linens to room 217 in hall B; then, he woke up next to a dead body in a pool of blood in 215 just before half a dozen police officers stormed the room. He was escorted to a police car under the flashing lights of a group of journalists who had just received word of a murder at the Coal Master Hotel. The news of Kenneth McGill's death spread faster than a flash flood. The major news stations began bringing up the breaking news with various titles: US Senate candidate, Kenneth McGill, has been murdered in a hotel room in DC; The leading Senate candidate from Texas, Kenneth McGill, was killed in a hotel room in DC.

Senator McAdams had just arrived home from the Capitol when he saw the phone call from Agent Murdock. He said, "Thank you, Corey," after the agent told him what happened at the hotel and what he did. "Where is she now?" he asked.

"She is with me here, sir," the agent said.

"Can you bring her home, please? Thank you. Did you take care of everything? The cameras?"

"I got it all covered, sir."

"Thank you, Corey, your actions will not be forgotten."

"Yes, sir," the agent said.

The senator waited in the living room for Corey and his daughter to get back. Lindsey rushed into her father's arms.

"I am sorry, Dad," she said, sobbing. "I didn't mean for that to happen, I just, I just . . ."

"Shh! You don't have to say anything, honey! Just breathe, take it easy."

"I just—I was mad at you and, I . . ."

"Shh! Stop talking," the senator said, holding his daughter tightly. The headline at the bottom of the TV grabbed Lindsey's attention: Kenneth McGill was murdered today in a DC hotel, suspect in custody.

"Suspect in custody!" she said, turning to Agent Murdock then to her father. Just as she was about to ask the agent what happened, the journalist announced that they had learned the name of the suspect,

"Kamao Ofando-Birama is currently in FBI custody. There are no other suspects at this time. We will tell you more as we get more information." Lindsey almost fainted.

"What—what is this? But . . . how . . . ?" She looked at her father, then at the agent, and back at her father, bewildered.

"Corey found him working at the hotel," the senator said. "It was either him or you. Corey had to choose, and I support him."

"You framed him? I killed McGill, Kamao didn't!"

"Again, it was either him or you. If you disagree, here is the phone; you can call the police or go to the station and turn yourself in." The senator took the home phone and gave it to her. She kept it in her hand, staring at the TV as a picture of Kamao popped up at the bottom of the screen.

"We will both be ruined; if that's what you want, go ahead and make the damned call. I am tired. I will call you tomorrow, Corey. Thanks again." The senator went to his room. Lindsey stood in the middle of the living room, her eyes still on the TV, the phone still in her hand. She took a few steps toward the TV. The phone fell out of her hand; she collapsed on the couch.

Chapter 23

"The trial will begin as scheduled in April," Mr. Vivaldi told Kamao during one of his visits. That was only a few weeks away. Kamao would not be graduating that spring; he knew it. He had planned to graduate in May, but fate had decided otherwise. He hadn't seen or heard from Lindsey since he was arrested; it was a strange thing, but he thought it would be better not to dwell on that. It was probably for the best, he thought.

"It seems like you have been eating lately," Mr. Vivaldi said. "You've been looking much better on my latest visits and that is very good. You have to stay positive and strong and hope for the best." Kamao nodded and smiled. For Mr. Vivaldi, there was nothing better to do in the few weeks before the trial than managing to keep his client's morale up; he knew he couldn't promise him his freedom in the end, but at least he would be encouraging, reassuring him so that he didn't look beat before the end. "The jury has been selected. It was a tough process, but we got that done. Some of your friends have come forward to testify on your behalf and to speak about your good character." He opened his folder. "Ayefumi, Lazo, and Ali are some of them. Let's hope that counts for something."

"Yeah," Kamao said. For a long time, he had fought the urge to implicate the senator in the set up that landed him in prison, but after realizing the potential outcome of his trial, he came to understand that the only chance he may have to survive his ordeal was to lay down all his cards. So he changed course and demanded that more focus be put on the senator because of his hatred for him.

"He's the only person I know who would exult in seeing me locked up like this," he had told his attorney back in December.

"Unfortunately, we found no connection to the senator with any of this," Mr. Vivaldi said. "He came out clean. There was nothing that linked him to the unfortunate event."

"What about the cameras? Someone must have tampered with them," Kamao said.

"Yeah, we had our expert look at that, but they didn't find any fault. Whoever did the work is no apprentice, that's for sure."

"What about the hotel manager? Kurt can help—he must know something!"

"Yeah, unfortunately, he is not your friend. He's going to testify against you."

"What? Why? I didn't do anything; he knows that!" Kamao punched the table and stood up, breathing heavily.

"You have been patient and calm from the beginning; I know I have encouraged you not to give up, but you must continue to remain calm and think about anything that can help your case. You don't want to give anybody a chance to question your character any further. Don't give them any reason to do that," Mr. Vivaldi said calmly.

"Sorry! I am sorry!" Kamao said and regained his seat.

"As I told you, the senator and his daughter were questioned, and nothing tied either of them to the murder. So we won't expect them to testify unless there is an evolution of circumstances that requires them to appear."

"Lindsey was staying with her best friend, Megan, when this whole thing happened; she might know something," Kamao said.

Mr. Vivaldi quickly wrote the name down. "Are you suspecting that Lindsey might have something to do with this?"

"No, absolutely not! I just wanted to give you everything I have, all the names I know. Maybe somebody knows something."

"Lindsey hasn't visited you, has she?"

"No, she hasn't. We broke up. I wouldn't expect her to, and to have her see me like this would only make things worse for me."

"I understand. Do you know Megan's address?"

"Yes, I do."

"I will see what I can get from her. I am glad you're willing to get your head out of the water now. For months, I wondered if it was worth it defending someone who was already giving up before the trial started, but now, I have something to keep me going." They both smiled.

"Thank you, Mr. Vivaldi," Kamao said as his attorney got up and shook his hand.

After leaving Kamao, Mr. Vivaldi went straight to the apartment building where Megan lived.

"Megan moved out of her apartment four months ago," the landlord said. "She was in quite a rush. I wondered what got into her suddenly."

"Do you know where she went? Did she say anything?" Mr. Vivaldi asked.

"She just zoomed out. She paid for everything, including the penalty for breaking her lease, turned in her key, and left."

Megan had been helping her grandfather on his ranch in the remote western Arizona countryside for a few months now. She had suddenly felt that the country life was what she needed. At least that's what she told her grandfather, Frank, who didn't believe a word of what she said, but he was happy to see his granddaughter and couldn't refuse extra helping hands. Her senior year in college didn't seem to matter to Megan anymore. She thought that if Kamao were an easy target, it wouldn't be long before she went down too. She was the only person who knew about Lindsey's plan that involved McGill, and the senator knew that Lindsey was staying with her, so Corey and his guys must have known too. She knew someone would be coming for her, so the best thing she could do was to disappear. Her grandfather's ranch in the remote countryside of Arizona would be a perfect hiding place, she believed, and she had been safe for months, so that was a good sign. She had been rather busy, every morning helping Frank feed the cattle and clean the hen house.

"You work like you were born for this, Megan!" Frank said. She smiled and continued scooping the pile of cow feces on the ground. "Your mother called again yesterday. She asked me if I knew where you were and guess what? I lied again. People are worried about you, Megan! Whatever or whoever you are running from . . . I don't think you can do this forever. Why don't you just tell me so I can help you?"

"You can't help me, Grandpa! No one can help me," she said, sticking the shovel into the feces as though to inflict them with all the pain she could get out of herself. Frank looked at her and sighed.

"When I went into town this morning, Harry from the coffee shop told me that two men came by yesterday asking about my ranch. He said he didn't tell them anything because he didn't like them. Are you sure you don't want to tell me anything?" Megan looked at her grandfather, leaving the pile of feces alone for a second.

"I can't tell you anything, Grandpa. That's the only way I can protect you; that's the only way I can protect all of you. I would never have believed this would happen to me. I see it in movies all the time." She started to cry, holding onto the shovel as her spasms became uncontrollable. Her grandfather rushed to her and hugged her tightly.

The next morning when Frank came back from town, Megan was nowhere to be found; her luggage was in her room, her clothes in the closet, but there was no trace of her. He called Tom, the local sheriff.

"My granddaughter just vanished, man! Her belongings are here in the room, but there is no trace of her."

"Megan disappeared," Vivaldi said when he visited Kamao to update him on his effort to find his ex-fiancée's friend.

"What do you mean she disappeared?" Kamao said.

"She was staying on her grandfather's ranch in Arizona. She has been MIA for a week now."

"Do you think there might be a connection? I mean, she is good at picking some crazy boyfriends, as far as I know. Maybe the one she has now is causing her some trouble, I don't know."

"She's the one you helped in that nightclub, right?"

"Yeah! Don't you think she might help me if she knew something?"

"Yes, I think she may want to help you if she knows something, but not if she's fearing for her life. And don't forget that the prosecution is certainly going to use that nightclub incident against you." Kamao sighed and said nothing. "Now, I know you've said before that you don't want me to ask Lindsey to testify, but her testimony is vital, in my opinion, and she will have a lot of good things to say about you, which you are going to need."

"But her father is McGill's opponent. Her support for me might hurt her father's campaign."

"Yes, I get that, but . . ."

"I prefer to leave that up to her; if she comes forward and offers to help, fine. If she doesn't, then please let it be. I don't want you to force her to do anything she doesn't want to do. If she still cares about me, she will come forward on her own."

Kamao's trial began on April 11, a Monday; it was expected to be the most-watched event for the entire spring. Kamao's attention was solely on the jurors during the opening statements. He tried to find a clue on their faces, in their appearance, for his chances of being found not guilty. He had watched enough shows that included trials to know that his fate lay in the hands of the twelve people sitting in the jury box. He scrutinized them, attempting to find a connection. Suddenly, color mattered, and it seemed to play a vital role in his fate. He wondered what would happen to him if all the jurors were Black, or all white. There were two Black people in the group sitting next to the judge, a man and a woman. Did they view him as one of them? Or was he, in their eyes, a mere stranger from across the ocean, an annoying presence that repulsed them? The others were white; he refused to see that as a bad omen. Would they let race cloud their judgment? Was he, in their eyes, another angry Black man, or an innocent immigrant who was probably framed for a high-profile murder? He knew the prosecutor's job was to blame him, and it was his defense attorney's job to prove his innocence. He knew there would be surprises, but he didn't think it would involve unpleasant acquaintances like Adeomi. He choked when the latter was called as a witness for the prosecution.

"Could you please tell the court what the defendant did to you only a few days after he came into this country?" the prosecutor asked. Adeomi cleared his throat and recounted to the court his unfortunate dealing with Kamao. "This is the first example we have of our short-tempered defendant," John Foster, the federal prosecutor, said. Kamao stared at Adeomi in his tranquil posture. When their eyes crossed, Adeomi didn't blush, unmoved by the fact that his former roommate's life was in jeopardy. Ayefumi was astounded by how low Adeomi had gone, to testify against Kamao in a federal criminal court where a death sentence was the imminent outcome. Who was paying him to do this? Ayefumi wondered. He knew Adeomi was capable of many dirty tricks for money, but this hadn't crossed his mind.

"I told him I didn't take his money, but he just kept punching me," Adeomi said. Two jurors turned to Kamao with an admonishing look, then back to the witness box.

"This is just one example of the kind of person we have before us today. He assaulted and seriously hurt another individual whose only fault was that he was sharing a room with him," John Foster said.

"Is it not true that you were digging into the defendant's suitcases—without his permission—a couple of days after he had arrived in the United States?" Vivaldi asked Adeomi when it was his turn to question the witness.

"It was j . . . just to get the bread he brought, and he was sleeping, so I . . . I couldn't wake him up," Adeomi said, starting to get a little agitated, as he knew the defense attorney's job was to get the truth out of him.

"Did you receive any visitors in your dorm within the first few days that my client arrived? I mean, did anyone come to your apartment before the money's disappearance?" Vivaldi asked.

"No," Adeomi said, "But he might have received visit—"

Vivaldi raised his hand, inviting him to stop talking with a smile. "So, tell me if I am wrong about anything that I am going to say, OK?" Vivaldi said to the witness, then he turned to the members of the jury. "Our friend here was digging into my client's bags and was asked to stop several times, but he didn't. That leads to the conclusion that he may have found the location of the money, all that my client came into this country with. When my client got home that day, the door was cracked open, and our friend here said he might have forgotten to close it. He went out for only thirty minutes to the nearest store; that's what he told the judge at the time. So another individual, who knew nothing about the money, entered the apartment within that thirty-minute window and went straight to the suitcase where the money was. All the suitcases, by the way, had locks on them. My client said he started to lock them because our friend here wouldn't stop digging through them, even in his presence. So the unknown individual knew exactly where the money was and broke the zipper on that suitcase to get it and left the apartment intact except for the broken zipper." Vivaldi turned to Adeomi and asked, "Is it true that you bought a car about a week after the incident?"

"Yes!" Adeomi said.

"How did you pay for that car? Was it with cash or with a credit card?"

"Objection, Your Honor!" John Foster said. "These questions have no connection to the case."

"Overruled," the judge said. "The counsel's effort is to find out if the witness's testimony can be trusted. I am sure you want to know that too since he is your witness. Continue, please," she said, turning to Vivaldi.

"Thank you, Your Honor," Vivaldi said. "Could you please answer the question? How did you pay for that car?"

"With cash!" Adeomi said. There was grumbling in the room.

"The car cost a little under four thousand, didn't it?"

"Objection, Your Honor! This proves nothing; the money could have come from anywhere, and the witness doesn't have to prove anything on that matter," John Foster said, realizing how hard the defense was squeezing his witness.

"Overruled," the judge said. "Continue, counsel!"

"Thank you, Your Honor," Vivaldi said, and continued. "If the actions of our friend here are questionable, because they are to me, should his judgment of my client's temper be taken into account? Without trying to defend my client seeking justice by his own hands, I don't see how calling the police and filing a report could have helped him get his money back. He was new to the country and was desperate; it was all the money he had, and he saw the witness go into his affairs without his permission, which in itself was a violation of property. I will let you make your conclusion and decide if any word this man is saying about my client's temper should be trusted." Vivaldi sat back down; the room was quiet for a few seconds. Kamao glanced at the jury box, wondering if Vivaldi's words had moved any of the people sitting there in his favor.

"Thank you!" the judge said to Adeomi. "You may regain your seat."

Kamao's anxiety grew by night. The quiet, empty cell added to the feeling of being a condemned convict locked away from society. The crowd in the courtroom gave him some hope, as he was confident he had a few supporters there, people who believed in his innocence. Ayefumi and Lazo were two of them, and seeing them every day was a relief. He thought about his parents every day, all the time. He thought about his father, Nana Ofando, whose words of wisdom took shape in his mind since his incarceration. He saw himself as that mackerel and understood what his father meant. He had indeed been preparing his own funeral by letting his guard down, by believing in his love for Lindsey, knowing too well her father's fierce opposition. He had dinner with them and even had lunch with the senator alone, which was unexpected and made him think that there was nothing to worry about; after all, they were just like us, he thought. But love couldn't be blamed; he didn't choose to love Lindsey.

Nana Ofando was suffering in his silent agony. He managed to present a diplomatic smile every day and showed up to work as if everything was well with
him. His collaborators and the employees at the health department tried their
best to show him their support; he politely thanked them for their kindness
and assured them that he was fine. But alone in his office, he could barely
pay attention to the files on his desk; he asked his secretary at times to read
or summarize the contents of the documents for his signature. His son had
become the prime suspect of a high-profile murder in the US, and he was
denied a visa to be close to him and show his support. There was no point for
him to consider the possibility of Kamao committing the crime. Although
he knew how the Western world, how America, changed people, it was out
of the question for him to doubt his son's integrity and to suspect any change
in his moral values. Nothing could make him believe otherwise, and that was
what hurt him most: imagining his son alone with no support, at the mercy of
strangers who had no reason to hold him dear, to be sorry for him. He wanted
to help him, but he didn't know how. He had called Lindsey's phone. It rang
the first day; then, it stopped ringing.

Mama Agatha was inconsolable. She cried every day for weeks, mourning her son, thinking she would never see him again. She wouldn't leave her
house; Adjoa and two other girls she had raised and mentored had joined
hands to keep her business going. Adjoa gave her a full report every week and
made sure all her accounts were up to date. Mama barely paid attention to the
report, sometimes locking herself in her room, refusing to open it to anyone,
including her favorite girl. Adjoa would talk to her from the hallway, wondering if her former protector was even listening. She asked Mama Agatha on the
few occasions she caught her outside the room if she had heard anything from
anyone, from Lindsey.

"That girl's phone stopped ringing since my son was arrested," Mama said.
"I have no idea what is going on. She hasn't called me. A good African girl
would have called. Nana said he gave her number to a good friend of his in
Washington, and he said he called too, but nothing. And he won't dare go to
the senator's house to talk to the girl. There are guards everywhere, like crazy dogs. Jesus help me, I trust You; You have never failed me, You never fail
Your children." Adjoa would leave Mama Agatha at that point, in her time of
connection with God. Most of her conversations recently ended in intense

prayers like that, and her interlocutors usually let themselves out, making sure not to interrupt her.

With Marvin still incarcerated and dismissed by the prosecution as a witness, Kurt remained the last person to talk about Kamao's temper and personality. He was also the key witness of the trial, the only person who had been in direct contact with the victim and the suspect before the unfortunate event. He sat in the witness box, trying his best to avoid eye contact with the suspect. Kamao still couldn't understand why Kurt would testify against him. They had gotten along since he was hired. Kurt told him regularly how he appreciated his honesty, dedication, and willingness to help whenever his help was needed. He stared at Kurt, who made sure to keep looking at the same group of individuals who were sitting in the opposite aisle from Kamao. Everyone knew that Kurt's testimony would weigh more than any other. Ayefumi and Lazo did their best to help their friend.

"Without Kamao's help and understanding, I would be more stressed now trying to pay the rest of the money my cousin and I owed him. He is a true friend: reliable, honest, compassionate, and empathetic," Lazo said during his testimony.

Kamao smiled at him and quietly said, "Thank you."

"Would you please tell the court what you noticed about the defendant and the contents of your conversation with him the day of the murder?" John Foster asked Kurt.

"He seemed tense and was complaining about a lot of things every time I walked into the break room. I know employees always talk about different things in the break room, which is everybody's right. But because he is a knowledgeable person, when he talks, everybody listens, even me. So when he says some things, that worries me a lot because it appears that people take what he says seriously."

"What did he say that day that worried you?"

"There was news coverage on the TV about a Senate hearing and other things related to politics, and he said that there's no one more dangerous than a politician. That you will hear them say one thing, but in their head, they're thinking something else, and they will stab you in the back if they get the chance." There was a commotion in the courtroom.

"Why did he say that?"

"I have no idea!"

"Did he have any encounter with Mr. McGill before making that comment?"

"Yes, he had taken some wine to Mr. McGill in his room. That room was in the hallway he was assigned to."

"So what happened next?"

"I went back to the break room a second time and told him that Mr. McGill wanted some more of the same wine he took to his room before."

"And what did he say?" Mr. Foster asked.

"He said that McGill was rude to him, that he didn't want to go back."

"Was that room 215?"

"Yes."

"And what did he say Mr. McGill told him?"

"He said Mr. McGill told him that he needed to get better training before serving VIP rooms because he was holding the wine or the plate wrong—something like that."

Mr. Foster turned to the jury box and said, "So the defendant already knew who Mr. McGill was and was already upset with him. He probably knew what he would be tempted to do if he had to go back to that room, that's why he told the manager he didn't want to go. And knowing the explosive temper he has exhibited from the beginning, it wouldn't be too hard to conclude that he didn't need any other motives than his pride being injured by Mr. McGill's comment." There was a murmur in the room that looked like people refuting that argument.

Mr. Vivaldi got up and approached the witness. He scrutinized Kurt and asked, "What was your relationship with the defendant before the sad event occurred?"

"It wasn't bad," Kurt said. "He's a hard worker, but his temper sometimes worries me."

"And for you, temper is a big enough motive to lead someone to take the life of a US Senate candidate, with no other reason?"

"Well, I don't know what was in his mind; I can only talk about what I noticed."

"OK!" Vivaldi said. "Now, according to the camera footage, my client was the last person seen going inside Mr. McGill's room. And he was holding the wine." Kurt nodded. "The next thing we know, he woke up next to the victim's body in a pool of blood."

"That's right," Kurt said.

"Now, to your knowledge as the hotel manager, did anyone tamper with the video recording to make it look like it was my client who committed the murder? Please remember that you are under oath, and there is a steep consequence for lying to the court."

"Objection, Your Honor!" Mr. Foster said. "The counsel is turning his questioning of the witness into intimidation. Experts have examined the tape and found no anomaly."

"Sustained! Counsel, please stick with the questions," the judge said.

"I—I . . . didn't see anything happening to the camera or the video recording."

"No one had tampered with them, to your knowledge?"

"No!" Kurt said firmly.

"Did you or anybody hear any commotion, a fight? Because my client seemed to have passed out and woke up next to the body."

"No, I didn't hear anything. Some of the rooms like 215 have some kind of soundproof walls."

"So that might be the reason you hadn't heard anything?"

"Probably," Kurt said. Vivaldi looked at him for a moment, suspicious that Kurt was hiding something, as his legs were unsteady.

"Are you nervous about something?" he asked.

"No! I am fine," Kurt said.

When the day's session ended and he was alone with Vivaldi in his cell, Kamao sniffed; the air suddenly seemed to be turning thick. "It's hard to breathe in here; do you feel the same way?" Mr. Vivaldi shook his head. "I could see in those people's faces in the courtroom; they hate me."

"Things are not looking good, but we should not despair."

"The cameras! Something must have happened to the cameras," Kamao said. "I am sure somebody messed with them; Kurt knows something, can't you see? He won't look at me."

"I know; something is going on. But our experts have examined the camera footage, and they found no anomaly. We have to use everything we have and get help from anyone we can get help from to get you out of this, and that includes Lindsey. You have to let her testify."

"OK, please do it," Kamao said, sniffling even harder.

"Just breathe," Mr. Vivaldi said. "You have to be strong; you can't give up!"

"I don't want it to end like this," Kamao said in a pleading voice as tears started falling. "I don't want this to be the end of me. I didn't kill anyone." He bowed his head and watched his tears fall on the brown table.

"OK! We will call Lindsey. She can help us," Mr. Vivaldi said as he got up and left his client's cell.

As the verdict was approaching, Kamao began to realize the grim fate that lay ahead of him. He realized how his chances of acquittal were fading away. He had no substantial evidence that would prove his innocence, and he saw nothingness when he looked in the mirror, his oblivion in the country he loved. His last hope, Lindsey, was nowhere to be found. He was astounded to learn that she wasn't going to be testifying on his behalf.

"What happened?" he asked Vivaldi.

"I don't know. If she's not here, she can't testify. It seems she is out of the equation, and you have no proof of all the things that you said her father did to you."

On Friday, June 13, the country's attention was on Kamao's trial. The jury was getting ready to deliberate. At 2:30 p.m., the court was back in session. Outside, a pool of journalists was waiting, impatient, hunting for any piece of information that could make breaking news. In the courtroom, Kamao sat next to Vivaldi as usual, placid, wearing a dark gray suit. The entrance of the jury into the room after the long waiting period gave him palpitations, and he held his breath when the foreperson announced that they had reached a verdict.

After a few seconds of suspense, he declared, "We have found the defendant guilty on all counts." Some people cheered, then there was silence.

The announcement of Kamao's death sentence caused both outrage and cheer across the country. A protest against his sentencing organized by a civil rights group in Baltimore died out in half an hour, as only a few people showed up, and the heat seemed unbearable. Mrs. Sterling was walking her dog in the parking lot when Ayefumi pulled up. He'd been moving Kamao's things out of the apartment one day at the time.

"The man is not dead yet; what are you doing?" Ayefumi didn't say a word. "How is he doing?" she asked, getting closer to Ayefumi.

"Not too good."

"Oh, God! I can't believe they're going to kill that poor boy," she said. "I haven't seen him since . . . you know! Someone committed that crime, and they are making him pay for it; that isn't right!" She wiped the tears on her right cheek.

"Why do you say that?" Ayefumi asked.

"Certain things you just know; you feel it. I would never believe he would do something so senseless. I mean, I didn't know him for a long time, but I can tell he is not the kind of person who would do something like that. I feel like there is something bigger behind that story."

"Like what?"

"I don't know! I just feel it, you know! That incident in the parking lot. The suits those people had on, the car they were driving . . . something is going on. That girlfriend of his, is she still around?" Ayefumi shook his head.

"You see! She must be the daughter of one of those people who think they are untouchable." Ayefumi scrutinized Mrs. Sterling, wondering if she was simply a gossip or a caring person with excellent puzzle-solving talent.

"She's Senator McAdams daughter," Ayefumi said.

"Aha! You see? And was he OK with the relationship?" Ayefumi quickly looked around and examined Mrs. Sterling some more, wondering if he should trust her. He thought at the same time that, with his friend's life at stake, it wouldn't be unwise to glean help where he could find it. There was an investigation that showed no proof of the senator's connection to his opponent's death.

"Can I talk to you inside?" he asked Mrs. Sterling and followed her into her apartment.

"You see? I knew it. It shouldn't be a guess. That incident in the parking lot was a hit. That asshole wanted to hurt Kamao because his daughter wouldn't break up with him. And where is that girl now?"

"Out of the country! In Brazil or . . . somewhere else, I don't know."

"I knew it, I knew it! We must do something about this."

"There was an investigation involving the senator, but it hit a dead end; there was no proof involving him in anything."

"Well, did the parking lot incident come out during the trial at all?"

"There is no proof that the senator ordered the hit on Kamao. We know he did it, but without proof, it is just speculation, and it won't lead to anything."

"But not if the right people are in on this. Now is the time to use whatever asset we have, right?" Ayefumi wondered what Mrs. Sterling was trying to say and who she meant by "we." Was she on their side? How did she make that decision? he wondered.

"Now, you certainly don't know this, but I have a nephew in Congress too—a representative from Illinois." Mrs. Sterling put the plate she brought out of the kitchen on the central table and handed Ayefumi a cup of hot tea on a saucer.

"Really!"

"Yes, his name is Mike Donohue."

"Ah!" Ayefumi said. "I know him . . . well, I heard a lot of things about him. I heard that he helps people seeking asylum and works on other immigration issues from his constituency. He's a good guy. You know him?"

Mrs. Sterling smiled. "Like I said, he is my nephew. I am going to talk to him. Since he's from the same party as McAdams, I don't think it would be too hard for him to find some allies who could join the case to find out what happened, and if necessary open a congressional investigation or something; I don't know. I just hope something gets done about this before . . . you know what I mean?" She got up, throwing her arms in the air, went into the kitchen, and came back with a box of crackers that she opened and offered to her visitor. "I will give you a call to let you know what he says, and we can go from there."

"Thank you so much!" Ayefumi said.

"Write your phone number here, will you?" She showed him a space in her notebook. "What's your name?"

"Ayefumi; but you can call me Aye."

Mike Donohue was finishing his cup of coffee, a newspaper in front of him. He kept glancing at the round clock on the wall. He had a meeting with Ayefumi at 9:30 a.m.; he didn't want to be late, and he didn't want to hurry either. He wanted to leave the house at the perfect time. It would only take him fifteen minutes to get to Nick's Café on Elm Street. It wouldn't be a good idea to receive Ayefumi in his office at the Capitol, he thought. Ayefumi and Lazo arrived at the café at 9:30 a.m. Ayefumi told the popular Illinois representative that he was coming with a friend who knew everything about the situation. In reality, Ayefumi needed a witness for all his encounters with DC's big fish. Donohue listened attentively, making sure not to miss any detail of Ayefumi's story.

"Even if all that is true, there's nothing really that anyone can do without any type of proof. I doubt that his daughter would testify against him." He paused and took a sip of his coffee. "A lot of people on the Hill would show little surprise if they learned about all the things you said the senator did to your friend. Many people question a lot of things he does and the motives behind them. All you need is some kind of evidence. Do you have anything all?" Ayefumi sighed, going through his thoughts. "Kamao said Lindsey told him about a Secret Service agent the senator uses to run his errands. Corey something, he said his name is Corey . . . Mur-something."

"OK, that can be a starting point: an agent named Corey Mur-something," Mr. Donohue said and wrote the information down. "I will let you know if something comes up, but you have to be discreet. You can't go around telling people about this. It is too big of a situation to be taken lightly. We all need to be careful, OK? Let's see if something comes up that could help your friend." Ayefumi and Lazo thanked the representative and left.

Two weeks had passed since he met with Mr. Donohue, and he hadn't heard anything back, but Ayefumi resolved to keep his hopes up for some good news soon. He had been trying to convince Lazo to keep the faith, but the latter wasn't hopeful about Donohue's handling of the situation.

"In this country, anything can get entangled into politics, and things can quickly get ugly. Not that I am negative or pessimistic, but it's hard for me to think that anyone on the Hill would like to see this through without worrying about their career."

"I know, but we have to try something. We can't just give up like that," Ayefumi said. He felt a buzz in his pocket; he picked up the phone. Lazo could hear the man's voice on the other end of the line but couldn't get what he was saying.

"It was Donohue," Ayefumi said, after he hung up. "He wants to see me tomorrow at a different location."

"He must be terrified, changing places like that," Lazo said.

"I am so sorry to tell you that there is not much I can do. We just don't have enough tangible evidence to work with, and many people don't want to push forward, which would give the impression that they have something against McAdams. He's a strong ally of the president; you probably don't know what that means."

"I do," Lazo said. Donohue looked at him, smiled, and nodded.

"So that's it, then?" Ayefumi asked.

"Yeah. I am so sorry. It seems like it is a closed case for your friend."

"What about the Secret Service guy?" Ayefumi didn't feel like giving up too easily.

"I learned from a reliable source that there's a Secret Service agent named Corey Murdock. It seems that the senator and Agent Murdock are good friends; asking for the agent's help on and off doesn't prove that there is anything wrong going on. I have to be honest with you: nobody wants to upset the senator by looking too deep into that. Unless there is undeniable, tangible evidence, nothing can be done right now that could suggest Senator McAdams's involvement in your friend's case. Again, I am very sorry! I wish I could do more, but I can't."

"Thank you!" Ayefumi said and shook Donohue's hand.

PART VII

MORNING COMES AND ALSO THE NIGHT

Chapter 24

Dania took her laptop out of the suitcase. She hadn't checked her emails for months. Her current phone was not the fancy smartphone she had in DC, on which she could do almost anything she would need a computer for. She had been working at the hospital for a while now, trying to readjust to life in her country. Her belongings finally arrived. Knowing that the valuable items might be stolen if he shipped them, Lazo waited until he learned that a friend was planning to visit his family back home, so he paid him for Dania's luggage. Dania's aunt called her at work to let her know that someone left her a suitcase. Lazo did his best to put most of her valuable belongings into one suitcase and took the rest to his apartment. Dania hadn't gotten the chance to say goodbye to her cousin; the ICE agents had shown up at her apartment that Sunday morning while she was brushing her teeth. They picked her up, and that was it. She leaned back on the chair as the computer was starting up to let her misfortune unfold in her head once again.

She smiled and shook her head as her memory took her back to her ordeal in the US. She wondered how things were in DC at that very moment. She looked at the time. It was 11:13 p.m. In Washington, DC, it would be 12:13 a.m. She would be just getting home from the Coal Master Hotel. She wondered if Celine was still there and thought she wouldn't be surprised if she still was, grooming other girls for Bradford's pleasure. She went and checked on Junior, who was sleeping peacefully. She went outside to breathe in the fresh air of the late-night breeze and clear her head. She came back in and opened her email. It showed 278 unread messages, 245 of which were from SMART TRACK. She wondered what that was and opened one. It was a video recording; she recognized room 213 of the Coal Master Hotel in DC. She wondered how those recordings ended up in her mailbox. Lazo might have added her email address when he was setting the cameras up without her knowledge. She smiled and came up with an idea: she would grab some snacks, stay up late, and watch as many video recordings as she could. At one fifteen in the morning, she was still watching the recordings, laughing at the variety of the contents, their gruesome explicitness. One showed a woman who knelt between a man's legs, moving her head up and down and back and forth. Another one showed a hairy septuagenarian with a huge belly, groaning as he discharged, then rolled on his back, panting as if he had run a hundred-mile marathon.

As she kept on, she got to a recording where the scene was quite different from the others. It was room 215; there was a man and a woman. They were talking, and suddenly, there was a struggle; the woman grabbed what looked like a bottle on the bedside table and hit the man on the head. He collapsed and became still. The liquid from the bottle soaked the floor mat, together with the man's blood. She gasped and froze.

Lazo's phone rang; he groaned and reached for it; he looked at the time: 3:16 a.m. The caller ID showed *Prima*. "*¿Está todo bien, prima?*" he said.

"*Sí, sí, todo está bien*, Lazo," she replied. "You remember when you installed the cameras at the hotel?"

"Yes," Lazo said.

"Did you set it up so the recordings can go directly to my email?"

"I . . . I think I did; it was an option, kind of like a backup. Why?"

"I just saw some weird shit, yo! A lady hit a man on the head with a bottle full of wine or something, and he is dead!"

"What?" Lazo sat on the bed and turned on the lamp.

"Yes! In room 215."

"Wait! Wait! Are the cameras still working? I thought they found them and took them down; that's why they deported you."

"No, no, the guy broke my phone, remember? He thought I was recording our conversations on it. I didn't tell Celine about the cameras. They are still working." Lazo got off the bed at that moment.

"Oh my God," he said.

"What is it?" Dania asked.

"Oh my God! Oh my God! Oh my God!" Lazo couldn't utter any other words.

"What is it, Lazo? You're scaring me now!" Dania said.

"Kamao!" Lazo said.

"Oh, shit!" Dania replied. "Was it in that room?" she asked.

"I don't know! But with the bottle of wine and the man dead, all of that sounds like . . . Can you forward the video to me please? I need to check something out to make sure."

"Yeah, sure!" Dania said. Lazo rushed into the bathroom, brushed his teeth, and cleaned his face. He looked at the clock; it wasn't even 4:00 a.m. yet, and he wasn't getting ready for work, so what was the point for him to brush his teeth and clean his face? he thought. But there was no way he could go back to sleep. He grabbed his computer and opened his email. The recording was there; he sat on the bed and opened it. He called Dania back.

"It was the murder, *prima*! It was the murder Kamao was sentenced for," he said in a calm but trembling voice.

"Are you sure?"

"Yes! I recognized Lindsey, Senator McAdams's daughter. It was her!"

"What!"

"Yes! I will call you back during the day, OK? Make sure the video doesn't get deleted, please! Kamao's life depends on it."

"OK," Dania said.

Lazo picked up his phone and looked for Mr. Vivaldi's number. He hesitated and gave up. What if the same people who framed Kamao had bugged their phones, somehow? They must be capable of it, he thought. He grabbed his jacket and looked at the time; it was 4:35 a.m. He took the computer and left. He arrived at Mr. Vivaldi's residence at a quarter to five and rang the bell. The front door camera flashed, and he heard Mr. Vivaldi's voice.

"Lazo! What are you doing here?"

"I need to show you something, Mr. Vivaldi," Lazo said, looking around, nervous.

"Are you alone?"

"Yes!"

"I'm coming." The seven minutes it took for Mr. Vivaldi to open the front door seemed like an eternity for Lazo, who was trembling, not from cold, and was looking around every five seconds. He almost dropped the laptop at one point and struggled to get ahold of himself.

"Are the cameras still in the rooms?" Mr. Vivaldi asked after watching the recording.

"Yes," Lazo said.

"Do you know who put them there?" Lazo told Mr. Vivaldi Dania's story.

"You put cameras in the hotel rooms?" Vivaldi said, indignant. "Well, brace yourself for some troubles ahead: you are trailing several violations behind you here, but if this recording is authentic, it will undoubtedly be a turning point in this case. I will show it to a few people and see what can come out of it. I will call you after meeting with the judge and the prosecutor about this new evidence. To be honest with you, I was hoping for something like this. Great work, Lazo! Kamao is lucky to have friends like you," the lawyer said, shaking Lazo's hand. "I'll see you out."

Ayefumi lay on the couch; his son, Ogumi, was watching *Sesame Street*, his favorite show. His wife Ayela was in the kitchen cooking lunch: rice with peanut butter sauce. He heard the breaking news alert on his phone: New evidence has surfaced in the McGill murder case. There seems to be a video recording that shows a different story from the case, the alert read. He jumped off the couch as if he was stung by a bug hiding inside it.

He called Lazo. "Laz, have you heard? They are talking about the recording."

"Yes," Lazo said. "Vivaldi called me. They have accepted it as evidence; I was going to call you. Kamao might still have a chance, but it's not over yet."

"Of course not."

"Vivaldi said he would go see him today. I wanted to go, but he said I couldn't. I'll call you later."

"OK!" Ayefumi said.

Chapter 25

Since her return from Brazil, Lindsey's days were filled with a void. Her friends, who knew about her relationship with Kamao, deserted her for fear of being linked to the case. She was engulfed by guilt, her sleepless nights endless. Her days were filled with an emptiness that grew and it was becoming an unbearable load. Inaudible voices were judging and condemning her, and she couldn't stop them. "Please forgive me, forgive me," she heard herself say at times, with no one around to hear her cry and comfort her. "I am going to turn myself in," she said to her father one morning during breakfast. "I can't bear it anymore."

"You can't do that," the senator said. "We've come too far to go back. You don't have to worry about anything. It's almost over. If everything goes well, he won't make it to Christmas."

"I can't take it anymore," she replied, crying. She went back to her room and locked herself in. She wanted to confess her crime to Kamao and ask him for forgiveness, but he wasn't receiving visitors. She came into the kitchen one afternoon to get a glass of water and looked through the window: five FBI agents were headed to the front door. She opened the door and met them on the porch.

"Lindsey McAdams?" one of the agents said.

"Yes!" she replied.

"You are under arrest for conspiracy and concealment in the murder of Kenneth McGill. You have the right to remain silent . . ." The remainder of the Miranda Rights sounded like an echo in the distance to Lindsey, who felt liberated as she was handcuffed and escorted to one of the armored SUVs. Journalists rushed to the Capitol after the news of Lindsey's arrest broke out.

"Do you know anything about your daughter's involvement in the killing of Kenneth McGill, Senator?" a reporter asked Mr. McAdams, who looked at her like a vicious bug he wanted to smash but restrained himself. He got into his car and the driver drove off.

Kamao couldn't believe it when he was told the charges against him were dropped and that he was free to go home. It was surreal even though he knew about the new evidence, the precursor to his unique and much happier fate. He left his cell and walked down the empty hall with two guards, a somber look on their faces. Vivaldi waited for him at the checkout and walked him to the gate. Ayefumi and Lazo were waiting for him outside, and so was a group of journalists.

"I thought I would never see you again, my dear brother," Ayefumi said, hugging Kamao as tears filled his eyes.

A young journalist, an intern at Southern Cameroon Broadcasting Corporation, approached Kamao with a smile and asked, "Mr. Birama, how does it feel like to breathe the air of freedom again after months on death row, awaiting your execution?"

Kamao turned to the camera and said, "I honestly don't know! It feels weird. I could have died if this recording never came out. My thoughts just go to all those innocent people who have been executed for crimes they never committed. I am humbled and grateful to all those people who believed in my innocence. Thank you all!"

"Thank you!" the reporter said.

"You are a celebrity now, bro!" Lazo said as he hugged him. "Wait and see how much easier your life will be now!"

"I am not going to bite into that bait again, Lazo," he said with a serious look on his face. "I promise you that!" He shook Lazo's hand firmly and hugged him. "Thank you for saving my life."

"You are welcome," Lazo said. Kamao got into Vivaldi's car, heading to his office for some paperwork.

"I was waiting for your official release to tell you this: Lindsey's attorney informed me that she wants to talk to you," Vivaldi said, laughing. "I don't know what is going through that girl's head, but she must be out of her mind to think you will want to see her after what she's put you through . . ."

"I will go!" Kamao said, quickly, ending Vivaldi's jabbering. "I want to hear what she has to say." Vivaldi looked at him, thinking he must be mad.

"OK! I will arrange it."

Kamao didn't feel like celebrating his release, as Lazo suggested. He went to his apartment and called his parents.

"God! I didn't think I would ever hear your voice again, my sweet boy. What have they done to you?" Mama Agatha said, sobbing with joy. "But I also knew my God never fails His children. You need to come back! You have nothing else to do in that country. You have to come back home, once and for all."

"Mama, it's not the country; only a handful of people were involved in this. That's all! Lindsey has—"

"I don't want you to talk about that girl. I don't ever want to hear you mention the name of that evil girl again, and you better stay away from her family, you hear me?"

"Yes, Mama; I hear you. I will come and see you next month."

"See me! I am telling you to come home once and for all."

At the announcement of Kamao's death sentence, Mama Agatha had ordered a weekly prayer session for her son at her church. Every Friday evening, she met with her friends and other members at the church for long hours of prayer led by the pastor. As the weeks went by and Kamao's case was still leading in the news, the number of the attendees of the special Friday prayer meetings—as they called it—grew to the point that a new tent was raised outside of the main building to accommodate newcomers. The pastor and his deacons were well compensated, so their dedication never faded.

Nana Ofando, on the other hand, was calm when his son called him. "Well! Wasn't that something?" he said. "How are you feeling?"

"Still a little shaken. I can't believe I am out, but . . . I am just grateful that a lot of people believed in my innocence and went above and beyond for me."

"Wish I'd been there to support you."

"I know! My lawyer said you were denied a visa. I am sorry to have caused you so much pain, Father! I can't imagine what you have been through."

"Yeah! It was quite an ordeal; but it is now over, right?"

"You'd warned me when I was there with Lindsey, but . . ."

"So you remembered!

"Yes, it took me some time to realize what you meant . . . I am sorry!"

"Well, you don't need to be sorry. Sometimes you learn better from your trials, and they become your best teacher; in your case, you almost lost your life. Just come and see us when you can. The president is impatient to see you."

"I'll be there next month." Kamao hung up and thanked God for his parents.

Mrs. Sterling, Ayefumi, and Lazo came over to keep Kamao company.

"I thank you all for what you've done for me," he said.

"There are a lot more people to thank than us," Lazo said.

"I know!"

"And there are going to be a lot of interviews—TV interviews—and you can't decline them all; that won't be right! A lot of people in this country believed in your innocence; they prayed for you and went to the street for you. They deserve to see you and hear you talk to them," Mrs. Sterling said, looking at Kamao with admiration. "You are so brave! When the jury"—she tried to hold her tears—"when the jury said they found you guilty, my heart stopped; but you sat there calm and took it all, all the curses, the hateful words. You took it all! I can't believe it." She pulled a couple of Kleenex tissues from the box on the table to dry her tears.

Ayefumi rubbed her shoulders. "Thank you for everything, Mrs. Sterling! We are truly grateful," he said.

Mrs. Sterling's phone rang; she picked it up, talked to someone, and said, "He's here!"

"Who is here?" Kamao asked.

"There is someone who wants to see you and who wants to share some information with you."

"Who's that?"

"Wait and you will see." She went out. Kamao looked at Ayefumi, then Lazo, then back at Ayefumi, waiting for an explanation, but both remained quiet, attempting to avoid his fierce stare.

Mrs. Sterling came back with a tall man in a khaki coat, his dark hair nicely groomed.

"Congressman Donohue!" Kamao said and stood up to shake the man's hand.

"Now, you will forgive me. I usually don't barge into people's places like this, but this is an opportunity not to miss. In a few days, when people find out where you live, we may have to fight through the pool of reporters to get to you."

"Yeah! You should hide for a little while before showing your face again," Mrs. Sterling said, with her usual smile. "Well, as you already know, this is

Congressman Donohue; he happens to be my nephew, and he's been trying his best to help us. So I will let him tell you why he is here," she said, turning to Donohue, who found a space on the couch between Ayefumi and Lazo.

"Thanks, Aunt," he said. "Well . . ." He cleared his voice. "I have used the information your friend here gave me and the description my aunt provided about your aggressors and the car they were driving the night you were assaulted in the parking lot. It turns out that a couple of other agents are on McAdams's payroll besides Murdock; one of them is Jim Bernic. He's been cooperating with the FBI and is willing to cut a deal. He confessed that he's been doing some side jobs with Corey Murdock, who, by the way, could not be found anywhere. The FBI is following several leads, and they might be questioning you and your friends soon, so just be ready for it and tell them everything you know. Whoever did this to you is going to pay for it, I can assure you."

"What about Lindsey? Is she saying anything?"

"She is trying to protect her father, putting all the blame on Murdock, from what I've heard. But she can't deny her knowledge of her father's treatment of you; it's only a matter of time before all of this leads to McAdams; the whole thing will come out soon."

"Thank you very much, sir!" Kamao said.

"You're welcome!" The congressman got up, shook Kamao's and his friends' hands, and headed to the door.

"What about my situation . . . you know . . . the camera," Lazo yelled, nervous.

"I'm not sure about that one, but . . ."

"My lawyer, Mr. Vivaldi, is looking into it; don't worry, Lazo. You'll be fine."

"OK!" Lazo said and smiled.

"Thank you again, sir," Kamao said as Donohue waved at them and left the apartment.

Since his testimony against Kamao in court, Kurt frequently had cold sweats at night from his persistent nightmares that forced him to jump out of bed in the middle of the night and kneel at the bedside and pray for forgiveness. Other times, he would suddenly wake up panting, in sweat, uttering some unintelligible words.

"What is wrong, honey? It's happening again! This has to stop," his wife, Ella, said one night. "I am tired of cuddling you every night so that you can go back to sleep. If you don't tell me what the matter is with you, I swear I will leave, and you'll be alone in this house with your devious demons. I have had enough."

"I ... I can't take it anymore. I am a good Christian," he said. "I ... I ..."

"What is it?"

"I ... I ... The guy is innocent."

"Which guy?"

"The guy, Kamao. Kamao. He's innocent."

"What are you talking about?" Ella said.

"He ... he didn't kill the guy. They paid me to lie; they gave me twenty thousand to testify against him." He jumped off the bed. "They gave me twenty thousand! The money is in the garage. I will give it back. I can't take this anymore." He started crying and crawled on the floor. "I am sorry, baby! I am so sorry; I lied to you."

Ella sat on the bed, bewildered, crying. "You testified against a man, knowing well that he was innocent! How can you do something like that? And all this time, you've been feeling guilty, but you didn't do anything about it." Kurt was still on the floor, crying. "I can't stay here. You better figure something out quick to redeem yourself before you rot in hell, monster!" She got up, went to the bathroom, and locked the door. The next morning when Kurt woke up, she was gone, with all her belongings. Kurt called her aunt's house, thinking she might have gone there; no one picked up. He looked inside his jacket pocket and found the folded piece of paper with the number that Agent Murdock gave him to call in case he needed help with anything. He called; no one answered. His breathing started to accelerate. The TV was on, and the commentator drew his attention when he announced that new evidence was surfacing in Kamao's case. Eyebrows raised, he stepped back and fell on the couch. He called the hotel and said he wasn't coming. That evening, he was fixing a ham sandwich for dinner and looked out the kitchen window and saw two FBI agents walking toward the house. He went to the door and met them outside.

"Mr. Kurt Bosewell?" one of the agents said.

"That's me," he said quietly.

"We have some questions to ask you. Could you please come with us?"

"Sure!" he said. He thought about the bag of money in the garage. There was nothing he could do about it now.

Chapter 26

Kamao sat on a chair in the visiting area of the women's prison. A thick glass separated him from the inmates' quarters, and a phone hung on a wall next to him. The place brought back recent memories he wasn't keen to dwell on. He was a bit nervous, gauging his word choices to find the least angry ones to use in his conversation with his ex-fiancée. Ten minutes had passed and felt like an eternity to him; he wanted to get out of that place—the waiting was becoming unbearable. As he began to reconsider his decision to talk to her, he saw two people turn a corner and walk toward the glass in front of him. Lindsey was walking in front, a female guard in a blue uniform behind her. Lindsey was wearing a gray and black striped jumpsuit. She looked exhausted, her face pale, her hair scattered, and she seemed depressed but peaceful.

She picked up the phone as she sat down. Kamao picked up the phone on his side too. Lindsey forced a smile, and said, "Hello."

"Hi," Kamao replied with an expressionless face.

"Thank you for coming! I didn't think you'd come. I wanted to see you and tell you I am sorry for what I did to you. I should have said something; I should have said that I did it, that I killed McGill." She stopped and managed to fight her tears back. Kamao didn't say a word; he didn't try to comfort her. "We had a beautiful thing going on, and I ruined it, and for that, I am really . . . sorry." She covered her mouth as if to prevent herself from screaming. "Will you ever find it in your heart to forgive me?"

"I don't know if I can forgive you, but I will try," Kamao finally said, feeling a bit sorry for her.

"I've prepared a check for you; my lawyer will contact you. It is not to redeem myself or absolve myself from my sins against you, but it's so that you can get back on your feet. Kamao, I loved and still love you, and I don't know if I will ever win your heart again, but my actions will haunt me forever, and that alone is killing me already. Please forgive me." She hid her face in her palms, sobbing.

"I find it outrageous that you're talking about giving me money; that alone is a sign that you don't really know me. Do you think I've ever wanted your money? I made it clear that I didn't want it. I never thought about it. Accepting it now will prove your father right; didn't you think about that?"

"I don't care what my father thinks anymore."

"And I heard you're protecting him; you are trying to cover what he did. Why?"

"My father is already facing his demons; I don't want to add to that agony. Please, take the money; that would grant me some solace, knowing that you are doing OK financially. If you ever need more, all you have to do is let me know and I will give it to you. My father had given me everything; he had put everything in my name. I just wanted a good life for us. Now, I want it for you; I want you to be happy. Please say you will try. That'll give me much comfort."

Kamao got up and said, "Goodbye, Lindsey." He hung up the phone and left. Lindsey sat there and watched him disappear through the door, the phone still in her hand.

"How is she doing?" Mr. Vivaldi asked when Kamao got back to the car.

"I don't know! She looks beat up, but I don't know what to think about her anymore. I think she might have some kind of mental issue. I didn't suspect that before, although I kind of questioned some of her childish and strange behavior."

"You know her more than I do, so that's your judgment. Now, you do know she may not stay in there for too long, right?" Vivaldi said.

"Why not?"

"Her father is a good friend of the president. I am pretty sure President Reynolds is going to pardon her before leaving office."

"Really?"

"Yes, it's very likely," Vivaldi said. "And besides, I don't believe her sentence is going to be too heavy either, because the killing itself was in self-defense; the cover-up that landed you in prison is what she will mostly do time for."

"So she might get out sooner than we thought."

"In a couple of years, yes." The drive back to his apartment seemed shorter than it was. Kamao always enjoyed talking to Vivaldi. Not only was he a great attorney, but he spoke to his clients as if they were old acquaintances, as a good friend who looked out for them.

Vivaldi pulled in the parking lot; Kamao sighed. "I don't know if I can ever thank you enough."

"Well, I simply did my job."

"Still, I appreciate you."

"Well, thank you! We are at the end of the road now. It was a pleasure working for you."

"Yup!" Kamao said with a smile on his face.

Vivaldi shook his hand and said, "Be well, my friend, and take care of yourself. Now you know that this is our America! If it doesn't kill you, it makes you rich and famous."

They both laughed.

"Thank you!" Kamao said, firmly shaking his lawyer's hand, and got out of the car.

"Oh, one more thing," Vivaldi said. "The hotel decided not to press charges against Lazo. They are too ashamed of the fishy business they had going on in there. And they are going to close anyway. So it's all good. And Bradford, the guy who abused Lazo's cousin—the FBI got him yesterday."

"I will let Lazo know. He will be delighted to hear that. Thank you!"

"You're welcome. Take care."

Senator McAdams's death came as a shock in DC and throughout the country. Even those like Kamao and Ayefumi, who expected an official announcement of his involvement in McGill's murder cover-up, didn't expect things to turn out that way. The news came out one evening as Kamao was spending time with Ayefumi's family. Since his return from Accra, he had been spending his evenings at his friend's apartment, enjoying Ayela's delicious dinners. Ayefumi was on a three-week vacation from work, so it was the perfect opportunity to spend time together with his friend, who was single again. Ogumi was playing a game on his tablet; his father subscribed to cable now and had monopolized the TV, keeping it on a news channel for the whole day. On the screen, a TV host and her guests were debating racial issues in the country.

"Since when have you become so interested in politics?" Kamao asked, his mouth full of a big chunk of chicken thigh.

"I just want to stay informed, that's all. I want to show you something," he said. "You won't believe this." He went to the bedroom and brought a newspaper to Kamao before pointing at an area on a page and asking him to read it.

Kamao read the piece. "What?" he exclaimed. "Adeomi is dead! What happened?"

"Well, do you remember when I told you he was going to die young? This is it." Adeomi's body was found in Lake Michigan, near Chicago. He was quickly identified thanks to the driver's license found in the back pocket of his jeans.

"Wow! This is sad, man! I can't believe he kept on with his devious tricks and died from it."

"You feel sorry for the guy who lied about you in court, who wanted you dead? What is the matter with you?"

"Come on, he was doing that just for money. You know it."

"Exactly! And that's what got him to where he is right now."

Adeomi had died the day he went to collect his money after his testimony against Kamao in court. He parked his car in the empty spot next to a large black SUV with the lights on. There were a few other cars in the parking garage with no occupants. Adeomi got out; the guy in the passenger seat pulled the window halfway down and handed him a brown bag.

"Here's is your money. Thank you for your help."

"You're welcome," Adeomi said. He opened the bag and removed the bundle of cash. He began counting the hundred-dollar bills without breaking the strap. The two guys looked at each other and smiled.

"This is five thousand! We agreed on ten," Adeomi said.

"No, we did not agree on ten; we told you we will see, but we offered you five grand," the driver said.

"No, no, no, I was expecting ten thousand, I want the rest of my money." Adeomi's persistence amused the two guys, who looked at each other and smiled again.

"Look," the guy on the passenger seat said, "all you did was say a few bad things about that son of a bitch. How many shifts would you have worked to get this amount you're holding in your hand, huh? Just take the money and get the fuck out of here before you really piss us off."

"Besides," the driver said, "our guy was done for anyway even without your help, so you shouldn't complain too much. This is easy money; just take it and go."

"Really!" Adeomi said. "You do know what would happen if I go back and say you paid me to say all the things I said about him, right? I lied because you asked me to; he'd never threatened to burn my car and—" Adeomi got caught off guard by a punch to his face before he finished his thought. He rolled on the ground, holding his bloody nose. The guy in the passenger seat came out.

"That was the stupidest mistake you've ever made, man! Threatening us!" Adeomi started crawling backward.

"I am sorry, I . . ." He put a hand up, begging for mercy as the guy walked toward him, putting a silencer on his Beretta 92. Two short sounds were heard, like punches on cardboard; Adeomi gasped for air, feeling the two holes in his chest. He lay on his back on the hard cement floor, his mouth open, eyes haggard, his head tilted to the left.

"He would have died sooner if he hadn't come into this country," Ayela said. "He would have been beaten to death or burned alive by neighbors if he was still back home."

"Yup!" Ayefumi said. "He was no good. People like that give us a bad reputation here, you know!"

They were still talking about Adeomi when the TV host interrupted a guest and put a hand to her ear and announced: "We have breaking news: Senator McAdams has been admitted to St. John Memorial Hospital. He has sustained a gunshot wound to the head and is in critical condition. We will let you know as we learn more." A couple of images of the senator came up on the screen. The room was quiet; no one knew what to say. Kamao couldn't find the right words; he sat back on the chair and sighed. His thoughts went to Lindsey.

The senator's death was announced in the late evening news the next day. A grim mood covered the streets of DC as thick dark clouds took hold of the sky. In front of the US Capitol, a reporter stood before the camera; behind him, the US flag was flying at half-mast.

"Today, a great US senator has died," he said. "The nation will mourn him and will miss him. May he rest in peace."

A few days after Senator McAdams's death, Agent Murdock was surrounded by FBI agents in a cabin he was hiding in near Virginia. He opened fire when the agents asked him to come out with his hands up. He wounded two agents and was killed at the end of a three-hour standoff.

Epilogue

When the midsized jet landed on the hot tarmac of San Salvador's airport, Kamao was only half awake. He had a good hour nap. He looked through the window; it seemed warm outside, from the look on the faces of the ramp workers who were unloading the luggage. He wondered how hot out it was; Lazo warned him about traveling there in April, but Kamao said it was the perfect time to tie the knot with Dania in the hope of bringing her back to the United States, legally this time. His summer class was starting in late May; he wouldn't have time to travel then. Dania was waiting for him in the arrivals' hall, a smile on her face, her sunglasses on, and another pair in her hand. Kamao hugged her and complimented her on how charming she looked in her green blouse and white jeans. They left the airport hand in hand.

Acknowledgments

I would like to express my sincere gratitude to a wonderful group of people, who, knowingly or not, directly or indirectly, have helped me get where I am today.

To God Almighty, first and foremost, for his everlasting Wisdom and Grace, for guiding me, for inspiring me, and for teaching me.

To my mother, Adzo Jeannette Tsédévia, who inspired me to become a passionate teacher and lover of books.

To my wife, Asséyé, and my children, Enam and Keli, who, by the way, wanted me to mention that she helped me write the book. I thank you guys for your support.

To my father, my brothers, and my sisters, who encouraged me on this journey, in particular my sister Béné, who read the very first draft and provided valuable feedback and encouragement.

To my American family who took me into their house and provided me with a place to stay for my first three years in the United States, who treated me like a son and a brother, and continue to do so to this day: Colin Younge, his wife Simone Younge, their daughters Temitayo, Anike, and Makeda.

To Monsieur Rigobert Yawovi Wotodzo, my seventh-grade French teacher who instilled in me the love for literature and reading with his amazing lessons and comments on books during class reading sessions and poem recitations.

To Monsieur Dogbé, my eighth-grade French teacher and Assistant Principal of CEG Kpodzi, Kpalimé (Togo), who prophesized to my class that they had a future writer among them after giving me my graded essay back. Two days after he made the announcement, I approached him and asked: "Monsieur, why did you say that I am going to be a writer?" He replied: "The way you write, the way you tell your stories," then he walked away.

To Eve Hermanson, writing coach and writer herself, for her support and encouraging words, and for reading the first few chapters and giving me feedback.

To all my fellow teachers (former and current) who sent words of encouragement and showed their support when I announced the future publication of the book.

To Ed Vogel, for his encouraging words, and for giving me valuable ideas in my quest for a mentor during my residency at UNO.

To Caleb Narva, who listened to me read the first couple of chapters and who gave me some organization ideas.

To those who read the full manuscript and gave me valuable insights: Miriam Andres (Spanish teacher), Jeffrey Stallworth (psychology and government teacher), Stacey Ruffalo (school psychologist), Brian and Deana Rainey (coaches and English teachers), Maria Perez Mozaz (world languages supervisor).

To Dr. Kate Gale, my publisher, for giving me a chance, for accepting my work. The United States is indeed a country of opportunity, but it is people like you who help turn the opportunity into real success. Thank you!

To Rebeccah Sanhueza, my editor, for reading whatever I send her way and giving me feedback with encouragement.

To the entire publishing team at the Red Hen Press, for the amazing work from start to finish.

To all the future readers of this book, thank you for allowing me to take you onto this amazing journey into the world of Kamao, Lindsey, Dania, and Brad McAdams.

And finally, to the country that I love and respect, the United States of America, for giving me a chance to thrive and take a shot at the American Dream. Thank you!

Biographical Note

Elom K. Akoto immigrated to the United States from Togo (West Africa). He earned a bachelor's degree in Education and a master's degree in TESOL (Teacher of English to Speakers of Other Languages). He is the founder of Learn and Care, a nonprofit organization that aims to promote Literacy and Adult Education, not only among immigrants but also among Native Americans who missed the opportunity to earn a high school diploma. The program offers ESL, literacy, GED preparation classes, and more. He published two ESL workbooks: *Ideal Companion, ESL level 1* and *Ideal Companion, ESL level 2*. He teaches French in a high school and ESL at a community college in Omaha, Nebraska, where he lives with his family.

Printed in the USA
CPSIA information can be obtained
at www.ICGtesting.com
JSHW021033280724
67171JS00003B/3

9 781636 281827